THE BLOOD-CURSED

The Blood-Cursed

Samantha Traunfeld

Copyright © 2024 by Samantha Traunfeld

Cover Art © 2024 by Diana Dworak

Map copyright © 2022 by Grayson Wilde

Sveva font ©2003 Andreas Seidel

Cover Design by Mandi Lynn

All rights reserved.

No part of this book may be reproduced in any form or by any electronic or mechanical means, including information storage and retrieval systems, without written permission from the author, except for the use of brief quotations in a book review.

Also by Samantha Traunfeld

The Legionnaire

To anyone currently lost, especially within their own minds this book is for you. There is a light at the end of the dark tunnel.

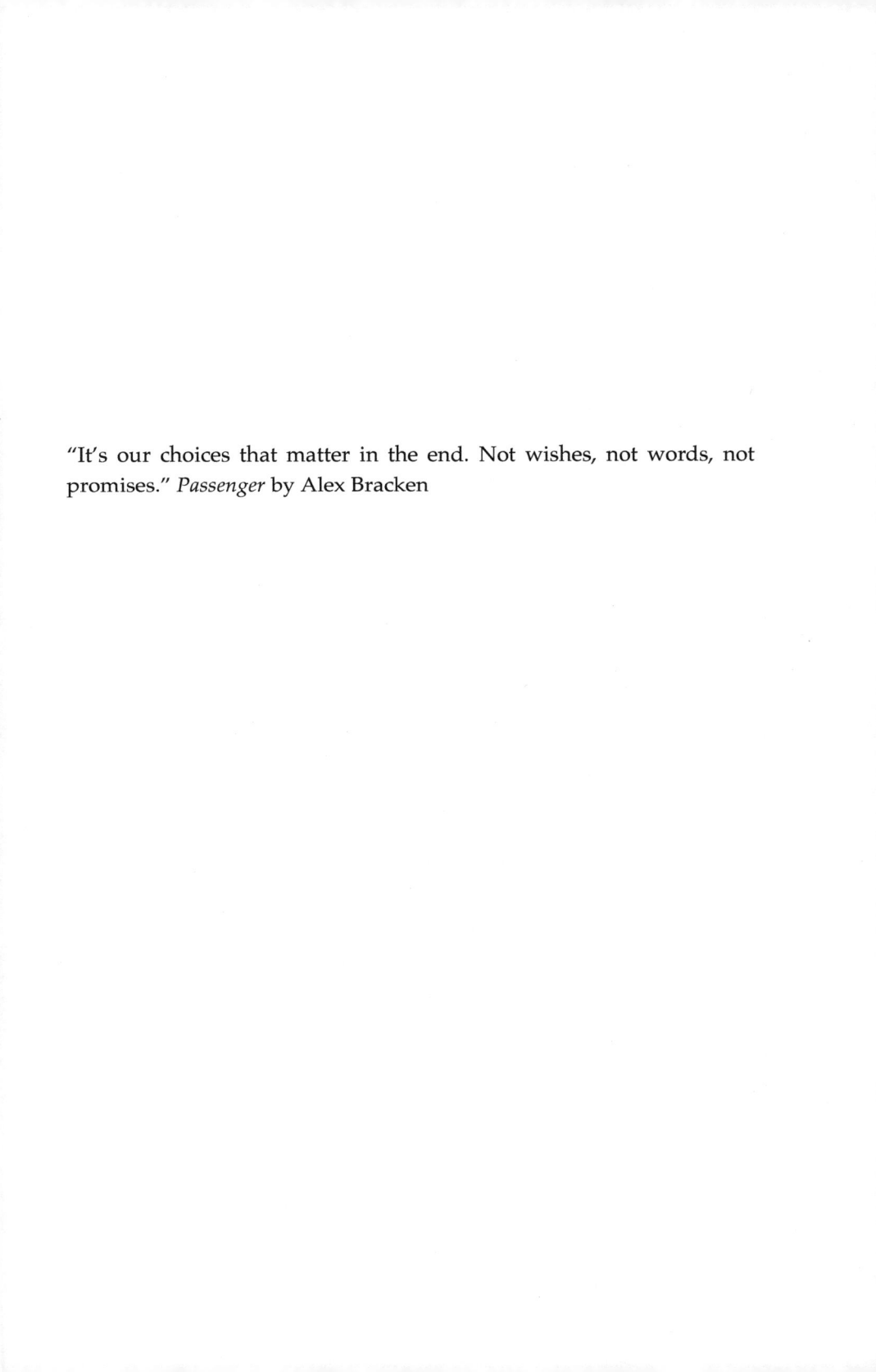

"It's our choices that matter in the end. Not wishes, not words, not promises." *Passenger* by Alex Bracken

TRIGGER WARNINGS

Trigger warnings include: Fantasy violence, death of a fictional character, graphic depictions of violence, mentions of infanticide, mentions of possible sexual assault, mental breakdowns, panic attacks and religious fanaticism.

I

SAIDEN

SAIDEN COULD NOT REMEMBER WHAT IT FELT LIKE TO BE FREE OF GRIEF. To not have the shadow of death walking only steps behind her. Her hands became more blood stained with every life she took. If she could see the aftermath now, she knew her hands would be dark as blackest night.

Inside, she felt hollow. The sense of purpose she had started to build, now crushed by the blades she carried at the base of her spine. Sweat pooled beneath them as the hot sun bore down on her and her mother where they knelt in prayer beside the small grave marker in the legion's cemetery. She ran her fingers over the letters she now knew by heart.

Our beloved general fallen before her time. May she rest forever in Ilona's peaceful embrace.

She tugged at the sleeves of her shirt, pulling them down over the still healing tattoos she had had inked into her skin only yesterday.

On her left hand, the one that would call Ilona, goddess of death, a bright red rose bloomed, the same kind Loralei had carefully tended to in her gardens. Sometimes the sight of it reminded Saiden of blood, and it was a reminder she needed. A reminder of the cost of her decisions.

On the right, on Keir's side, a brilliant lily, the kind only Saiden knew Nakti loved. Something no one else would ever learn from her, because Saiden had killed the woman who had raised her.

Her mother had come with her, not willing to stray too far from her daughter's side. Saiden wondered if Magdalena felt the same way—that if they separated, if Saiden were out of her sight, she would realize it was all a dream. Or a nightmare.

Saiden still wasn't sure which one she was living.

Silent tears slid down her cheeks, cool against the sun kissed warmth of her skin. The newly sprouted grass swallowed them up. Even her grief taken from her before she was ready. She couldn't reconcile all that she had lost with what she had gained—the chance she had to be with her mother. The mother who loved her so much she had been willing to spend the rest of her days rotting in a living crypt of a prison cell below the castle. Yet she yearned for the stern reprimands that had been a constant all these years since she had last been with her parents.

Saiden rested her hands against the hot stone, bowing down so her forehead rested against them. The first day she had visited Nakti, she had burned the skin on her forehead, a band of blisters marking her, a visible sign of the pain that tightened her stomach. But her mother had seen them, and she had cried, holding Saiden to her chest until she agreed to see a healer. She tried now to hide her pain better, to keep the burning confined to her palms, where only Mozare would see when he forced her to use healing balm each night before sleep.

She wondered if her mother could tell from her spot behind her, how much it hurt to have Magdalena in her life again at the same time as she was mourning the woman who had raised her. As she was also hiding the grief she felt for failing Loralei. Could her mother hear the same screams that bore through her mind whenever she was silent?

Saiden stood, turning the corner to find the small stone she had buried, hidden from the normal path through the cemetery. Loralei's death had not been given the same honor as Nakti's. There was no headstone for her to weep over. She didn't know that it was what she was missing in order to grieve, until her mother had placed the uneven stone into her palm, and wrapped Saiden's hand in both of her frail, bony ones. She had cried again, and they had come to the cemetery together to honor a fallen queen.

Her mother came up behind her, footsteps quiet, though the creak of unused bones could still be heard if Saiden listened closely enough.

She placed one hand against her back, not rushing, just letting Saiden know she was there.

Saiden said her last prayer, bowing over to touch her forehead to the small stone that was the only proof Loralei had lived. Then she wiped her tears with the cuff of her long-sleeved shirt and standing, turned to her mother with a sad smile on her face.

"Little Maus," Magdalena said, reaching her other hand up to cup her daughter's face.

Saiden flinched, though she tried hard to keep it from Magdalena's notice. Too much of her was still waiting for the other shoe to fall, waiting for her punishment to find her hidden here with everything she could ever want. "I think your friend is waiting for you."

She was right, of course. Saiden had known that Mozare had been there for the past few minutes, silently waiting at the top of the hill for her to be finished. A guard at his post once more, always watching her back. Despite the fact they were meant to be safe now. That they had supposedly brought a better life to the people of Kaizia.

She stuck out her arm, waiting for her mother to tuck her hand into the crook of her elbow so they could walk back to the castle. They had all been given rooms there, presumably so they were never too far if Revon wanted them. She didn't care about his reasons, only that she had her loved ones close, where she could protect them from the punishment that would eventually come for her.

Mozare smiled down at them, rushing over to offer Magdalena another arm.

Saiden worried that his smile didn't quite reach his eyes anymore, but she didn't push it. She wasn't sure she could bear another person's pain when she was already drowning in her own.

He nodded at her. "Saiden, Mama Maggie," Mozare had taken to using the nickname not long after their reunion during the coup, and it made her mother smile whenever he used it. Mozare turned to speak directly with her mother, "Revon planned another session for you with the healers, he wants to make sure we get you back into perfect health."

Her mother made a small sound in the back of her throat. It had been a fight to get her to attend the healing sessions at all, but Saiden could see how color was coming back to her mother's cheeks, how her arms weren't so thin anymore. There was strength in her grip that hadn't been there the first time they had embraced since Saiden was a child.

"He needs us to look over some troops, make sure everything is still falling back in order after…" He paused, and the weight of it sank onto her shoulders. "Everything that's happened in the past few weeks." The death permeating the cemetery pushed its way back into her heart, the heaviness pulling at her from every direction. Mozare knew that her mother didn't like being far away from Saiden, so letting her know that they'd be tending to their own responsibilities while she went to her healing session was smart.

"Besides, I heard Cassimir was going to be at the session," Mozare added.

Her mother smiled at that. She had taken an instant liking to the foreign ambassador, which made everyone smile. There was an extra pep in her step as they made their way back to the palace, escorting her to the healers.

2
MOZARE

MOZARE STOOD WITH SAIDEN AT THE TOP OF ANOTHER HILL, OVERLOOKING the lines of soldiers that stood in the palace courtyard. Other higher-ranking members of Revon's newly reorganized military walked through the lines, pushing at stray boots or criticizing a sloppy uniform. They were men and women Mozare knew from the early days of their rebellion. Revon hadn't made time to officially appoint any of them as new generals to make up for the three who had died raiding the barracks, so Saiden and he were the only soldiers truly in his close confidence.

Revon much preferred they be his eyes, Saiden's tattoos a stark warning to everyone who would oppose him. Mozare wasn't even sure how Revon had become privy to that knowledge, a secret he would've taken to his grave. He knew that she blamed him for Revon using her that way, but he was just as angry that Revon knew and was using Saiden's vulnerability against her.

He was worried that there was more to it than what he could see.

Now that he was king, Revon had taken to privacy more than he ever had before. There were no more public speeches, no more demonstrations of his gifts, bolstered by Mozare's own strength. Revon wasn't a man who liked to rule from the shadows. At least he hadn't been before and the change unsettled Mozare.

It was almost worse when he did make a demonstration, using Saiden to make a point to anyone who dared defy him. Mozare's blood burned at the thought of her standing on that podium on full display, once again a threat she didn't want to be.

They marched down the hill, keeping to the shadows, always listening for any sign that the people were rising against Revon. The king was paranoid now that he had committed a successful coup, worried that their success would be copied. His only claim to the throne had been bought with blood. It could be undone by it, too.

He thought he had known what he was doing when he had turned against his country, but he was stuck now at another precipice, torn between what was right and what was his duty. He looked at Saiden next to him, at the small scrap of bloodied fabric she had taken to braiding into the base of one of her buns. The embroidered flower, now so stained by blood its original colors would not be remembered.

But *he* remembered what the dress had looked like, and the girl who had worn it. He remembered what it felt like to watch her bleed and to have to keep Saiden from reaching out to her. He remembered the fear he had felt that if his partner stepped too far, she could be next.

They reached the bottom of the hill. The gathered soldiers didn't speak, so Mozare relied on what their faces were saying, on the fear or joy or pride that pushed its way across their expressions. He smiled at Rhena, the only one in the yard to have noticed that he and Saiden had joined their ranks. She was clever and that only worried him more. Revon wouldn't tolerate cleverness in his ranks, would never be able to see it as anything more than a threat to his new throne.

Revon had moved all the gifted soldiers to the palace. The palace guards still left alive had been moved elsewhere, although Mozare was unsure of the specifics. Hopefully, they were in the barracks themselves, and time and distance would heal the wounds left on their bodies and minds.

He could only hope the same would be true for himself.

Mozare tripped, something that ordinarily would've shocked him, but the lack of sleep over the past few weeks had made coordination more of a struggle than usual. He turned the trip into a roll, standing up and grabbing one of the soldiers by the shoulder, pressing a blade to his neck. The others in line around them moved back, reaching for the weapons they were all starting to acquire.

"What do you do now?" He asked, voice steady despite the yawn building in his throat. He watched them move aside, whispering to each other, panic flying across their faces. Rhena pushed through the crowd, always ready. They had trained her well.

"Your leg is vulnerable," she said. She was the only soldier he was certain was not carrying a blade. Saiden had promised to give her a one when she had earned it, and Rhena had stuck to that standard despite change of leadership. "So is your hand."

He smiled and released the boy, who quickly returned to the comfort of his friends, fingers searching his neck for any sign of blood. Mozare had been careful, despite his shaking hands, to keep the blade a safe enough distance, so he knew the soldier would be fine once the shock wore off. Those higher-ranking soldiers started yelling orders, unsure of how to deal with the interruption and their own lack of say in the disruption. Rhena bumped his shoulder as she walked past to rejoin her line, adopting the habit from him and Saiden.

Saiden had a funny look on her face as he walked back over to her. "You totally almost fell," she said, and he realized that her expression was barely contained laughter. It faded all too quickly. "Still not sleeping?'

"You know me," he said, turning and leaving the young soldiers behind him. "I'll sleep when I'm dead."

"Which will be soon if you keep acting like nothing hurts you."

"And then, I'll come back to haunt you. Can't let your days be too peaceful now."

He knocked into her again, ready to make their way back to the palace, when they heard something out of the ordinary. There was rustling in the trees on the path to town, footsteps and the sounds of people trying to be quiet.

He pulled his axe free from its sheath, stepping forward and trusting that Saiden had his back. It felt good to fall back into the normal routine, into something certain. He pulled his shadows down around them as soon as they had stepped through the tree line, keeping them hidden from sight and bending them to help cover the sound of their own footsteps.

They didn't have to search for long when they found two men hiding in the undergrowth, weapons strapped everywhere he could see. He was sure that they had quite a few weapons he couldn't see as well. They wore old, ripped military uniforms. Under Revon's orders the old black and white uniforms of the chosen queen's army had been replaced with new plain black gear.

The smaller of the two men grabbed for the handle of a short sword where it rested over his shoulder, pushing himself from the ground and aiming the pointed tip at Saiden. She stepped to the side, body moving to avoid the worst of the damage as she reached for the longer of her kindjal blades. He didn't realize she hadn't already pulled them.

Mozare couldn't watch, didn't have time to help her, as the second soldier pulled free his own weapon, a crude twist of blades that he knew would hurt. He pushed himself forward, not giving his opponent time to think, to go on the offensive. He swung his axes in wide arcs, keeping the rebel distracted from his friend. He only needed long enough for Saiden to sneak around and knock him out.

He would kill this man if he had to, he thought, which startled him just enough that he was pushed back, slamming into the rough bark of a tree. Mozare used the handles of his blades to catch the rough metal of the weapon just before it completely impaled him. He strained to push against the soldier, who was solid through the shoulders. Mozare didn't have the advantage of the upper ground, so had had to deal with the weight of his opponent bearing down on him.

Then the burden was gone, and he was pushing himself forward, collapsing on the ground and taking a deep breath. His arms ached, though it was better than the emptiness he had felt only moments before.

"You really need to get better sleep, Moze," Saiden said, reaching down a hand to help him back to his feet. "You should have been able to take him with no issues."

She was right, but he knew it wouldn't matter. Words were not going to keep his nightmares away.

3
SAIDEN

Saiden and Mozare brought the prisoners to Revon, who barely uttered three words before sending them to jail, so she and Mozare were free to meet up with Magdalena for lunch. Normally Saiden liked to have these meals alone, but she figured that she wasn't the only one who could use a little bit of her mother's contagious peace today.

She was more worried about Mozare than she had ever been in the past. Deep bags had taken up permanent residence under his eyes, and his hands shook whenever they weren't firmly fisted at his sides. The few times she had tried to bring it up he had dismissed her, claiming that it was only a few nights of sleeplessness. As soon as he got used to the palace pillows, he would be fine.

But they had been at the palace for weeks now, and he was definitely not fine.

When he went to leave her at the door to her mother's suite, she grabbed his hand, pulling him back to stand next to her and giving it a tight squeeze. She kept her grip until they had been let into the room, when she knew that Mozare would not be able to back out of lunch.

"Hello Little Maus," her mother said, smiling brightly. Cassimir was seated at the table next to her, sitting a lot straighter than the last time she had seen him. He had received a nasty slash to the side during training, and was healing much slower than he should have been. Still, it made her mother happy to have someone to keep her company during her own sessions, and she couldn't help but wonder if perhaps that was why it was taking him so long to make progress.

When they came inside, he tucked a letter under his leg, trying to smooth the worried lines from his face before she could see them. Saiden made a note to ask him about it later.

She smiled at him quickly before turning to kiss her mother's cheeks. She could already see how much of a difference the healers had made today, and it brought a genuine smile to her face.

"I thought Mozare could join us today Mama," she said, the last word coming out more forced than she would have liked. "I think he would like to hear you talk about the butterflies."

"Of course dearest, we'll have a small family meal. Nothing would make me happier." The servants that waited in her mother's rooms jumped into action, bringing small plates of different dishes out for them to share, the last plate piled high with different fruits. Saiden loved that most about living in the castle, there was so much fresh fruit for her to snack on.

Her mother grabbed the spoon, ladling it all out to them as if they were small children, instead of the deadly warriors they were. And when she sat, she watched as her face shifted the way it always seemed to when she was going to tell another story.

"Saiden is so much like her father, strong willed and loyal just like he was. And fiercely loving, though I'm sure she hides it well," she said, reaching over and squeezing Cassimir's wrist conspiratorially. "When Saiden was first born, we weren't sure what to do, we wanted nothing more than to give her a normal life."

"We tried everything to get rid of the marking," she ran a finger down the loose pieces of hair that framed Saiden's face, "but nothing would do. So, we took to hiding her instead. But she was a curious young child, restless just like her father. And she wanted nothing more than to see the outside world."

"Her father and I, we were terrified that someone would find her, so we were forced to keep her inside, though it broke both of us to keep her from something she so desperately wanted."

"One day my husband set out, bag full of jars of all different sizes. I remember how they all clinked against each other with every step he took, the sound like music in our small kitchen. Saiden had desperately wanted to go with him, convinced she would fit in the bag if he only removed all the jars, but we had to refuse her."

"You loved your father more than anything Little Maus," she said, turning to speak directly to her, "and he loved you more than life itself. It tore his heart to see you so upset, so he brought something back for you."

Her mother had already told her this story once, though she felt the same giddy wonderment at the small pieces of her life she had lost in the years since she had stopped being a child.

"Each of his jars held a butterfly, vibrant in color and waiting to be free, just like Saiden. He closed all the windows and one by one he let them go, filling the house with their beautiful colors. You laughed every time one came near you, and when one landed on your nose, you went so still, and there was a peace in you that we had not seen before."

Her mother reached over and squeezed her hand. Lunch was almost over, the warm dishes gone cold as they had listened to her mother. Cassimir and Mozare both stood up from the table, excusing themselves and giving her a moment alone with Magdalena. She had never wanted to be alone with another person before fate had given her mother back, but she found these moments brought her a semblance of serenity. It was a taste of what her life would have been like if she had been born without her curse.

"Your friends want to be there for you little one," her mother said. Saiden loved that she called her little one, despite the fact that Saiden had long since outgrown her small frame. Her father must have been a tall man, because she had certainly not gotten her height from her mother. "You need only to let them in. You are young still, and though you have lived a life harder than most, you should know that the weight of the world isn't yours to hold alone. There are people here who would be happy to share that burden with you."

The words hit Saiden, each one a tiny scratch in the armor she had slowly been rebuilding for herself. The armor that kept her from being hurt the same way she was in that castle hall when death had surrounded her. She was only now realizing that she was truly alone on the other side of her shields.

"Plus that ambassador, he's not too bad on the eyes you know."

The indignant "mama" that left her lips that time felt more natural, and she smiled only because of that.

Cassimir was waiting for her outside the door to the suite she shared with her mother. Blush rose to her cheeks, a sensation so new she almost couldn't believe it was possible. "How much of that did you hear?" The question was out of her mouth before she even had the time to try and play it cool.

Cassimir rested a hand over his chest, "you accuse me of listening to your private conversations? Mistress, truly, you must think so little of me."

She bumped his shoulder as he stood up from against the wall, laughing gently. He might look indignant, but the small smile tugging at the corners of his mouth showed her that he had heard her mother's every word. At least he wasn't as obnoxious as Mozare. A comment like that would have left his ego inflated for months.

"I thought maybe you and I could go for a walk?" He extended an arm to her, but like always, he waited for her to initiate contact. He always gave her a choice. Saiden didn't know if he could truly grasp how much that meant to her with the way everything in her life had changed so quickly.

"Only if you tell me what about that letter had you so worried." She didn't want to use the news against him, and if he pushed back she wouldn't force him to share, but Saiden wanted him to know she was there for him.

"My uncle writes of some unrest in the islands bordering the empire. Technically they are under his control, but they do not want to be there. Fortunately, he has not yet requested my presence, but I feel the day is rapidly coming when I will be forced to return home."

Saiden watched him speak, pain clear on his face. When he offered his arm to her, she didn't hesitate to reach out to him, his answer more than enough to sate her curiosity.

She rested one flowered hand in the crook of his elbow, silently relishing the warmth of his body as he tucked his arm back in close to his chest. The smell of cinnamon that always lingered was mixed with the healing salves from his earlier session.

She secretly loved the way he smelled, and had to stop herself from leaning in closer to him. She had never felt so fluttery with anyone else before, and she wasn't really sure how to behave when inside she felt such chaos.

Luckily, it seemed Cassimir was content to just walk with her. She doubted she would've been able to hold up her side of a conversation when her thoughts were still wound around how he smelled and how being here with him in the open made her feel seen in a way that was safer than anything she had known before.

Then, when the quiet felt like it might make things worse, Saiden asked Cassimir the first question that popped into her head. "Where's your favorite place to go when you are home in your kingdom?"

Cassimir looked at her, and his face split into a smile so bright, Saiden felt like she was looking at the sun itself. "When my sister, my cousins and I were all smaller, we used to get in a lot of trouble exploring places we weren't meant to be." He laughed, and she felt like he was letting her into some kind of personal joke. Warmth bloomed within her, easing the chaos in her chest. This was a feeling she could easily get used to.

She listened intently as he told her about the hall of relics. "Deep inside the main palace of the emperor, there is a room where they store treasures from times past. Most of them from the reign of my ancestors, others from lands and people that the Taezhali rulers absorbed into the empire. Eleni and I would tell stories, imagining the different kinds of lives they lived and where each piece came from."

He almost smiled more when he talked about his sister. They were obviously very close, something that a few weeks ago would have made her insanely jealous. But now the small circle of people she considered to be family had grown, to the point where one day she might even get to meet Cassimir's sister. It was wishful thinking, with all her responsibility to her kingdom, but there had to be a reason Cassimir stayed, even after they no longer desperately needed his aid. And in her secret desires, she hoped that she was the reason.

"Obviously your life here was very different from mine. I can't imagine they keep relics like that in the barracks." He was giving her a chance to share something in return, and the opportunity to choose how vulnerable she wanted to be. The sounds of their footsteps on the marble floors echoed as she tried to decide how much she was willing to share with him.

She figured that he had shared something that made him happy, perhaps she would be able to do the same. She changed the path of their walk, circumnavigating around Loralei's gardens so she wouldn't have to show him how viscerally she reacted to the sight of the flowers now.

"Do you think you are able to ride a horse?" She was already leading them towards the stable, but she could change the path if he didn't think he was up to the jarring experience of getting in the saddle.

"The healers say I am mostly healed. I think a horse would pose very little risk to my health, though it would perhaps be safer if we took one horse."

Her blush returned with a vengeance. She pulled her arm out of his, turning away and pretending to busy herself with getting the saddle. She couldn't understand why this was happening now, with Cassimir, and why she couldn't get the racing of her heart under control.

"You'll have to sit in front though, since you're the one with the injury."

He laughed, but he didn't argue.

Having him in front of her was almost worse than she imagined having him seated behind her would be. At least, seated snuggly behind him, he couldn't see the blush that had taken up permanent residence on her face and was spreading down her neck as well.

She took it slow, worried despite his reassurances that she would somehow re-injure him on their way to the oasis. She left their horse to wander, only briefly wondering if the horse was trained well enough to stay close, or if she would end the afternoon having to chase it down in the woods.

She knelt at the lake and splashed water on her face before she even said a word to Cassimir, hoping the cool water would help lower the heat in her cheeks. She didn't look at him when she spoke.

"This place brings me peace. At one point it was the only thing I had."

She didn't realize Cassimir had come to kneel next to her until she heard him speak. "I am honored that you have shared it with me." He reached over and briefly squeezed her hand. "Perhaps we could go swimming."

Saiden assumed teasing was the best course of action when she couldn't tell if he was being serious. "Do you even know how to swim? I can't imagine there were a lot of opportunities to learn in the desert."

She finally looked at him, and immediately regretted it as he was pulling the loose fabric of his tunic over his head. She quickly looked back to the water.

"One day I will have to take you there, if only to prove you wrong." She heard the smirk in his voice without having to look at him. The water splashed in her face as Cassimir dove into its depths, reappearing with his face only a few inches from Saiden. Only her training kept her from jumping out of her skin.

After the displays Revon had already made of her in his few days as king, Cassimir had already seen most of the tattoos that covered her back and climbed down her arms, so she had no problem peeling the sweat soaked long sleeve shirt off, leaving it in a pile with her boots, pants and the various weapons she kept concealed on her body.

In one graceful move she dove into the water, leaving barely a splash in her wake. The water instantly cooled her, and she was grateful for the relief from Kaizian summer sun. Though she was sure this heat was nothing to Cassimir.

She grabbed his leg from under the water, not realizing until she surfaced how close that put them. She sucked in a deep breath, trying to hide how fast her heart was racing. They both kicked gently in the water, doing their best to stay afloat without hitting the other. She wasn't sure how he managed to pull one hand from the water without disrupting his balance, but he did, tucking the loose strands of her hair behind her ear.

His hand was warm, and without necessarily meaning to, she closed her eyes, leaning her head into that warmth. Impossibly, Cassimir got even closer to her, until she could feel his breath on her cheek.

"How come I didn't get an invitation to come swimming?"

This time as Mozare spoke, she really did jump, putting a few feet of distance between her and Cassimir before turning to face her partner. She had been so absorbed in the sensation of being here with him that she had lost all awareness for their surroundings. She looked at Cassimir, hoping she hadn't hurt him by jumping apart, but there was a smile on his face, and a look in his eyes that suggested he wasn't going to give up that easily.

"Because no one likes you." She teased, trying to keep her voice light.

"You wound me." Mozare was already stripping out of his clothes, pulling all the straps of his harness loose so he could leave his weapons in a matching pile to hers.

In the end, she didn't mind Mozare joining them, as the weight of their responsibility rested on shore, and they could enjoy just being. For a few hours at least.

4
MOZARE

After their lovely impromptu swim, Mozare was still left with a long list of tasks he was responsible to complete for Revon. At the top of the list was inspecting the new troops, something that seemed like a never-ending task these past few weeks.

He was glad that Cassimir had decided to join him, leaving Saiden to her own devices for the afternoon. He didn't feel the same sense of responsibility for the ambassador's wellbeing. Technically he knew Saiden could take care of herself and he didn't *need* to feel responsible for her, but he wasn't going to out grow his protectiveness of her anytime soon. Not when he saw the way Revon tended to watch her.

He felt lighter after listening to Magdalena's story and taking time off for their swim, but his nightmares were never far from mind. Even now, with the sun high in the sky, his demons still danced in the shadows around him.

Cassimir spoke, ignoring the looks from recruits. "You don't look so good my friend," his accent was like rich music.

"I look a lot better than I feel," Mozare replied, doing his best to hide the grimace from his face. Twice in one day he had been called out on his general well-being, which meant it was probably time for him to face it. "At least I haven't been stabbed recently," he teased, resorting to humor as he always did when things got uncomfortable.

A cautious look passed over Cassimir's face, as if he was unsure whether or not he should push the issue. He nudged Mozare and smiled, though it didn't quite light up his face the same way his smiles did when he saw Saiden. "I will have you know I was not stabbed," he said, pulling himself straighter, "just lightly grazed."

"I'm pretty sure your insides were outside for a few moments there."

"Apparently that trainee really did not understand the exercise." Neither of them brought up the other reason why the recruit might have targeted Cassimir in that way. "Your healers will have me back to new in a few days. I doubt even my sister would be able to tell that something has happened, and she tends to be very observant about those kinds of things."

The soldiers were no longer being forced to stand in their long lines. Revon had decided that soldiers needed more than constant training, they needed enrichment to grow the mind as well. Classes were being offered to soldiers in the royal libraries, though not many of the soldiers took that offer seriously. For the most part they returned to their barracks in the afternoon, either for games or to catch up on much needed rest.

Mozare still thought it was valuable to watch them, to see who took the offer seriously and who might be hiding secrets. At one point, he would have done it for Revon, because he believed in the cause, but now, he mostly did it to help assuage his own anxiety.

He needed all the information he could get to keep his friends safe. It was the only thing that mattered to him anymore. Cassimir kept quiet behind him, but as much as they stalked through the hallway, they didn't overhear anything useful.

That meant he was probably missing something. At least that was the spiral going on through his head. It was all he could think about. Missing something that would get one of his friends killed.

When the sun finally set later, and Cassimir had retired to his own bed chamber, Mozare paced the halls restlessly. He knew what he had to look forward to if he turned in, and he was not yet ready to face the horrors that waited for him beyond sleep.

He stopped at his room briefly, only taking enough time to switch the light shirt he had been wearing for one of his heavier black hooded jackets. Shadow bending was something he excelled at, but he knew there was no point in being cocky when he could use his clothing to his own benefit. Especially because he was going to have to sneak out of the castle before he could even start a night patrol.

One of the first orders Revon had put in place after killing Loralei had been a curfew inside the palace. He couldn't stand the idea of someone using the cover of night to slip into his new home without his knowledge, and his meager talents could not help him see in the shadows the way Mozare's could. He was paranoid, even more so than when they could have been considered traitors. Only victory had stood between them and the executioner.

Mozare was starting to worry they had been traitors, the thought making dinner rise in his throat.

Luckily, everything he had done to prepare for their coup had given Mozare the knowledge he needed to get in and out of the castle without anyone knowing. He wasn't sure he would have been able to survive the restless jitters that accompanied his sleepless nights otherwise. It felt almost normal to him, to be sneaking out of bed without telling anyone. He had already been doing so for the better part of two years, and the habit seemed to have stuck with him.

He slipped into the queen's old bedroom. While Revon had already redecorated most of the queen's old rooms, Mozare wasn't sure why he hadn't taken her bedroom as his own. Maybe it haunted him, like it did Mozare or maybe Revon had decided that they were useless to him. Either way he had left it to gather dust. The carpet was stained a rust color, the puddle of blood that had spread from Cara as she lay dying. He felt his chest tighten, and he reached over to grab the edge of the dresser, still covered in different trinkets and pieces of jewelry.

He forced himself to breathe, counting in and out until the pressure in his lungs released and he could see straight again.

He couldn't risk his own panic here, not when the rest of the rooms Revon had claimed as his own were so close by.

He wondered briefly why Loralei had owned so much jewelry, when he had hardly ever noticed her wearing any of the more extravagant pieces in her collection. And why Revon hadn't taken some of it, if only to sell. Without truly understanding why, he picked up one of the stones, a small purple one, and slipped it into the inside pocket of his jacket. He stepped over the reminder of death that had settled in the room, and opened the back entrance Revon had used to gain access in the first place. He had been surprised that those secret tunnels hadn't been boarded up, but their secrecy seemed to have put them low on the list of Revon's priorities, which was an issue Mozare had no plans to rectify.

There were so many things that no longer made sense to him, but at least this one had its benefits.

He slipped through, his feet silent in case there were any soldiers sleeping outside the tunnels he walked through. He couldn't afford to wake anyone who might get suspicious about footsteps in the palace walls.

When he was free, when he could breathe the cool night air of Kaizia and see the swirling midnight skies where they peeked through the trees, he felt the pressure in his chest relax, the grip of his own anxiety letting go for the night. Despite the fact that he was potentially putting himself in danger, he felt much more comfortable on the streets with a weapon in his hand.

He went back towards the woods, curiosity teasing him to understand what made those soldiers abandon their posts, and what made them think hiding in the woods outside the palace fully armed was a smart choice. Despite the previous leadership, he doubted there were soldiers in the Queen's army who would be that unnecessarily foolish.

He cloaked himself in shadows as he stepped past the wall, hiding from the light of the sentry towers that had been updated in the recent weeks. He doubted they would notice another dark spot against the night, but he crossed his fingers regardless as he ran through their line of sight.

In the woods he was able to release his hold on the shadows, relying on the trees themselves to keep him covered. He traced the broken sticks and rearranged dirt path from where they had dragged the two men to the place where they had been hidden. They'd left an obvious trail dragging the men back for questioning, but it took more of his training to track their path back to their hideout in the woods.

What he found there surprised him. There was a small cottage, likely a hunting outpost if he had to guess. That wasn't anything unusual, many of the residents of the capital survived off what hunters could provide for them. What was surprising was that there were candles lit in every window, the light pushing through the thin curtains. Hunting sheds like these were usually abandoned in the summer, when nights were still warm enough that you could sleep under the stars. He crept around, careful of each step he took, until he could place his ear against the rough wooden wall.

The grain of it scratched his face, but he couldn't be bothered to move away. He could blame it on shaving later if it left a mark. Inside, voices spoke in hushed tones.

"The boys were meant to back already," one of them said, a quiet woman whose voice shook as she spoke.

A gruff man answered her, cutting off any further protest, "they knew what they were getting themselves into." He said. Mozare heard him pause to drink then rest his cup back on the table. "They knew what it would mean to try and regain the country."

Mozare froze, unable to move from the house if he wanted. He wondered if they had sounded like that, paranoid and huddled in their underground bunker. And then he wondered what he was going to have to do to bring them to justice.

5

SAIDEN

Saiden woke up early the next morning, and had a quick breakfast with her mom, who would likely spend the morning tending to the flowers in Loralei's garden. She couldn't bring herself to go out there, not when she knew how much those flowers had meant to the Queen, not when she had a reminder of them permanently tattooed to her right hand.

She did however have another morning ritual, one in which she and Rhena snuck off to the small training room they had set up when Saiden was going to be training the Queen, and they fought until both of them were sweating. Rhena was an excellent student and she had taken to her lessons as fast as Saiden had at her age.

Rhena was waiting for her, lacing her boots tight in one of the corners where she had a clear view of the doorway. That was a lesson she had learned the hard way when Saiden had snuck up behind her during one of their first training sessions in the palace. Now she always waited where she had a clear vision of everyone coming and going.

Rhena smiled when she saw Saiden, and she returned the smile with equal happiness. She was relieved that she had found Rhena in a time where she had thought Mozare was going to be the only person she let close to her. Now she had him, and her mother, and Rhena, and possibly even Cassimir, and she still wasn't entirely sure how she had managed it.

She went to the small lineup of weapons and picked up two pairs of tonfa, testing the weight of each pair, before handing the lighter ones to Rhena. They tended to train with a variety of weapons, she never wanted Rhena to be in a situation she couldn't get herself out of, and she used this practice to give Rhena her best chance. She held the grip of her pair tightly in each hand, keeping one of the staffs out while the other she kept close to her forearm to block incoming strikes.

Rhena mirrored her, favoring the right side for blocking while Saiden tended to favor her left. She waited a second before swinging forward, aiming the heavy wooden staff at Rhena's head. Rhena moved fast, pushing back against the strike, and swiping at Saiden's now exposed ribs. She dodged, pulling her own body to the side, and waiting for another strike to come. Saiden blocked, the loud thud of wood connecting echoing through the room.

They went back and forth switching between offense and defense more times than a normal observer could have kept track of. Saiden wanted to push Rhena to the limit, to see what she would do if she were backed into a corner.

It turned out that the corner worked better for Rhena than Saiden would have thought. She used the advantage to push herself against the wall, spinning over Saiden's head and swiping her feet clean out from underneath her. Saiden hit the floor hard, curling her spine in to protect her head from most of the damage, unwilling to go visit the healers. And then as quickly as she had fallen she was back on her feet, clapping before pulling Rhena into a big hug.

The younger girl stiffened, and Saiden had the delayed realization that this was the first time she had ever initiated contact that wasn't involved in a fight. She squeezed harder, her pride for Rhena overwhelming even her own awkwardness. When Rhena reached around her to squeeze back, she smiled slightly, before she noticed Mozare standing to the side of the hall.

He walked in, slowly clapping between each of his near silent footsteps. "I've been wanting to see that practically forever," he said, clapping Rhena on the back. "And now you get a weapon little sister." Mozare had no siblings of his own, at least not any that he knew of, and Saiden knew he had the same fondness for Rhena that she did. It made her happy that they were able to share that connection with her. And she loved the idea of a little sister, although she had never thought about it before Rhena.

Saiden led both of them out of the training room, to the suite of rooms she shared with her mother. Magdalena smiled at the small parade of mercenaries who walked by where she was having morning tea with Cassimir. Saiden pulled at her sleeves, a blush creeping up her face as she continued to the room where she slept.

Inside, resting sheathed on the small chest of drawers where she kept most of her clothes, was the short sword she had commissioned for this moment. The handle was crafted to look like a flowing river, and there was a stone of the lightest blue at the end. Inscribed down the middle of the blade were the words that she had picked out to guide and protect Rhena whenever she would need to use it.

"So you have finally met your match then?" Cassimir called from the small gathering of people.

"Someone had to beat me eventually," she was careful to keep her voice steady.

"I still want another try," he said, stretching before he flinched as he pulled at the stitches in his side, "once my, as Moze puts it, insides aren't at risk of being outside."

She laughed quietly, went and knelt down in front of Rhena, who copied her and waited to see what Saiden was going to give her. This was a monumental occasion for both of them, Saiden had never imagined having the honor of gifting someone's first weapon. She remembered Nakti, and the small celebration they had held in the back of her office when Saiden had been only 11, and she had been given her kindjal blades.

"May you raise your blade only in the aid of another. May you never draw blood without righteous cause," she paused, Nakti's voice ringing in her ears. She wondered if she could say that she had kept the oath she had made over her own blades, but she tried not to let that worry settle over Rhena's oath now. "And may you live a life where it is drawn very few times."

She pulled the silver blade from its sheath and laid it on Rhena's upturned palms, then she leaned forward and gently kissed the young girl's forehead. She wasn't sure if that had been an actual part of the ceremony, or just a short moment where Nakti had shown her affection for Saiden. Either way her heart swelled, and Rhena smiled proudly at her.

Magdalena put a small flower from the garden in each of their hair, which Saiden was quick to remove and place on the table next to her, hoping she didn't offend her mother in the process. Then she looked at Mozare when she realized that there was no reason for him to have met her at training.

"What is it that you wanted anyway Mozare," she asked unceremoniously. She didn't used to be so blunt with her words, but she found herself feeling more comfortable with these people, and settling into that comfort more with each passing day.

"Oh right," he said, and it wouldn't have been out of place if he had smacked himself in the forehead. "Revon needs both of you," he gestured to her and Cassimir, "he's called an emergency meeting."

6
MOZARE

Mozare took Saiden's ridicule about forgetfulness, but he still felt relieved. Just last night, while they had all been sleeping, he had managed to lure each of the four people who had ended up being inside that cottage away, trapping them and one by one returning them to the palace for questioning. Despite the fact that he had not even gotten into bed that night, and he was even still wearing the same clothes as the day before, he felt better than he had in weeks.

Revon was waiting for them in the hall of wisdom, the room where Loralei had sentenced each of her advisors to hang for crimes they had not even committed. The hatred and agony still hung in the room, though he wasn't sure if anyone else could feel it.

"We're having way too many issues with the counter-revolutionaries." Revon said as way of greeting. He had taken a great liking to the term counter-revolutionary in the past few weeks, turning the light on those who wished to return the country to what it once was and making them seem villainous for it. The three of them were the only ones gathered early, Revon had yet to decide which of his other high ranking soldiers he trusted enough to promote to general.

Mozare noticed as Saiden sat down next to Cassimir that he handed her a mug, steam still billowing over the top. Mozare suppressed the desire to smile at them.

"Although Mozare had no business being out of the palace last night, and I will no doubt have to punish you later for that," Revon interrupted himself, speaking straight to Mozare for a quick moment, "I am glad to have these prisoners in custody. They hold invaluable information about groups gathering to challenge our reign."

It was always our reign, as if they had each been granted a crown and an equal decision in the fate of the country. Cassimir was not even technically a general, though he sat in on these meetings because of his ties to the southern kingdom of Taezhali. They all knew that Revon would get rid of anyone who was the slightest threat to his control over Kaizia. Without hesitation. They had already seen it happen once, a reminder he did not need.

A reminder that sent him from his sleep and had him emptying his stomach more nights than he could count.

"Were you able to learn anything vital since their capture?" He wondered if Saiden asked the question because she could tell that he could not, or because she was desperate to take the attention away from him and the punishment Revon promised.

"Nothing yet. But I have a few of my best men down there with them. It's only a matter of time." Mozare had first-hand knowledge of what it meant to be one of Revon's best men, and he didn't think it was an exaggeration.

"Was there anything else we could be of assistance for?" Cassimir asked, his thick accent cutting through the room. Maybe they were both on his side, or maybe he was reading too much into it, but he appreciated them being there, nonetheless. He hadn't realized before how difficult it was to have Revon's undivided attention, but he was grateful they were there to share it with him.

"There will be a state dinner tonight, you will all need to be in attendance and on your best behavior. We have to present a united front now more than ever. There will be some important lords and ladies there this evening who are getting their first chance to take our measure." The lords and ladies he hadn't already sent them to kill that is, Mozare thought with an almost imperceptible grimace.

"I got you a gift Saiden dear, I believe the palace staff delivered it to your room while you were out and about this morning. You boys should both wear your finest as well." Mozare didn't miss how Revon had singled Saiden out as the recipient of his gift. Or the way her face had paled. Had the dress been in there a few moments ago when they'd all gathered to celebrate Rhena? It was unsettling enough to think that someone had been in their chambers, but to think that none of them had even noticed? He really didn't like that thought.

He knew that Cassimir and Saiden had also picked up on the weirdness of the situation but none of them argued. When they stood he and Cassimir sandwiched Saiden between them as they filed out of the room, his punishment all but forgotten.

Still he didn't like the way he could feel Revon's eyes follow them from the room.

7
SAIDEN

Saiden headed back to her room as late as she possibly could and still be on time for Revon's dinner. She'd unwrapped the package on her bed almost twenty five minutes ago now, but she couldn't bring herself to put the dress on. It was worse than anything Revon had made her wear before, and the idea of having that much skin on display made her itch. She wondered briefly if she might even vomit. She had known the dress was going to reveal her tattoos, the constant reminder Revon gave that she was to fear. But this dress had long slits on the thighs, and there was a crisscross of cut out sections through the abdomen.

She panicked, locking her door before pacing back and forth in the small open space of her bedroom. She was fairly certain her mother was on the other side of the door, trying to ask her what was wrong, but there was cotton in her ears, all the sounds she could normally hear from her room were muted.

When she felt like she could look at the dress again without fainting, she opened the door and let her mother in. Magdalena took one look at her and Saiden realized she must have been as washed out as she thought, because her mother was quick to wrap her in a bear hug.

Despite the height difference, it was amazing how protected she felt in her mother's arms.

She looked at the dress over her mother's shoulders, steeling her nerves to ask for help putting it on. She had to listen to Mozare's advice from weeks ago, to be careful how she pushed back against Revon. As much as he brandished her as a weapon, he was afraid of her too, and she knew it. Mozare knew it too, which was why she had never been left alone with their new leader.

Her mother rested her hand against Saiden's golden tan skin, and she gave herself one last moment of weakness as she leaned into it briefly. "Mama, I am going to need your help spinning this web of a dress, so I don't give it any new holes." She tried to laugh, but the sound was forced. She was glad her mother didn't call her on it, glad that even after all these years her mother's intuition still won out.

She stripped down as her mother laid the garment out fully on Saiden's small mattress. She stood and spun and lifted her arms as her mother said, waiting for her instructions, and doing everything to keep out of her own head. There was no mirror in her bedroom, the space hadn't really allowed for it, and she wasn't normally worried about her appearance. Part of her was relieved, while another part of her wanted to see how ridiculous she must look in the shreds of a gown Revon had picked out for her.

If she had not been marked the way she was, if her scars weren't so much deeper than her skin, she might have enjoyed wearing the dress. The stitching was neat, and the front of the gown was embroidered with red roses. She might have even thought they were pretty if they weren't the same color as the ones Loralei had grown in her garden. The same color as her blood spilling across the palace floor.

It did match her hair however, which her mother carefully pulled free from its braids, pulling and tucking the pieces until they were all behind her head, with only two small tendrils hanging around her face. She was sure she would spend most of the night tucking them behind her ears.

"Are you going to come to dinner Mama?" She asked, turning to look at her mother, while Magdalena dug through the small pile of cosmetics she had brought with her. She didn't know what made her mother think she would need makeup for a state dinner, though she had to admit she also didn't know why the dress was necessary.

"I think I will rest Little Maus, it is far too late in the evening for me to be getting ready for such an affair." She had a gentle smile on her face as she tilted Saiden's head back and ran something cold and wet across her eyelids. She reached up to touch it, only to have her mother gently slap her hand away.

"I want you to listen well my daughter," she said, her voice taking on a much more serious tone than it had in the weeks they had been getting to know each other again. "There are times when you need to take your armor off, to be vulnerable with your friends." She waited, pulling Saiden up from the bed and leading her to the mirror in Magdalena's own suite. "And there are other times where you should use every piece of armor you have. The difficulty is knowing when to let your guard down, and when to carry an extra sword."

She had to admit that her reflection in the mirror looked fierce, despite how vulnerable the dress made her feel. And she took a deep breath, because although her mother wasn't coming with her, she knew that Mozare and Cassimir had her back, that neither of them would let her go through the bad stuff alone.

Saiden met the boys at the formal dining hall, partly relieved that neither of them had come to pick her up. She doubted Mozare, in his anger at Revon for playing his games, would have even let her leave the suite. She knew they were both going to be as uncomfortable as she was, and none of them could do anything about it. At least, beneath the dark skirts of her dress she could still wear her boots. She wasn't sure if she could survive it if Revon tried to make her wear fancier shoes. And the boots had flowers, so at least they matched somewhat.

Cassimir and Mozare were both waiting at the door, Mozare dressed head to toe in black, standing at great contrast to Cassimir, whose Taezhali clothing was embroidered with golden suns and deserts that looked like they reflected the color of the sunset. It was an amazing effect, and she stared for longer than she probably should have. When they noticed her, they both stood up straight, moving off the wall they were leaning against.

Mozare clenched his fists at his side, releasing them and then pulling them tight again as he took in the sight of it. She did her best to stand in a way that reduced the slit up her leg, which reached fairly high up her thigh.

"Let me give you my jacket," Cassimir said, already reaching down to undo the line of buttons.

"You know that won't work out well for any of us." She said, her voice quiet. She waited for them to understand the look on her face. "Just stay by me, otherwise I might stab someone for getting too close." She made it sound like a joke, but she had tucked a dagger into each of her boots, and was prepared to stop anyone who tried to bother her. Cassimir moved to stand next to her, offering her his arm, and she tucked her hand into the warmth of it.

Mozare walked in front of them, no doubt trying to use his own body to shield her from view as they walked through the hall to take their seats near the head of the table. Before Mozare could sit next to Revon, Cassimir took that seat, keeping Mozare and his barely contained rage away from the source of his anger. The two of them took their seats next to her, keeping her guarded on either side.

Revon leaned towards them across the table. "How do you like the dress Saiden? I thought it would be perfect for the occasion."

She moved her hand to gently grab Mozare's thigh, keeping him from jumping across the table and killing the current king. She wasn't sure blood would make this dress any better. "It's beautiful, perfect for the warm weather we're having." She lied, but he must have believed her because he smiled slightly before taking a large sip from his glass. Behind him, taste testers waited for each of the courses to be brought in.

She turned to Mozare, "if you jump across the table and start another coup, I am going to have a really hard time backing you up in this dress." She looked at him until he released his tight grip on the arms of his chair, and sank against its cushioned back.

Cassimir leaned into their conversation, "I'm sure he will leave in a few rounds anyway, he doesn't want to have his face out where anyone can stab it."

"Now children," Revon said, startling them out of their little huddle, "secrets don't make friends."

She plastered a demure smile on her face before turning back around. "We were just checking on Mozare, he wasn't feeling well earlier this afternoon." She was lying again, the politics of their recent lives tainting her morals. She didn't like how easily the lie came to her lips, and she waited for someone to see through her, to see her for the liar she was and to remove her from the room. From the palace where everyone she cared about was. But Revon only nodded and continued his conversation with the man seated to his left.

The first dish they brought out was on a delicate plate, far prettier than food ought to be, and when she bit into the small disk, bursts of citrus and spices that reminded her of Cassimir's cooking danced on her tongue. She finished hers, and then reached over and stole Mozare's since he was still too busy brooding to properly enjoy it. Cassimir smiled as he leaned to whisper in her ear.

"You like it?" She nodded. "I gave the chef my recipe for them this morning."

She knew they reminded her of his cooking. "I think I could eat these for the rest of my life and never get tired of them."

"I picked this recipe specifically because I knew you would like it." He reached up and tucked one of the pieces of hair she had forgotten about behind her ear. "I like what your mother did with your eyes." He leaned closer to her.

"How did you know it was my mother?"

Cassimir winked at her. He didn't have a chance to answer before Mozare was interrupting them.

"You two need to break it up before I lose the rest of my appetite." He pretended to vomit before taking a drink of water.

Cassimir's smile felt like they were conspiring to do something they shouldn't. It was a secretive smile, but one that she still trusted. And despite Mozare's supposed nausea, she felt perfectly at ease between the two of them.

The rest of the dishes passed by in a blur, people talking all around them as they remained in their small group and shut out the rest of them. As the night passed, people left the hall, most of them paired with someone else for the evening. She watched them, looking for anything that might set them apart, that might make them dangerous.

Sometimes she wished she could turn off the part of her brain that was always on high alert, always seeking out an enemy, but it was as much a part of her as her blood red hair. As much as her curse.

None of the courses compared to the first, to the recipe Cassimir had delivered to the chef just for her. To the spices that had danced across her palate. When the main dish had been cleared away, Revon stood from the table and excused himself from the room. Within minutes warm fabric hung over her shoulders coating her in the smell of the sunshine and warm spices. She had to resist the urge to burrow into the fabric, turning to smile at Cassimir instead.

She felt a weight lift off her shoulders. Without the pressure of Revon's gaze always hovering over them, she was able to enjoy the desserts the chef brought out. She felt full, though she still wished for them to bring her another.

When the sun had long since passed the horizon, and there were very few people still up, Cassimir and Mozare escorted her back to her suite, each leaving her with a gentle kiss on the cheek. She felt loved, and she wanted to share the feeling with her mother, but her lights were off, and she figured her mother must have retired to her bed long before the party was finished. She would tell her about it in the morning, there was no reason for her to rush.

8
SAIDEN

When Saiden woke the next morning, her mother's room was empty, and she assumed she was in the garden already. She had taken the morning to sleep in, since she had given Rhena the day off training, and they had been out so late last night. She went down to the kitchen to get whatever food was laying around for a quick breakfast before going on rounds.

The chefs avoided her in the kitchen, but she was used to people shying away from her, worried about her curse, that she might transfer her bad luck. It didn't bother her this morning.

A soldier slammed the door to the kitchen, startling the kitchen staff and almost getting hit with one of the head chef's wooden spoons. His eyes were wild, his breath coming in heavy puffs.

"You're needed in the main hall general." He said, turning down his eyes as the words rushed out of his mouth. The title still had her looking for Nakti briefly before following the orders. He turned before she even had a chance to reply, running back up the stone steps, his boot thuds making her heart pound heavier with each step he took.

She found Mozare in the halls, breakfast long forgotten, but even he didn't know what had called for such a sudden and rabid summoning. Especially so early after a state dinner.

She froze when she saw her mother, pale faced, her hair bunched in one of Revon's fists. Mozare pulled one of the axes from his back, moving forward while her feet felt cemented to the floor. He stopped as Revon pulled a dagger from the sheath on his thigh.

"What are you doing?" Mozare spoke, echoing the words that she had desperately tried to push out, to force her mouth to form. Her body refused everything she asked of it, waiting for whatever was going to happen next. For whatever nightmare today would bring her.

"You know, I expected that there would be a certain resistance to my rule, people who were still in the dark, who refused to see the truth I was offering them. I was prepared to spill blood, to sacrifice soldiers for this cause, to bring about the kingdom we were meant to have."

He walked around the throne, pacing with Magdalena's hair firmly in his grip.

"I knew that their sacrifice would be honored, that Ilona would bathe them in riches and glory in the next life. But I wanted to preserve as many gifted as possible, so I was searching for a way to give us a benefit, to put us ahead of anyone who might contradict our control."

"You would be surprised to find out that the archives had a very interesting solution to my problem. A curse," he looked at Saiden, and waited for her to react, but she was still frozen, even her face refusing to move. "That could be a blessing."

"There wasn't a lot of information about how I could use that power, buried so deep inside you, dear, that you couldn't feel even a tendril of its strength. But there was one way, one key that would unlock the power that lies dormant in you, for our cause."

Her heartbeat filled the silence, the thud in her ears nearly deafening. Mozare was still between them, still looking for a way to be the hero, to stop whatever Revon had in mind.

"The blood curse is only released if the blood of the last living kin is spilled." His voice fell flat, spilling through the room. Whatever it was lacking, it was enough to release her from her trance, to push her into action. But she was too slow.

Revon pulled her mother against his chest, her back pressed to his. And he swiped the dagger across her neck. Saiden saw her mother reach out to her, the room spinning and her vision dotting as her body hit the floor. She was crying and she was watching Mozare run towards Revon only to be blocked by incoming soldiers.

And she was screaming, her throat already raw with the pure terror that she pushed through. Her body felt strong, and she pushed herself, using the stone steps to propel her body up through the air, flipping over the black and white throne that haunted her. Her brain couldn't think past the need for vengeance. Past the overwhelming desire to free this power growing inside her, past the fire burning through her veins.

Cold metal slapped over her wrists, hands burning where they touched her, the smell of blistered flesh filling her nostrils. She was wild, uncaged despite the chains and the several guards pulling her from the hall. Away from her mother where her body lay dying on the stone steps only feet away from where Saiden had been unable to save Loralei.

Darkness swirled at her fingertips, pooling in the divots of her knuckles, wrapping around her wrists. She could feel their darkness around the cuffs, a gentle caress where the metal had already torn at her skin. Her blood dripped on the floor as she was dragged away. As her body sagged and gave up on her. As she slipped into the blindness of sleep

9
MOZARE

Mozare pushed at the soldiers, hitting those closest to him with the handle of his axe, knocking them unconscious where he could. He needed to get to Revon, needed to make him pay for this. Needed to fix what he had done that lead to this, to make things better. His first instinct had been to run to Saiden's mother, to do whatever he could to get her to a healer, to save her life. But he had seen enough dead bodies to know that there was no saving her now.

Saiden had been swarmed by guards, who had dragged her away to wherever Revon would keep his weapon until he was ready to wield her. Every step away from him was another black spot in his vision. Mozare wouldn't let him keep her for long, no matter who he had to kill to get her freed. Although he hoped there would only be one life to pay the price, he didn't care if others fell getting in his way. Let anyone who tried to stop him pay the same price.

But Revon had shielded himself behind layers of soldiers, all of them heavily armed and prepared to die for their king. He hadn't realized how much of a coward the old man was until today. The sun was shining bright in the hall, despite the darkness he felt burning around him. He needed time. Time to figure out a plan, to get them somewhere safe where Saiden could rest until she was whole again. Until the wounds new and old that scarred her body and soul had time to heal.

He ran, hearing the footsteps of armored men chase him as he turned down corridors, pushing himself to run faster than he ever had before. They were all supposed to be on the same side, but this wasn't what he thought it was going to look like. This wasn't the country he thought he had been fighting for.

He could feel his legs burning, but he knew Saiden would do the same for him if their roles had been reversed, knew she would be smart about it. He was careful to wipe his eyes, pushing away the tears that threatened to block his vision. He would need time to mourn, but he could not afford the disadvantage of tears in the fight that was brewing. He slipped down narrow hallways, remnants of the palace from decades ago, until he could no longer hear the heavy thumping of following footsteps.

Then he let himself breathe, hunched over with his hands on his knees, his heart in his throat. He had thought they were done losing people, done having their small pieces of happiness ripped away from them, but he had been wrong. As long as they remained in Kaizia they would continue to be in danger. He was done with this life, this destiny that had been forced onto him.

INTERLUDE

Saiden woke up for the first time in a world where her mother was truly dead locked inside a room with rotting walls. At least she thought they were rotting. Her brain didn't seem to fully register what she was seeing, and her hands moved of their own accord, at odds with her body.

Every time she tried to move her finger, she found herself reaching for her own throat, bloody nails clawing at the metal that stopped her from taking a deep breath.

The room was cold, but her body was burning with fever or power or madness, she couldn't tell what. Only that lying on the floor with her shirt pulled up to her chest, skin making contact with the damp stone, seemed to ease the heat that threatened to turn her to ash.

She couldn't tell if time passed at all while she was in there. Night and day looked the same through the cracks in the wall where the wallpaper had long since shredded. Saiden wondered if someday she would look just like this room, with cracks that exposed all her secrets to the daylight. If anyone would appreciate what she had been through to get there. If she would ever grow older than she was right then in that cell.

Her mind could barely hold on to a thought, and as soon as she tried to focus on one it was gone, slipping through her fingers like water in a stream. Her fingers, that never seemed to be able to grab anything, even her collar, though blood from her fingernails striped her chest with flaky stains.

She thought she heard voices, but she never recognized them, and no one stayed long enough to check on her. They seemed to ask questions, to demand answers but her mouth, when she remembered that she had one, was unable to form words.

She was only her power, stuck in a body that could not contain it, lost to fates her gods had abandoned her to.

10
MOZARE

REVON BROUGHT SAIDEN OUT THE WAY YOU MIGHT HAVE DISPLAYED A fighting animal at a ring. She had been redressed in a short sleeved, nearly see-through top, Revon once again putting her tattoos on display. Mozare and Cassimir had been ordered to be in the front row, though Mozare wasn't sure if it was meant as a sign of solidarity or a reminder of what happened if they stepped out of line. Part of him knew it had to be a punishment. This is what he got for fighting back, for running away.

He didn't realize that he had taken a step forward, a step towards Saiden and Revon, until Cassimir's hand was around his arm, tugging him quickly back into place. He wasn't sure he would be able to withstand this demonstration if it weren't for the foreign advisor at his side, helping to keep his head on straight.

Aside from the new shirt she was wearing, Saiden also seemed to have acquired some new jewelry in the time they'd been apart. Wrapped tightly around her neck was a thin collar, the shining metal a mix of black and white. Chains were looped into either side of it, connecting to matching manacles, one black and one white on her wrists.

Revon barely had to speak and he was already pissing Mozare off.

"Today is a glorious day my friends." His friends, but never his subjects. Despite the fact that he stood at the front of the crowd, his dais raised so they were all forced to look up at him. Despite the fact that he had never lived like them and didn't care about any of them the way he had always claimed.

Despite the fact that he had turned Mozare's best friend into a monster, Revon still claimed to be their friend.

Mozare was sure that they were no longer friends, no longer even allies, and as soon as he could manage he would get Saiden away from him. He would keep her safe the way she always did for him.

"The gods have blessed our general, and have given her the gifts she needs to protect us." Mozare swore he could see Saiden flinch, but he was so tired, and he so badly wanted a sign that she was still herself, that he couldn't trust his own mind. "Centuries have passed since the last Anointed graced this earth, coming into their gifts without the madness of the curse."

Mozare's hands kept fisting at his side, no matter how consciously he tried to keep them flat against his legs. "This should be seen as a blessing to our reign, and to the prosperity of the kingdom of Kaizia for years to come. The gods have not abandoned us, and they send signs of their forgiveness for years of rulers that turned away from their gifts and teaching."

Not only was he a murderer, but a blasphemer as well. "Let us rejoice together in the glory that is to come."

The crowd around them took that as a sign that they were dismissed and began to fill the hall as they returned to their duties around the palace. Mozare tried to use the crowd as an opportunity, passing by people in an attempt to make it closer to the stage where Revon still stood, Saiden as motionless as a statue beside him.

Cassimir grabbed his elbow again, stopping his progress through the room. He had been so focused on Revon and Saiden that he hadn't even realized he was being followed, which he normally would have recognized within seconds.

He pulled them into a shadowed space, and Mozare struggled against Cassimir's grip. "I need to save her." He hissed through his teeth.

"Just watch." Cassimir lifted one hand towards the dais. Saiden wasn't as still as he had originally thought. She was watching everyone, eyes scanning the crowd with a predatory gaze. Mozare felt his shoulders deflate, his hope bursting out of his chest. "If you try to get to her like this, while she's under his control, she's just going to kill you."

Mozare kept his eyes glued to Saiden's face as she stepped towards a man who had veered too close to the dais, a growl tearing from her mouth that wasn't human. "When she comes back to herself, she will never be able to live with being responsible for your death. She'd never be able to forgive herself."

He liked that Cassimir said when instead of if; he was entirely confident they would be able to bring Saiden back. That she wasn't as far gone as she seemed to be right now.

But Mozare's hope was still missing, as if it had gone for a walk and forgotten its way home. "We can't even get her away from him. And what the hell is that collar?" Mozare's voice was stuck somewhere between rage and the beginning of tears, though he was careful of his volume considering the number of people who still lingered in the hall.

"You don't think that between the two of us we could figure out a plan?" Cassimir's optimism felt so light, but he couldn't bear the thought of agreeing and having things go wrong.

Instead, he just walked away without saying anything, relieved that Cassimir didn't touch him again, otherwise he might break in front of everyone left.

II
MOZARE

A WEEK WENT BY BEFORE THEY WERE CALLED TO ASSEMBLE AGAIN. THE arena was crowded, yet Mozare had no problem getting to the front. The fact that the over eager crowd split so easily to let him through made his stomach uneasy. Cassimir was waiting in the front, his skin unusually pale. Everything about this set his teeth on edge, made his hands itch for a weapon.

Across the stadium, he picked Rhena out in the rows of recruits. The new sword Saiden had just given her was strapped across her back, the detailed hilt peaking over her left shoulder. She looked as terrified as he felt inside.

Saiden was walked out in the middle of a large circle of guards, her new chains jingling slightly with each step. Her hair was in tangles, no sign of her usually neat braids. And her face was blank, as if the body she now inhabited had no memory of who she used to be. He balled his fists at his sides, but his anger was useless here, there were too many people, too many guards for him to even get to her.

In the center of the arena there was a large metal cage. Someone must have set it up in the early hours of the morning, because he was sure there had never been anything like it there before. The guards led

Saiden there, shoving her roughly into the cage without even undoing her chains. The Saiden he knew would have fought back, would never have let guards handle her so. But this version of his best friend just silently stared at the crowd. The collar around her neck and the two thin cuffs at her wrists seemed almost to glow, though he attributed that to his lack of sleep.

From the other side of the arena, a single guard brought in another man. While Saiden didn't look clean, compared to this man she looked pristine. His face and the ripped clothing that barely hung to his body were covered in a dark mixture of dirt and blood.

Mozare had a sinking feeling in his gut as he watched the prisoner limp towards the cage, paraded through the crowd at sword point. A dark part of him almost wished the prisoner would throw himself on the sword, to save himself from what Mozare could now see would be a horrid execution. He doubted Revon would allow it. Even if he couldn't find the man in the crowd, he knew the newly crowned king was watching closely. It wasn't enough to parade Saiden around as a weapon, he was going to give them all a demonstration.

He was going to show them all exactly how much they should fear him.

The other man might have once been strong, but he already looked like the world had beaten him. Then Mozare caught his eye and realized he was one of the men he had encountered in the forest. One of the men he had lured back to the palace for punishment. He had no idea how the man already looked so much smaller, as if the few days he had spent in the dungeon were more like a few years.

When Revon finally showed his face to the crowd, Mozare wasn't surprised to see him walking through, head held high, enjoying the spectacle he was creating of this man's death. If Ilona deserted him now, there would be no one he could blame but himself.

Revon walked into the cage before the prisoner, presenting himself to the crowd as a fearless man. As a man in control of the god's gifts and their vessel. But Mozare knew it was a message for him, that Saiden was no longer his and that Mozare had failed to protect her. He wouldn't fail her again.

The King took a small key from around his throat, one that must've been tucked under his blood red tie. Mozare wanted to choke him with that tie and dye the white half of his split suit red with his blood. But Cassimir had been right before when he said that Mozare couldn't make this a public rescue, and he couldn't approach Saiden with anger. So, he reigned it in, keeping his hands uselessly balled at his sides.

Revon used the small key to release the chains that kept Saiden's cuffs attached to the collar at her neck. For someone who wanted the world to think he was the one in charge, he required a lot of chains to keep Saiden leashed. He didn't remove the cuffs or the collar, so the chains hung from all three pieces of her new accessories as Revon leisurely exited the cage, shoving the prisoner in behind him. At least when Loralei had executed her advisors, she had given them a blessing first. And a quick death. He already knew Revon wouldn't afford this man either of those luxuries.

Revon said only one word. "Kill."

Saiden's reaction was immediate. Energy pulsed out around her, although he wasn't sure if it was hers or if it came from her new gifts. He shuddered at the power he could feel coming from her, despite the barricades that kept them from getting too close to the caged fight.

Cassimir was praying next to him, whispering words in a language Mozare had never heard before, despite intense linguistic training in his legionnaire days.

Calling this a fight was generous. The old man tried to fight against Saiden, but even without her new power he wouldn't have had much of a chance of beating her.

The people around them were screaming, but he couldn't tell if they were enjoying the spectacle or terrified of it. The man tried to fight back, but Saiden was stronger, she was trained, and she had her gifts overpowering her. He reached an arm out to punch, and she grabbed him by the wrist pulling his arm straight and using the forearm of her other arm to swing up underneath his elbow. The man cried out, tear tracks visible through the dirt on his face even from a distance.

Mozare knew that move, had practiced it countless times with Saiden without the force necessary to do damage. Now though, the man's arm hung limp at his side, the bend at his elbow suggesting it had been dislocated. She pulled at the arm again, and he heard the pop of the man's shoulder as it came out from its socket. Saiden stopped just shy of ripping the offending limb straight off.

He couldn't tell what was happening to her. If Saiden even knew what pain she was inflicting on this man, if she could feel the blood that ran down her fingers as she slashed them into his chest. Mozare felt tears on his own cheeks that had nothing to do with pain.

Cassimir's words next to him dulled the screams from the crowd, his voice its own kind of power. "This isn't who you are." His voice was barely above a whisper, and yet inside the cage he saw Saiden hesitate. "Mistress, you are stronger than this." She turned to look at them, finding them without having to search, despite the fact that she had walked into the arena without ever taking her eyes off the cage. "Saiden, you bear the strength of all who came before you. You bear our strength." Somehow Mozare felt included in that statement. He would give Saiden all his strength to see her overcome this darkness. "You have to fight this."

The look on Saiden's face didn't belong there. Even in the most strenuous fight, even against the most horrendous foe, Mozare had never seen rage burn on Saiden's face the way it did now. She looked like a predator, yet at the same time she seemed like trapped prey. Either way she was preparing to bite. She said only one word, "lies" her voice hoarse, before she stepped behind the man, and ripped his head clean from his body.

Mozare had to use his full body to hold Cassimir from jumping the barricades weapons drawn. He had sparred with the ambassador before, but he had never felt this strength behind his efforts. Revon returned to the cage, but Mozare could feel his eyes on them, on their struggle. He heard the key re-lock the chains, and the guard's footsteps as they surrounded the cage opening, waiting to escort the now blood-soaked Saiden back to wherever Revon kept his weapon when he wasn't using her.

Cassimir slumped against him, warm tears soaking the loose fabric of Mozare's formal uniform shirt. He held him there as he cried, as people stared at them as they emptied the arena to resume their responsibilities. He held Cassimir until they were the only ones left, until the man's blood had been cleaned from the floor, and the ragged pace of Cassimir's breathing had once again slowed. Then together they left, and he knew neither of them could stand to see her used that way ever again.

INTERLUDE

Something tugged at Saiden's memories, but it wasn't her name. In the darkness she knew nothing. Not her name, or where she was or what she was doing. She had known those boys, but only for a fleeting moment before the clarity was gone.

Back in the room she only sometimes recognized, her sensation was limited to the cool metal circling her throat and the chains that connected it to her wrists. She turned her hands in front of her, marveling at the small red flakes that fell to the floor when she bent her fingers. She wasn't sure where it had come from.

Power swirled inside her, just beyond her reach, and every time she thought to call it to her, the small bracelets, one black and one white, glowed slightly, another cage to contain her.

Then she couldn't even feel the bracelets, there was no cool metal against her fevered skin. And she couldn't see the water dripping slowly down the walls of the room, staining the wallpaper.

It was at this time that she heard the voices. But she couldn't tell who. She wondered if those boys had tried to reach her again. She thought maybe her mother would place a cool cloth to her forehead and sing the sweet lullabies that brought her back to her childhood.

"She is not a weapon to be wielded by some ungrateful…" the

voice cut off, or her ability to hear it did, she wasn't sure. The woman's voice sounded like lava, all burnt whispers and rage. She liked the way her voice sounded.

But when the man spoke she felt more at peace. "She is ours still, we must put our faith in her now." Then she would swear she could feel phantom fingers in her hair, gently unraveling the tangles from where she didn't realize she was pulling at it.

And then darkness would consume her so completely not even they could find her.

12
MOZARE

Mozare found Rhena waiting for him in his quarters. He had no idea how she had managed to escape her training, or how she had made it past the guards in order to access the room. But those thoughts didn't matter because she was laying in his bed crying so hard her tears had dampened his sheets.

He sat down in front of her and pulled her to him, careful not to hold her too tight. And then, because blurred memories of his childhood suggested it had once comforted him, he started gently rocking her side to side.

She didn't pull away from him when she started speaking. "Saiden would've never done something like that. She's gone. He might as well have just killed her when he killed Maggie." Mozare never thought to even check in with Rhena about Magdalena's death, but the older woman had slowly become an integral part of all their lives, and of course she would miss her. And seeing Saiden like that, when they had been so close, it had devastated him, he could only imagine she felt the same.

But it wasn't time for his feelings. It was time to act the big brother he wanted to be for her. "Saiden isn't gone little sister. Only lost." He felt far too young to be holding her, far too inexperienced to know what to do in this situation.

Rhena's tears quieted a bit, and he worried that he had said the wrong thing. But when she looked up at him, tears silently streaming down her cheek, there was the beginning of hope in her eyes.

"You're going to save her." There wasn't a question in her voice, in the voice that had been trembling just seconds ago. "I'm going to help you."

Mozare flashed back to Cassimir's words. Saiden was unhinged, possibly completely lost to Revon's control, and she didn't know them. If she hurt Rhena, she wouldn't be able to live with herself. If they were even able to get her back to herself.

"You can't little sister. I need you to do something more important." He could feel the shift in her body as he whispered his plan to her. Understood how purpose could dull the worry she still felt for the small family they had carved out for themselves.

"Do you think you can manage that?" He asked her.

Rhena didn't speak, just nodded her head, and then silently slipped from his room.

Later Rhena was waiting for him outside the training rooms, her eyes still swollen from tears. Behind the sadness there was a resolve that only he could see because he was the only one who knew to look for it.

"You are sure that you can handle this. I don't know if I will be able to come back for you once we have Saiden." He hated the idea of leaving her behind, but he had to be honest with her when he was asking her to put herself in danger.

"No one will suspect me if you tie me up and leave me behind." She suggested. He was somewhat proud of her, at the same time as the thought made him nearly sick to his stomach. It reminded him of beating Saiden up to send her back to the palace. He nodded, and they started moving through the halls.

Mozare made a show of being louder than normal, but not so loud as to draw suspicion. He only wanted to make sure that the other soldiers placed on guard shifts around the palace heard him talking about training sessions and going on with his life as if nothing were out of the ordinary.

He led the way to a small training room Saiden had created for Loralei, the space where she had been rigorously training Rhena in between her regular recruit duties. Where just a few days ago Rhena had earned her first blade the same way he and Saiden both had.

That life felt like it belonged to someone else now.

They were quiet when they entered the hall, as if the doorway had been some kind of switch and their ability to make noise had been turned off.

Mozare went to the wall to get rope. There was no use prolonging the inevitable when they both knew what was going to happen.

"You're going to have to hit me you know." The words hit him like a punch to the stomach, and then suddenly he was laughing. Rhena just stood at the opposite end of the hall, staring at him as if he had grown another head. "I may be a recruit and all, but I'm still top of my class."

He shook his head at her misunderstanding. "You sound just like Saiden. She said the same thing to me when we were sending her back to the palace." The nostalgia felt heavy, but he was willing to bear the burden if only to prevent himself from forgetting what they were fighting for.

"She must be rubbing off on me." Rhena said with a too casual shrug of her shoulders, but Mozare could see how much the words meant to her. "Now hit me and tie me up already."

Mozare gave Rhena a quick salute. When she braced herself, he took one solid swing at her face, avoiding her eyes and her nose, using just enough force to bruise.

Mozare was surprised by the variety of curse words that flew from Rhena's mouth, something she must've been picking up from barracks life. He winced, and apologized, but she just shrugged him off, holding her hands out to him so he would do what he needed to.

When Rhena was tied up and gagged, he pressed a small kiss to her forehead and then headed into the tunnels, looking for a way to Cassimir's room.

Cassimir must've heard the door hissing open, because he greeted Mozare with a sharpened chakra blade to the throat. Mozare hated to admit it, but he felt almost jealous of the way tears still slid down Cassimir's desert golden skin, a contrast to the fierceness of his blade.

Cassimir removed the blade once his brain processed that Mozare had been the one to come into his room from a seemingly invisible hole in the wall. "I have a plan." He had been up all night trying to reason with himself, thinking through every possible thing that could go wrong, every misstep, and finding a solution until he was almost positive his plan was airtight.

Cassimir took a moment of time to collect his thoughts, absorbing the information before he was whirling into action. He grabbed a bag, stuffing it with clothes and other odds and ends from his small bedroom.

"Lead the way." He motioned at Mozare; his voice steady despite the obvious emotion on his face.

He pushed into the hidden passageway, deciding on the best spot to start looking for Saiden. Unlike in the underground bunker, he wasn't sure where all of Revon's hiding places were. He let instincts guide him through the dark tunnels, pushing at the shadows to tell him their secrets.

They lead him to a smaller door, one through which both of them had to duck to get into the room beyond. Saiden was in the far corner, bloodied wrists still held in chains, her hair free of its braids and matted at her neck. Her eyes were wild, roving back and forth in the dirty shadowed room. His heart bled. He didn't know how to get her out of the chains, how to free her from this prison cell.

What she might do to them when they freed her.

Cassimir had been so unbelievably right when he had warned Mozare about Saiden earlier, about how different she was now, and how she would be capable of things in this state that she would regret later.

He was frozen in horror, in fear. He never thought he would be afraid of Saiden. He had already put his trust in her a long time ago, until Revon had ripped her humanity away.

Cassimir put a steady hand on his shoulder, then walked past him, his steps slow and quiet. Approaching Saiden the way you would approach a caged animal. He pulled two thin pieces of metal from a pocket on the inside of his wrap.

He knelt before her, and she watched him, leaning into the empty hand that Cassimir pressed to her face before reaching for one of her injured wrists. Whatever it was that was blooming between them seemed to still be able to reach her, just like Cassimir's voice had interrupted her rampage in the arena. He brought her peace, even if it was fleeting.

He slipped the lock picks in, and had the chains free in a matter of seconds. Saiden stood, snarling, stepping towards them. And then she fell, her entire body sagging, stopped from hitting the ground by Cassimir's quick reflexes.

They carried her through the tunnels, and waited for it to be dark enough for them to smuggle her outside. To find some way to get them to safety. When there were no more cracks of light sifting through the old stone walls, they pushed through the doors, once again fugitives in their own country. He heard the alarm start ringing through the city and cursed under his breath. There was no going back. He prayed for the safety of his little sister, as he pushed them to move faster through the edges of the city.

In the end, they had to steal a cart, since Saiden still hadn't woken, and there was no way they could get through the city street carrying an unconscious soldier. He kept looking behind them, waiting for legionnaires to start flooding the street, for people to start hunting for them. They needed to be far away before that happened.

INTERLUDE

All Saiden could feel was heat, burning in her veins, tightening her skin around her bones until it became a cage. She was trapped inside her own body, her mind a foreign entity, her every thought and movement a traitor to who she was. She wanted water, needed something to drink to settle the coal spitting sparks in the deepest part of her belly.

Every once in a while, from wherever her body had sent her to protect herself, she could feel cool hands press against her temples, fingers reaching to check her pulse at her throat. She wanted to tell them, "I'm here", or "I'm alive", but the fire ate every word before she could push them through her chapped lips.

In her mind, she was forced to relive memories, some that she had long forgotten, and others that had been constant reminders of everything she had fought not to be.

She remembered the first life she had taken. She had been only eleven. She was on a patrol with Nakti and a few of the older recruits when their group had been attacked. She hadn't even thought about it, she had just stepped into the fight to protect one of the older boys who had been frozen by the sounds of clashing weapons. She had pulled one of the daggers from his belt, and stabbed the attacker, and his blood had stained the sleeves of her tunic.

She had cried for days after that trip, until Nakti had found her curled up in the back of one of the stables and coaxed her to go for a ride. She had seen the leaves, studied the trees and decided on her tattoos, each meant to honor a fallen life.

She remembered the first time a villager had spit at her feet. He had seen her as a smaller child, huddled beneath Nakti's cloak. Had seen the shocking red of her untucked curls and had cursed her life to anyone who would listen. She had not understood his cruel words then, only that the General had moved to stand between her and the man, weapon unsheathed and back taut.

She remembered the little cottage that she had lived in before her life in the legion. The floor was packed dirt, cool under her often-bare-foot feet. Laughter filled her ears, and the smell of baking bread filled the one room that had been her whole life. Her father came home, and she had jumped at his feet until he scooped her up in his arms, leaning over and smooshing her between him and her mother as he leaned down to kiss her forehead.

Magdalena was humming a quiet song as she mended his clothes in a seat close to the fireplace. She could hear it ringing in her ears, but she couldn't remember the words. The fire in the house grew stifling hot, burying the memory before she had a chance to grab onto it.

She remembered the day Mozare had arrived at the legion, all skin and bones and big gap-toothed smiles. She was there when the new recruits were presented to Nakti. Though she was younger than most of them, she was a feared member of the legion. In the fog of her mind, she wondered if this had been a way for Nakti to try and protect Saiden, to make the others fear her so they wouldn't hurt her. But she also remembered how much she had longed for a friend.

When Mozare had found her alone in the hallway later that evening, she had carefully placed a hand within reach of the dagger at her waist, an easier weapon than the blades she had recently earned that were strapped in the new sheath at the hollow of her spine. But he didn't try to hurt her. He only smiled, one of his front teeth still hadn't grown back in yet. And she had felt oddly at ease, though she hadn't moved her hand from the dagger.

Later, when he had sat with her at her solitary dinner table, she had taken a deep breath, savoring the company before warning him away. But he had not left.

She felt the pressure in her chest build. Somewhere ice and cool water fought to overpower the heat burning through her. A cool cloth was pressed to her forehead, the smell of cinnamon and citrus filling her nostrils.

Her thoughts were consumed by Cassimir then, of long nights in the kitchen when she had listened to stories of his childhood, and his love for his younger sister Eleni. When he had practiced cooking different dishes from the regions of Kaizia, and she had sat judge to his experiments. She remembered the worry that had flooded her thoughts when she had heard about the training exercise, and the relief when she had seen him open his eyes again on the too small cot in the new infirmary.

She felt the peace he brought her, and her body slipped into the calm numbness of true exhaustion.

13

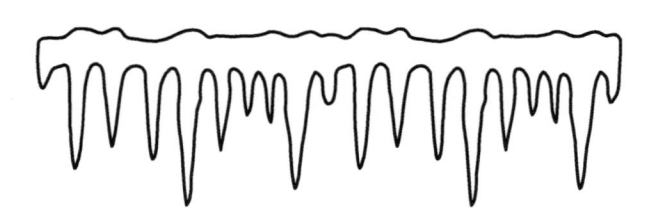

RHENA

Two recruits from Rhena's class eventually found her tied up in the training room where Mozare had left her. She hadn't wanted to yell, she didn't know how much time it would take Mozare to get to Saiden and get her out, and she couldn't risk them getting caught. So when she heard the footsteps heading in her direction, she did the first thing she could think of, and pretended to be unconscious.

A gentle hand touched her shoulder and she wanted to break into tears. She didn't think they were going to end up being able to come back for her. At least the tears weren't out of character for the story she was going with.

Neither was the cold that filled the room around her as she pretended to startle awake.

"What happened?"

"We were hoping you could tell us." Rhena tried to look confused, but without overdoing it. She wasn't sure how to react, and she couldn't risk giving anything away. There was no one left in the palace that she trusted, not even her fellow recruits.

She hadn't picked up on Mozare and Saiden being rebels before, she wouldn't trust anything her eyes showed her now. It wasn't a risk worth taking.

One of the recruits pulled a small blade from his belt and made quick work on the rope tying her up. Rhena just hoped he didn't notice that they weren't tied very tight.

The girl who first touched her ran a finger over her cheek. "I'm not very good at this yet, but I can take down some of the swelling."

Rhena could feel the power pressing under her skin, but she also understood that she wasn't a trained healer yet. Still, it felt better to be able to breathe fully again, so she appreciated the difference.

"Do you know who did this to you?" The boy asked, leaning back so he was perching on his ankles.

"It was Mozare." The shake to her voice was fake, but they didn't seem to notice. The two of them looked at each other, and she couldn't tell what passed between them, but it didn't matter much. The two were clearly in each other's confidence, and there was no including Rhena in it.

"You should go see a trained healer." The girl said. "We'll make the report for you."

Rhena nodded, looking dizzy as she stood. The numbness in her legs that made her stumble a bit wasn't faked.

She raced back to her room as fast as she could, and only once she was alone did she really let it settle in. Rhena was stuck here, and she wasn't exactly sure how she was going to survive it.

14

MOZARE

Mozare watched Cassimir fuss over Saiden, using the collected river water to wet one of his spare shirts before pressing it to her forehead. He was tender and gentle, the kind of person Mozare wondered if he would have been in a life where he couldn't call the shadows of death. Where his parents hadn't given him up without a single look back. Where he wasn't burdened with the same nightmare night after night.

He pushed the horses forward, turning away from what suddenly felt like a private moment. He didn't know when exactly Cassimir had made it into their inner circle, but he had thought of the southern ambassador first when he needed help rescuing Saiden. It had been just him and Saiden against the world for so long, it was nice to have someone else they could rely on. Although the knowledge of how he proved his loyalty was something Mozare could have lived without.

"She has settled." Cassimir said, coming to sit beside him at the front of the cart. "The fever seems to be subsiding slightly, though I am worried about whatever might be causing it. She has no physical injuries, no infections, so it can only be her mind, at war with itself."

Mozare thought over the words. He didn't know what his friend was going through, but he hoped there was a way for her to come out of this fight victorious. He hoped that whatever she was battling, she was strong enough to do it on her own. He could take on her enemies when they came at her swords raised, but not when they were trapped within her own mind.

"She would not want you to blame yourself." Cassimir added, looking at him in the dark of the woods. He had given up trying to hide what he was feeling, he just didn't have the energy to care. Not about being vulnerable, not about the tears silently streaming down his face since they had reached the deep cover of the trees.

"I doubt she would want to be completely delirious in the back of a cart as we run away from the only country either of us have ever known. With no direction or plan." Saiden always had a plan for everything, and he felt lost without her guidance.

"I will bring you to my country," his words left no room for argument, so Mozare did not bother arguing. He doubted even the sandy deserts of Taezhali would keep them safe once Revon started searching for his weapon. "My uncle will shelter you both. To ride against you would be an open declaration of war on the empire."

His words, though confident, did little to fill the hollow that was growing in Mozare's chest. He didn't know what Saiden would do if she woke up in a foreign country. He didn't even know if she realized that her mother was truly dead now, her body long since gone cold, and her blood staining the steps not far from where Loralei's blood had been spilled.

He pulled tight on the reins at the sound of tree limbs snapping in the woods beyond their cart. He could see in the dark, his shadows helped him discern shapes and figures in their cover, but Cassimir could not, and so they had compromised by lighting a single lantern in the back so he could tend to Saiden. He reached for it, bringing the light forward so he could look into the woods, his other hand resting on the handle of the ax in his lap.

He saw Cassimir reach for his weapons as well, his body rigid in the seat next to him as they waited, careful not to make a sound. Beside him another branch broke, and he stood in time to see a hand reach out to grab him. Mozare jumped from the cart, trying to keep the raiders focused on him.

He dropped the lantern, and the underbrush caught fire, lighting enough of the woods beyond what even his night vision could see, and revealing at least eight men, all armed and ready for a fight. He pushed towards them, doing his best to keep any of them from reaching the cart where Saiden still rested.

The fact that Cassimir had not moved to his side of the wagon told him that these assailants were not the only ones in their group, and he worried for a moment about how many were out there. When the first one swung at him, he pushed forward, using the side of his axe and his shoulder to knock the man off balance and down the small hill. Two others reached forward, trying to rid him of his weapons or his arms, he wasn't entirely sure. He turned dancing through the woods so that he remained always a step out of reach.

But he knew he couldn't keep this up for long. He had barely eight hours of sleep in the last week, and his body had suffered greatly as a result. His energy levels were low, and his brain wasn't as sharp as it was when he took care of himself. A blade slashed deeply into his arm, blood running from the wound and dripping off his fingertips.

He adjusted his grip, then went on the defense, prepared to die if he had to, to protect Saiden and Cassimir. To give them a chance to get out of there alive.

"Take the wagon. Get her to safety."

He could barely hear Cassimir over the ringing in his ears. "You'll die."

"And you'll live." He yelled, pushing one of the fighters into the other, "that's the point of heroic sacrifice."

He heard a voice then that he hadn't been expecting. "That's why you're an idiot Mozare, a hero gets everyone out." Saiden had risen in the cart, her voice a distant likeness to its normal tone. And without another word, she was on her feet and fighting

INTERLUDE

Saiden wasn't sure exactly what had pulled her from the curse's fevered sleep, but she was awake, and for the moment, whatever powers she had been granted seemed to be cooperating. The woods rang with the sound of fighting, though she couldn't imagine how they were standing against so many fighters.

She shot to her feet; hands empty as she reached behind her for the two blades she always carried. When she found that spot on her back empty as well she paused, then moved to get a weapon from Mozare. She pulled a dagger from his waist, throwing it at the first man she saw and watching as it landed right between his eyes.

The power in her grew hungry, heat burning in her chest. She pushed through the masked fighters, some kind of band of thieves if she had to guess. She didn't know how to harness her powers, though that hardly seemed to matter. Around her, vines grew at a single thought, pushing through the guts of two of the fighters.

She moved faster than she had in any fight before, flipping over the cart and bashing one man's head against the side. She was delirious with the power of her gift, racing from one assailant to the next, killing each of them more violently than the last. She made child's play of them all, despite many of them being bigger than her and armed.

The inside part of her, the part that had not given into the monster in her blood revolted as her hand reached inside a man's chest and came back out bloody, holding his still beating heart. Her conscious slammed into the walls in her mind that kept the reasonable part of her contained. That forced her to watch herself commit these atrocities.

Then the monster was moving too fast, she couldn't even see who she was killing, though she felt each of their lives pull at hers for the briefest moment. She didn't know how, but her body seemed to circle around Mozare and Cassimir, who both watched her now, harbinger of death that she was. She could not tell if their faces were washed with horror, and the monster did not care.

She pushed through the pile of corpses, her brain seeking out one other person, another life she could sense in the depths of the woods, hiding and watching and waiting.

The monster did not kill this woman, only grabbed her by her braided hair and pulled her the rest of the way back to the caravan, no doubt staining her clothes on the blood of her fallen comrades. She deposited her on the ground, the fire in her belly growing so hot she could barely breathe.

When the woman turned to look up at her, the monster in Saiden's skin turned her head, watching them with the curiosity of someone who had encountered something entirely foreign. A girl she knew from a past life who had already passed on to Ilona's embrace. Her last thought before the fire consumed her once more was that perhaps she too had died.

15
RHENA

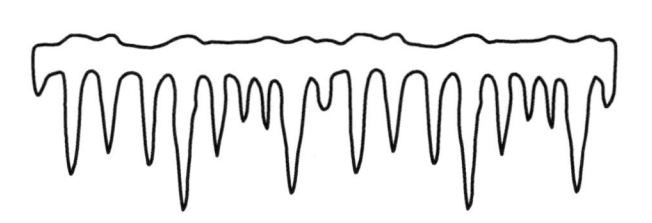

Someone came to pull all the recruits from their beds just before dawn. Rhena was already awake of course, so she was fully dressed, unlike the rest of her comrades who were paraded to the hall in various states of undress, most of them still in pajamas.

Rhena had been expecting this. Between his public showing of the gods blessing their reign, and Saiden's execution of the prisoner, Revon couldn't avoid making an equally public statement about them leaving.

He didn't look nearly as put together as he had when he'd presented Saiden to them as his weapon. His hair was messed up, and Rhena could've sworn something flickered at his feet, before the ocean of soldiers blocked her view.

His hands twitched at his side. If it were Mozare, she would've seen shadows around his fingers, but she was one of the few who knew that Revon's claim to the goddess was too weak. She had her own thoughts on the matter, and none of them were nice.

No one spoke. In a crowd this big, she would have at least expected whispers, but the only noise in the large room was the sound of footsteps as everyone filed in to wait.

"I have terrible news for you my friends. Just after we received a holy blessing to our reign, counter-revolutionaries crept their way into the castle and stole our prize from us." He paused, making sure everyone took his words to heart. "Saiden has been taken from our care, escorted away in the middle of the night. If anyone has any news of her whereabouts, they should report directly to me. Any information will be rewarded."

There was a desperation to his words. He'd unleashed a monster on this world, and now he was worried because he couldn't control her. He couldn't use her. Rhena pushed against her own feelings of relief, making sure there was no possibility of someone in the crowd catching her.

Fear spiked through Rhena at his next words, "I'm not sure where you are darling, but Rhena I expect to see you in my office first."

Rhena did her best to keep the chill that flooded through her from being noticeable by any of the others pressed in tight to her side. Her feelings triggered her powers, Mozare had taught her that much, and she couldn't clue the others into how tumultuous she was feeling inside. Not when it could be the thing that tipped the scales against her.

She felt a pressure against the base of her skull, a comforting hand that soothed the ice building at her fingertips. Rhena felt her breathing steady, and she sent a grateful thought into the universe for whatever force helped to keep her power in check.

The soldiers around her stared, but with her powers under control she no longer had to worry about them catching a glimpse of guilt on her features. She knew how to be composed, how to keep herself steady. She wouldn't be the piece of this puzzle that got her friends hurt.

As the room started to empty, Rhena stood perfectly still, letting the lines of soldiers flow around her. She was the unmovable stone in the hurricane, she would not allow herself to be forced out of the way.

The entire time she could feel Revon's eyes on her, even as he turned and lead the way from the hall. Something, some part of him, was still watching her, a pair of eyes flashing against the darkness in her mind.

She took her first step to follow him, keeping that darkness contained to the corner of her mind so she wouldn't lose track of it. Rhena might not have Mozare's talents for shadows, but she could feel Ilona's gifts being used against her, and she knew exactly how to keep it at arm's length.

Revon's office looked exactly how Rhena expected, but at the same time, somehow different. She didn't know how much of it he had changed from the last reign, but the dark wood suited Revon. It spoke of elegance and control. The scattered papers and stacks of opened books however didn't. It was a peek inside the messiness of his head, and the chaos he was trying so desperately to hide.

Rhena ran through her own thoughts, making sure she didn't leave him any clues to her own chaos. "You wanted to see me my king."

"No need for formalities here my dear. Please sit." He waved a hand to one of the chairs, both covered with their own piles of papers he didn't seem to acknowledge. Rhena gingerly lifted one pile, depositing it into the next chair and took her seat.

"I wanted to see how you were doing child, since I know how close you are to the traitors." Rhena didn't let her face move even a bit. "With everything that's happened lately I knew you must be in agony. Though you hide it well of course."

He turned away from his papers, and glared at her, something hidden just underneath his gaze. He didn't trust her, and she wasn't here because he wanted to check on her. She was here so he could test her allegiance. Rhena was suddenly glad she hadn't gone to see a healer.

She let her voice tremble, "Mozare hit me. He made me think he was my friend, but he left me tied up." She broke off in the middle of her sentence, like she was too overcome with emotion to keep going. Even with her eyes downcast in her pretend sadness, she kept her peripheral vision trained to Revon's face, to his reaction.

They were stuck at a stalemate, each of them waiting to see if the other would cave first.

"I couldn't expect you to put up a fight against him." His words were meant to sound caring, but she felt his disappointment, though she wasn't entirely convinced she was the cause of it all. "You've only been with us for a few months and Mozare is one of the best." She was surprised Revon used his name this time. "Clearly he did quite a number on you. But I trust you."

Rhena nodded her head, like that was exactly what she had hoped and worried she wouldn't get from him. He came round the table separating them and placed a hand on her shoulder. "If they reach out to you, come to me. I can keep you safe."

She let a single tear roll down her cheek bolstered by powers she was still figuring out. She just hoped his mind wouldn't react to the rise in hers. "Thank you."

He let her leave his office, but that trace of his power, those eyes watching her, they never quite went away.

16
MOZARE

Loralei sat in front of them around the small fire Mozare had built. He had no idea what to do with her, why in all her apparent bloodlust, Saiden had been able to recognize the fallen queen and spare her life. He had even less of an idea on what they were supposed to do with her now, so he'd just made camp near the smoldering ruins of the fire he'd set during the fight with Lorelei's raiders. Saiden was sleeping again, curled up on a thin blanket they had grabbed from Cassimir's room, her head resting against one of his legs.

He couldn't manage to tear his eyes away from Loralei as he wrapped the ripped strips of his own tunic around the deep slash in his bicep.

"I could heal that for you, you know," the traitor queen spoke. The sweetness of her voice did little to hide the venom behind it. "That is the reason you wanted me dead after all. My gifts are an abomination, much like your little friend."

He gritted his teeth, "don't talk about her."

"You don't get to give me orders shadow boy." She spit at the fire, the embers hissing. "No one gets to give me orders anymore."

"You're lucky I don't kill you now and get it over with."

"I'd like to see you try." She snarled, inching towards him.

Cassimir interrupted their fight, and he realized that Loralei had not been the only one to inch forward.

"Both of you stop. We have had enough fighting for one night. Call an armistice or a temporary ceasefire or whatever you want to call it. We need rest, you can kill each other in the morning."

Loralei huffed, but surprisingly she followed Cassimir's advice, turning her back to the fire and resting her head on her folded hands.

"I'll take the first watch." Mozare said, "there's no knowing what else might be lurking in the woods. What other creatures of the night might decide to make us its next target."

Cassimir nodded. "Wake me up in a few hours, and I will cover the next watch."

Mozare nodded, but as the hours passed, he did not move to wake Cassimir where he slept, body curling slightly as if he desired to protect Saiden even in sleep. He stared at the dying embers of their hastily lit fire and tried to wrap his head around everything that had happened.

He had both lost someone and gained someone within the span of a few days. Both of their blood had been spilled on the same floor, yet Loralei was here, alive and fighting late night travelers.

He stiffened as he heard light footsteps walk towards him. "You were supposed to wake your friend hours ago idiot." She said, sitting down beside him. He didn't understand why she had moved to his side, when they could not stand each other.

"They need rest."

"Judging by the bags under your eyes, you are in need of rest as well. Sleep, I can keep watch for monsters."

He shook his head, waiting for her to leave, to decide to just use the few extra hours to get her own sleep. But she waited, eyes staring into the same dying fire.

"What happened?" She asked, nodding her head at Saiden. "She was a talented fighter before, but what she just did should've been impossible."

"Beware the secrets of kings," he said. "Your last words have haunted me for weeks. I thought we were getting rid of a line of monarchs that hid secrets and plotted against their people." Loralei flinched next to him. "But I gave power to an even worse demon. He used the information in the files to release her blood curse." Mozare couldn't even bring himself to say Revon's name out loud.

"Magdalena," Loralei whispered. She had been the only other one to have access to the files Revon read, and he knew when he said it that she would know exactly what had happened to release the curse. The silence afterwards hung heavy between them.

"She never gave up on you." He whispered, though he wasn't entirely sure why. "She never stopped fighting to protect you."

He felt as both of their attention shifted to where Saiden slept. "She was meant to protect me, and she betrayed me."

"She felt she had no other choice."

"Choice is the thing that turns us into monsters." She replied, "you will find there is always another way if you look hard enough."

"Saiden only ever wanted to do what is right. She is a good person, if there had been anything that could have been done, she would have stopped at nothing to do it."

"Why are you trying to plead her case to me?" Loralei asked, "You had an equal part in the assassination attempt. In the coup. But you want me to forgive her. Why?"

"Because I am every bit the monster you think I am." He didn't wait for her to answer him, pushing himself off the ground so he could pace around their campsite. As the sun came up, he looked for game. He was surprised to see that Loralei had maintained her spot looking over Saiden, a guard standing at her post once more.

INTERLUDE

Saiden was haunted by the ghosts of her own sins. In the darkness that trapped her inside her mind that was the only explanation that made sense. Or she was dead, and the afterlife was forcing her to face the fact that she had been unable to save the Queen when she had been sworn to do so.

This was her retribution. Her suffering. Her path to atonement. After killing those men, her powers had surged-regaining control of her body, and without the collar, Saiden had even less awareness of what was going on around her.

Her mother's lullabies echoed in the empty space, never once letting up. A constant reminder of the comfort she had lost. Of the mother she would never see again.

She didn't even get to bury her. There would be no stone to mourn over, no prayers for her mother's soul. They would be lost together, torn apart by fate's cruel hands.

Her skin burned, made worse when they touched her. The cool cloths on her forehead were only sending her powers spiraling back into herself. But she couldn't speak, didn't even know whose fingers brushed against her brow, combing the sweat soaked strands away from her face.

The taste of copper coated her tongue, no matter how much they forced her to drink. The lives she had taken, their blood demanding payment. Their souls required recompense, and this was the way they intended to get it.

Lightning cracked behind her eyelids, her whole body trembling as if she'd been struck. She tried to escape its reach but she couldn't move. Couldn't force her limbs to cooperate with her mind.

With the mind that was betraying her every moment it fought against the power inside her. Two forces both too strong to allow the other space. Neither could flourish while they were still at odds.

She spent the entire journey this way, caught somewhere between sleep and waking, far away from any kind of peace. Forced to endure her torment without any reprieve.

17
SAIDEN

THE NEXT TIME SAIDEN WOKE, THE SUN WAS SHINING BRIGHT ON HER SKIN, and she lay mostly covered in the back of the same dirt cart she had woken up in, that night when she had fought all those ruffians. Her lips were chapped, and her throat ached as she sat up, trying to speak.

She froze before she could even try and pass the words through her lips. Sitting next to her in the cart was Loralei. Saiden's heart raced. She thought she had dreamed of seeing her in the forest that night, her guilty conscious reminding her of another of her past sins. She was only now beginning to understand that she had been seeing the truth.

"How?" It was the only word she was able to say before she was bent over coughing. She didn't understand why Mozare and Cassimir weren't there, why neither of them had come to her side. Why they had left her with the one person who might want to kill her, who had more reason than anyone to want her dead.

Instead, Loralei handed Saiden a canteen, the outside covered in a rough woven fabric. She unscrewed the top, bringing it to her lips and drinking greedily of the cool water inside. She felt it dripping down her chin, but she couldn't bring herself to stop. It was only Loralei's hand against her own that brought her out of it, forcing her to stop drinking.

She waited for Loralei to use her gifts to grow something to impale her, or to pick up a blade and bleed her the same way her mother had died. Horror grew in her heart, the memory of Loralei was real, and that meant she hadn't been imagining it when she saw her mother bleeding out on the palace stairs.

"The guard was still loyal to me." She said, as if it were the simplest thing in the world. In a way it was. Their lives were both so much more complicated than loyalties could describe. "He hid me away until I was able to heal the damage your beloved rebellion leader caused me."

There was an underlying malice to her tone, though something about it made her feel that she wasn't the recipient of such venom. She reached forward, her sleeve slipping up past her wrist. Loralei gasped at the brilliant rose, shaded and fully bloomed on the back of her right hand.

"One of my roses." She said, awe spreading across her face. Saiden pulled her arm back, hiding the tattoo under the tattered sleeve once again.

"Where are the others?" She asked, her voice still hoarse.

"They are negotiating with the ambassador's uncle. I drew the short straw and got stuck babysitting you."

Saiden's mind reeled. The capital of Taezhali was at least 3 weeks journey from the capital of Kaizia, and that was riding at full speed.

"You've been passed out for 23 days. You've come in and out of consciousness a bit, but never long enough to really talk." Loralei answered the question she was sure was written across her face.

"Why did you come with us?"

"You killed my band of thieves," Loralei said, anger lacing her words, before adding, "and I have nowhere else to go." The last words were quiet, as if there was shame in admitting that she didn't have a home. Saiden could barely even remember the cottage she was born in, and the palace and the rest of her life had never seemed farther away than they did now. The uncertainty of her own powers and the distance between them did nothing to help her feel settled.

Loralei just watched her until the boys got back, each taking time to hug her gently. She knew that three weeks without decent food or any exercise would leave her weak, but she hadn't imagined that she would fall as she tried to step out from the cart. Mozare and Cassimir were both by her side, carefully guiding her down, and each offering an arm to hold on to.

"We are to bathe," Cassimir explained, "before you are properly introduced to my uncle and the rest of the ruling family. The ladies can stay in the guest room in my apartment, and Mozare can bunk with me."

Saiden wanted to protest. She was in no state to be meeting any foreign rulers, her hair was snarled, her fingernails torn and bloody. Besides, she could still barely stand on her own two feet. She tried to protest, but she simply did not have the strength to argue.

Loralei reached out towards her. "Give me your hands Saiden." Hesitantly, she stretched out both of her shaking palms, watching Loralei's face as she fully took in both of the flowers on the backs of her hand. She ran a finger over the lily, "she would have liked this."

Saiden felt the moment that Loralei sent her healing into her body, helping the muscles in her arms and legs feel stronger, and clearing some of the fogginess in her mind. What was strange, what she hadn't ever felt before, was the sense of recognition. Something inside her knew the magic that moved through her and called back to it, the long-forgotten melody of a tune she knew by heart.

She tried to pull back, rejecting the idea of her magic calling out. Of her power being there right under skin when it had already cost her so much. But she knew that she wanted to be in fighting condition, needed to be able to defend herself and her friends in this foreign land, so she let Loralei finish.

When she was done, when her muscles felt much stronger than they had moments before, Loralei let go, wiping her hands on the side of the long gauzy wrap she was wearing over her tunic. When Cassimir offered her a hand out of the cart, she accepted, and she didn't try to pull away when he tucked that same hand into the crook of his elbow.

He led them through the open hallways of the emperor's palace, the wide arches of clay shaping sections of the balustrade so they almost looked like windows. Cassimir looked like he belonged here, the beauty and freedom of this place was exactly what she had been expecting of his homeland.

She kept walking by people whispering in the hallways, and she was surprised when she actually understood what they were saying.

"Why do all the people of Taezhali speak the language of the middle kingdom?" She asked Cassimir, leaning in towards him conspiratorially. She wasn't sure if she would have been able to speak louder than a whisper if she tried, even after Loralei's healing.

"The language of Taezhali was gifted to us by our gods. It is considered sacred and is therefore not spoken before foreigners. They teach all the common languages to children while they are still at school."

Saiden was amazed. She couldn't believe that the people spoke so many different languages. In the legion they knew enough of the language of the north, what was required for their duties, but she never would have learned them if it weren't for her service. Especially not as a child.

She stiffened as she heard light footsteps running down the stone hall, chasing after them. But Cassimir smiled, turning them around and opening his arms without releasing her hand from where it rested in the crook of his elbow.

"It is good to see you, Miri," the girl said, and she realized that this must be Eleni. The younger sister Cassimir had told her so much about. She wore the same bright colored clothing that Cassimir did, and her head was wrapped in a bright red prayer scarf, almost the same color as Saiden's hair. She ran a self-conscious hand over the tangle of her own hair and wished she had had that shower before meeting Eleni.

She placed a hand over her chest, and bowed, a bright smile lighting up her face. "You must be Saiden," she laughed and reached in to hug her. "It is a pleasure to finally meet you, *sahadi*."

Saiden looked curiously at Cassimir. The last word Eleni had used was not one she was familiar with, but he refused to answer, a slight blush coloring his cheeks pink.

"Come, I can bring you to the bathing hall and help you into fresh clothing. My uncle is waiting for Cassimir with my cousins, and he will likely not want to be delayed any longer."

Saiden hated the idea of leaving Cassimir and Mozare when she was already surrounded by so many unknowns, but she trusted Cassimir wouldn't leave her with someone she wasn't safe with. And she felt like another part of her already knew Eleni. Cassimir's sister was someone she could trust, and she was going to do her best to show him how much she believed in him and his family.

18

MOZARE

MOZARE WAITED PATIENTLY IN CASSIMIR'S APARTMENT BEFORE BEING GIVEN a chance to clean up and change. He had not been allowed to meet the emperor as he was, and so although Cassimir had been summoned, he had been left in the wide room to wait for someone to return. In the end, a servant came and lead him somewhere to change, and then escorted him back to the rooms. Cassimir was there and cleaned up by the time he got back, and they sat and talked while waiting for the women to be finished.

Saiden and Loralei came in a few minutes later, both dressed in colorful Taezhali fabrics. Saiden had a loose fabric wrapped around her arms that was dark green and embroidered with silk flowers. Her pants were simple, but the look was so different he was amazed. Loralei was back in skirts, the style similar to what Cassimir's sister Eleni was wearing, though the skin at her waist was bare and she didn't have the same head scarf. He wondered if the skin at her stomach would be soft to the touch. He swallowed, forcing himself to look away from her.

"How are you feeling?" he asked Saiden instead, reminding himself of why they were in the southern kingdom to begin with. Reminding himself how afraid they had been on the road when they were intercepted by Loralei and her band; when they weren't sure Saiden would survive.

"Strong," she answered, though she didn't sound sure of it. "What happened with Rhena, did you send her somewhere safe?"

Mozare blanched. In the chaos of everything he hadn't stopped to think about how Saiden would react to his decision.

"You forgot her?" Saiden had only watched him, and her voice came out low and cold. He stood from the cushioned seat, spreading his legs and waiting for a fight. They had fought before, usually it was a good way for them to blow off steam. Even in the wrapped clothing, he was sure Saiden could still throw a killer punch.

"You watched him kill my mother, and then you left her there with him?" Her voice rose in pitch as she stepped forward. Everyone around the room was tense. "How could you forget about her? She was ours to protect. She is ours."

Saiden was yelling. She stepped towards him, arm pulling back to punch him. But the hit didn't connect. She had pulled it at the last minute, staring at the skin around her knuckles where it glowed with the flickers of fire. She shook her hands, but the flames remained. She had no control over her own powers, and the fight had caused them to take control again. Mozare watched the panic on her face grow and she tried desperately to put out the flame.

"Listen to me Saiden," he said, stepping forward with his palms up. "Listen to the sound of my voice. You control it. You are in charge of the power." Mozare took another step towards her, and watched from his periphery as both Loralei and Cassimir moved to step to either side of her.

"You have to breathe," Loralei said. They were the only two who could properly understand the panic Saiden must be feeling. "Listen to your heart and control the beating. Your gifts will subside only when the panic and fear does."

Saiden pulled her hand into her chest. He could see that the flame was not burning the gentle fabric of her wrap, or the skin exposed above it.

"You are stronger than these gifts Sai," he said, taking another step forward and reaching for her. "You control them." He reached out and took hold of one of her wrists, and watched as Loralei took hold of the other. The fire that danced at her fingertips slowly burned out, returning the power to the well inside Saiden.

He reached forward and pulled her into his chest. Taking the time while she could not see his face to let the panic show before he carefully reconstructed the mask of calm. Her powers were stronger than anything he had ever seen, and the elements, the parts of her gifts that were like Rhena's ice and were tied to emotion, were going to be hard for her to control.

"I could have hurt you Moze," she whispered against his chest. "I could've burned you." He realized with a delay that the cold spots against his chest were tears.

"You won't hurt the idiot." Loralei said, her voice flat. "You are still you, even with the powers."

Saiden turned to look at the disgraced queen, wiping at her face. "You don't know that."

"I know more than you think I do World-Ender." He felt Saiden flinch at the old nickname. "You killed my men like they were children's toys despite the fact that they were all hardened warriors. You were lost inside your power far deeper than you were just now. There was no reason why you shouldn't have just killed me in the woods that night. But you didn't. This," she pointed at Saiden's hands, "this was nothing."

Mozare wasn't sure if the words helped or not, but when Saiden was ready to be let go, he stepped back, giving her space.

"We were supposed to go meet with my uncle," Cassimir spoke up, "but if you are feeling unwell, perhaps it would be wise to wait until the morning."

Saiden shook her head. Cassimir offered her his arm again, only to be pushed out of the way by Eleni, who tucked Saiden's hand into her own arm.

"We will be right behind you," Loralei said, motioning for Mozare to sit back on the cushion. He didn't understand, but with servants and who knew what other spies watching them he listened.

Loralei walked up to him and pulled at the bandages he had carefully rewrapped around his wound when he had gotten out of the shower. He hissed as the wound was exposed to fresh air.

"You are a fool," she pressed a hand flat over the cut, ignoring the way he flinched. "Stepping into something you know nothing about. What if you had touched her and her power reacted to yours? What if you caused her to overload?"

To be honest, Mozare hadn't thought of Saiden as this new person with gifts, despite the flames on her fingers. She was just his friend, and she needed him. "You are going to get yourself killed," she slapped the backside of his head with her free hand, "if Saiden doesn't do it, I might just run you through myself."

He stood, forgetting her grip on his bicep. He was taller than she was in the flat sandals they had given her, the top of her head resting right below his nose. "I would like to see you try," he said, his voice deep.

"You would do well to remember, you are not the only one with teeth shadow boy. You are not the only one who had to be scary to survive."

When his staring match with Loralei had ended in a stalemate, and his arm had fully healed, they both rushed to catch up with the others. Mozare didn't want Saiden going anywhere without him, not when their history with monarchs was shaky at best.

The throne room of the emperor's palace was vast, the walls open in the same way they were in the hallway, letting the warm desert air float through the room however it pleased. The inner facing sides of the stone pillars were painted in scenes that hadn't faded, the gold paint bright against the dark blues and deep browns. It was so different from the cold throne room of the palace of Kaizia.

Saiden was also looking around, her eyes wide with wonder. Mozare's parents had taken him outside of the middle kingdom as a small child, but Saiden had never been this far from her homeland's borders. He wished they could enjoy this trip, instead of pleading to a foreign ruler to grant them asylum.

Cassimir stood at the front of their group next to his sister, and both dropped into deep bows at the feet of the emperor. At the emperor's left side was an older man, one he knew immediately was Cassimir's father. On his other side were two young men, the crown prince of Taezhali, a golden circlet resting atop thick dark curls, and another boy he guessed to be the prince's younger brother.

Mozare pulled at Saiden's sleeve, and they stepped in line with Loralei, before sweeping into low bows.

"You may rise," a deep voice echoed through the chamber. His voice was rich, the words accented more heavily than Cassimir's speech. "Welcome to Taezhali, may you find peace among the sands."

The emperor stood. "Allow me the honor of introducing my brother, high lord Rami. His wife was the late honorable princess Sanora,"

The room echoed with dozens of voices saying "long may her spirit sail through the desert's winds."

He pointed to the other side, "my sons, the crowned prince Akil, and my younger son, the honorable Khari" Mozare watched the crowned prince, whose eyes had not strayed from the three of them since they had entered the room. He took the slightest step forward, doing his best to hide both Saiden and Loralei from the prince's line of vision. He was also letting the prince know that he saw what was happening, and no gold circlet was going to intimidate him.

The emperor motioned to the cushions stacked around the low table in the middle of the room, stepping down from his dais as he invited them to sit. "Please, I have sent for refreshments. My nephew tells me you have come a long way with very little."

"Your imperial highness," Mozare spoke and waited to see if he was going to be corrected, "has your nephew told you the reason we have been forced to seek your aid?"

"I am aware of the circumstances that bring you to my door. Never has a soul in need been sent away from these palace steps. I do not intend to break that tradition today my son." Mozare flinched slightly at the familiarity that the emperor used, but he did not correct him. He could not afford to slight the man who was their only chance at staying out of Revon's control.

"Uncle," Eleni spoke, pressing the side of her hand to her forehead and bowing her head slightly before continuing, "I would like to have Saiden join me in meditation in my gardens in the morning. I believe the practice will help bring balance back into her life."

Mozare stared at the girl, wondering if they had decided this together, or if Eleni was taking things into her own hands. He hoped Saiden wasn't going to be pressed into a corner, unable to control even her own schedule.

"Gifted child, do you swear to never harm my darling niece?" The emperor looked at Saiden. There was a thin layer of panic behind her eyes, and Mozare wondered if he was the only one who saw it.

"If it is within my control to protect and honor your niece I will do so." The words sounded rehearsed, but the emperor turned back to Eleni and granted her the permission she was seeking.

"She may join you in the gardens as long as you desire my heart." He wondered if the emperor used names with everyone. And why Eleni was his heart. They were questions he would have to leave for another time.

"Do you have guards here? Perhaps I could talk to them, let them know about some of the drills the middle kingdom soldiers might use if there were to be an attack."

"What a generous offer. If my nephew believes that is prudent then he can take you with him to his training session in the morning." Someone came into the room, bowing briefly before slipping up to whisper something in the emperor's ear. The emperor stood, but when they went to follow he tutted. "I have many things to attend to, but I would be honored if you spent time with my sons, they will teach you about Taezhali, and our ways." He didn't like the brief expression of panic that flashed over the emperors face.

The young royals and the exiles talked for a while as various cool dishes were brought to their table. The spices here were much richer, the food similar to what Cassimir had cooked for them back home, but bursting with even more flavor somehow. Every once in a while, Mozare would catch the crown prince staring at Loralei, or asking

Saiden another ridiculous question about gifts she didn't even understand herself, and he would clench his fists under the table.

He understood that people outside their kingdom were curious about their gifts, about the favor they had been granted by their gods. But Keir above, he was a few moments away from reaching across the table and pulling the crown prince's tongue from his mouth.

Underneath the shallow table, Loralei placed a cool hand over his tightened fist, long fingers squeezing and warning him against whatever violence was running through his mind. He forced himself to breathe, and he waited for their meal to finally be over.

19

SAIDEN

SAIDEN WAS SURPRISED TO SEE HOW FAST THE HALL COULD CHANGE FROM the harsh simplicity of the Emperor's throne room to an elegant court for a feast. She would have had a hard time reconciling the two images if she hadn't watched the servants transform the space. Though it was just her friends and the two young princes, they didn't lack in the decor or the food.

"Is he still worried about the Island of Severed Key?" Cassimir asked the younger of his cousins. Prince Khari simply nodded, and neither of them said anything more than that. Saiden wanted to press the issue, but it didn't feel like her place.

Cassimir lead Saiden to a cushion on one side of the table while Loralei and Mozare sat down on the other. On Saiden's other side, Eleni tucked her legs up underneath her. Although the table was more round than square, the two princes managed to sit at what was most like the head of the table.

She didn't mind. Not at first. Servers started bringing out plates of food, and Saiden's stomach rumbled. She'd never seen so much color on a plate before, even with all the fruits she'd pile on her plate at every opportunity back home. Rich warm spices fragranced the air, the tang of citrus a note in the background.

Even with Lorelei's help, her body couldn't deny that it had been neglected while her brain had battled itself and the new presence of her gifts.

When Cassimir reached across the table to start piling food onto her plate she smiled shyly into her lap, feeling the blush rising to her face. She appreciated that he wanted to take care of her, but she was unused to the care in public. She didn't want the princes' first impression of her to be weakness, especially when they were already in a position where they needed to ask for help.

She could feel the older prince's eyes on her, and did her best to ignore him. Everything in her, every sense she'd honed through her years in the legion was screaming to get out of there. But this was Cassimir's family, and she didn't want to offend them on their first meeting.

His sister at least seemed lovely. She was so warm and open, it made Saiden's heart hurt a little for the family she was missing. To keep herself from spiraling at the thought, she took her first bite of the food Cassimir had piled on her plate, barely stopping herself from moaning when the rich spices burst against her taste buds. She couldn't help but close her eyes at the taste, so many layers of flavor combining to create something she'd crave for the rest of her life.

Next to her, Cassimir's face mirrored the same shy smile that had just been on her own. She leaned into him, relished his warmth and whispered "you were right about the spices. Nothing in Kaizia could compare."

"Taezhali is home to a number of plant species that can't be found anywhere else in the world." The younger prince started, eager it seemed to talk to them. "We have amazing programs to supplement farming and planting, mixed with scientific research, we've been able to preserve and enhance thousands of species on the brink of extinction."

He was enthusiastic, and Saiden could see him gearing up to continue when he was cut off by his older brother. "No one cares about your plants Khari."

The younger prince visibly shrank in his seat, as if making himself smaller would save him from his brother's ire.

Akil did his best to moderate his tone, but she doubted any of them would forget the way he snapped just a second ago. "Besides, these are our guests, we should be asking about them, not prattling on about useless nonsense."

He looked at them like he'd given a command, but he hadn't actually asked a question, so none of them answered. She knew through the years they'd spent together that Mozare was reading this the same way she was. The crown prince was unstable, and they would do better to keep their cards close to their chest.

"Cousin you haven't asked a question." Eleni's voice hangs somewhere between motherly and reprimanding, like she was used to this behavior and knew exactly what to do to curb it.

"My apologies, there's just so much we don't know about our neighbors to the north, it's difficult to know where to start. I supposed the most interesting thing would be that which sets you apart from our own glorious empire."

The way he spoke sent shivers down Saiden's spine, and only her training kept her from showing her discomfort on the outside.

"Your religious tendencies differ so greatly from our own. I'd love to hear your opinion on the matter. Especially the nature of your gifts. I understand they're given to the truly faithful. Though I have to admit I don't understand why everyone wouldn't be faithful if you consider the gifts manifestations of your gods, isn't that enough proof of their existence?"

Though he asked for their input, Akil's rambling continued on, the time dragging slower with every sentence. He'd clearly done a lot of research, his interest in their religion bordered on the fanatic. With the way he was monologuing he would have fit in well with the Enlightened.

"Our gifts are given to those who believe, but also those who are worthy." Mozare interrupted the prince, much to his blatant disbelief. Akil looked like he had forgotten there were even people in the room with him.

Saiden watched curiously as Loralei leaned over and placed her hand on top of Mozare's. It was unusual enough that she had been willing to help heal Saiden, but seeing her offer grace to Mozare meant so much more. They had been so wrong about her.

"Of course." The prince had to force the words from his mouth, but luckily the interruption seemed to have derailed him enough that they got to finish the rest of their meal in quiet.

Panic woke Saiden in the middle of the night. In the darkness of the room, she couldn't tell where she was, and she feared her escape had been only a cruel trick of her imagination. Only her fingers against the soft cotton of her sheets reassured her that she wasn't still locked in Revon's dungeon, waiting to be used as his executioner again.

A voice spoke through the room, and Saiden finally realized that the darkness around them wasn't natural, it was coming from her. There was a chill to the room she hadn't expected, and then she realized it was just another manifestation of her own panic.

"Saiden, listen to me." Loralei's voice was firm, but the darkness was too disorienting for her to know where it was coming from. "You're in Taezhali. You are free of whatever that horrible man did to you. Listen to me. We're alive, we're safe."

Slowly the shadows started peeling back from the walls. Loralei sat on her own cot, the thin blanket wrapped tight around her shoulders as she tried to keep out the bite of the cold air. There wasn't anything appropriate in their room for cold temperatures, everything in Taezhali was made to endure the heat.

Saiden's voice came out barely above a whisper. "Are you hurt?" She wanted to ask if she herself, had hurt Loralei, but she wasn't brave enough to voice the words.

"I'm fine and so are you. The chill is nice, though I wish it came in a setting beside freezing. Do you think you could turn that down." Her teeth chattered, but she could tell Loralei was doing her best to hide that from Saiden.

She tried everything she could think of to pull the coldness back out of the room, but she was so far out of her depths, she didn't even know where to start. The shadows were one thing, they had receded on their own, but the cold seemed to be there to stay.

"Maybe I should get Mozare." Saiden said, her own voice muffled by her shivering. Ice and water did fall under Ilona's gifts after all.

"We don't need that idiot. Elemental gifts are powered by feeling. Whatever dark thoughts are swirling through your head, it's time to get them under control. I didn't survive having my spine nearly severed to freeze in a country made almost entirely of deserts."

The image of Loralei being stabbed didn't exactly help the situation. Her powers flared again, and she could see ice forming on the doorway, creeping its way across the floor.

In her bed she started whispering to herself, "think calm thoughts. Think happy thoughts."

"Breathe Saiden. If you hyperventilate it won't make things any better either."

Saiden took a deep breath, watching across the room as Loralei raised and lowered her hands indicating each breath. The exercise felt silly, but it worked, and the ice started creeping back to wherever it came from, the air in their room slowly warming back to comfortable temperatures.

"How did you know that?" Saiden asked.

"Know what?"

"The stuff about elemental gifts."

"You didn't think I was the only one in my band who had gifts did you?"

The thought hadn't really crossed her mind. She had killed all of Loralei's companions while blinded by her powers and her need to save Mozare and Cassimir. She hadn't considered whether or not they had born gifts. They were certainly no match for her newly awakened power.

"I killed them all without even considering it." Her voice was empty, and she was mildly surprised the image didn't bring a cold bite back to the bedroom.

"But yet you spared me. Seems like a miracle."

"You are not an easy person to kill. I have to believe the gods have more in store for you."

"Did you know it was me?"

Saiden paused to think about it, she hadn't really had the time before now, and she didn't realize the answer would be important. "I think, when you made me swear that blood oath to you, it connected us. I didn't know you, not the way I do now, when I can see you across from me. But inside I recognized you. I don't know if that really makes sense." She wasn't sure any of this really made sense.

Loralei didn't answer her. They stared at each other for a long moment before Loralei simply rolled over, her back now facing Saiden, and told her it was time for them to go back to sleep. "I may not be a queen, but that's no reason to start looking like a troll."

20

SAIDEN

THE NEXT MORNING, ELENI WAS WAITING FOR SAIDEN OUTSIDE THE bedroom she had shared with Loralei. She was wearing another beautiful skirt, the hem embroidered with patterns of jumping gazelles. The prayer scarf around her head this morning was a deep green that matched the base color of her skirt. Saiden had been nervous to share a room with Loralei, but when nightmares had woken her and her powers had gone haywire, she was glad that Loralei had been there with her.

"I was reading late into the night in the imperial library. I think the biggest issue with your gifts is that you lack balance." Saiden waited for Eleni to continue, eating the breakfast Cassimir's sister had brought her, eggs tucked into soft, still warm bread. "Your body grew up without these powers, and now your normal consciousness is at war with this foreign intruder."

The idea of her body being at war made sense with everything she had known about the blood curse before she had joined Mozare and learned about anointed rulers.

"It's like if you were to wake up one morning with two extra arms. Your body would not know what to do with them right away."

"You figured this all out in one night?" Saiden didn't understand her dedication to helping. She was friends with Cassimir, but his sister certainly didn't owe her anything. "I've had my whole life to consider this and I've never gotten this far."

"The libraries here are very extensive. They contain histories from before the beginning of Kaizia. Besides, I know about your powers, you have had to guess all this time about what they would be like. I think we should take this conversation to the garden, I've cleared space for us so we won't be interrupted."

She and Eleni walked down different hallways, discussing the different possibilities of her gifts, of what she could do to get them under her control. She avoided the idea of praying. She was not sure the gods would visit her here, or that even worse they may not want to visit her at all now that she was an abomination. Eleni seemed to notice her hesitation and moved past the topic, walking down a hallway that seemed to go nowhere.

She pulled a thin string from under the tight neckline of her shirt, pressing whatever hung at the end of it into a tiny hole in the wall. Behind them, the end of the hallway shifted, leaving enough space for the two of them to pass through before the entrance way closed again.

Saiden stared at the space where the door had been in awe. They had hidden pathways in the Kaizian palace, but none so sophisticated it could be locked like that. Eleni pulled the ring out to show her, "this was my mother's ring. My uncle gave these gardens to her when they were both still children. She wanted to leave the palace, but he couldn't stand to be parted from her."

They stepped through the thick leaves of different exotic plants Saiden knew instinctively would not grow in Kaizian soil. "He gave this space to her as a getaway. Somewhere she could escape court life without ever being too far away. There are only two rings, my mother's and my uncle's. He gave me hers after she died." Eleni held the small ring tightly in her fist before slipping it back under her shirt.

She reached up to start unraveling her prayer scarf, and Saiden turned away, careful to give her privacy. Eleni's voice behind her was startled. "What's wrong?"

"Your wrap, I read that Taezhali priestesses keep their head covered at all times, and to be seen without it was a disgrace." She waited, "I did not want to impose on your generosity by offending your beliefs."

"You are right about the Taezhali priestesses, but I am not a priestess. I don't follow the rules that they do. My mother was, and I wear the prayer scarf to honor her. It is okay for others to see me without it if I permit it. I would not have taken it off if I was not comfortable with you seeing me without it."

Saiden carefully turned around, going slow so that Eleni had time to change her mind if she wanted to. But Eleni did not change her mind, seated underneath an arch of plants, her scarf on the ground next to her. She had dark brown hair tied in a bun at the nape of her neck and when she moved it reflected the desert sun.

Eleni motioned for Saiden to sit down, so she crossed her legs and faced Eleni from the ground of the garden. She remembered the days she would spend with Loralei in her rose garden and her chest tightened. "Take a deep breath Saiden. Let the pain in and then breathe back out."

Saiden looked at her, confusion spreading on her face. Eleni just pointed to her hand. Thin black coils of shadows raced through her fingers. At least they weren't on fire this time. "The priestesses of Taezhali are special because they can connect to nature on deeper levels than normal. That's how my mother grew this garden. She taught me enough to keep it alive. It is all about give and take, the world in balance. Too much of any one thing, and the scales tip."

She held her hands in her lap, both palms up. Saiden copied her, then froze as she felt the earth shift the way it always did in the temple. She hadn't done anything to call the gods, had only rested her hands on her knees, but it seemed they were keen to visit her.

They brought her to another garden, the perfume smell of flowers overwhelming her. Keir and Ilona both had crowns of woven flowers in their hair, the colors a vibrant red, contrasting to the dark black of Keir's short curls and the blinding white of Ilona's flowing hair.

"I didn't think you could find me here," Saiden said, as Keir walked behind. This time there were no braids in her hair for him to undo, only the night's worth of tangles. He ran gentle fingers through them, pulling the knotted pieces free.

"We could find you anywhere my child," Ilona whispered, a gentle hand on her cheek. "Especially with your gifts free now, to us they shine like a beacon."

"Why have you come?"

"We know what happened, what that man did to you." Keir said, moving to stand beside Ilona once more.

"We wanted to check on you." Ilona finished.

"To see if I'd gone mad? To see if you finally managed to kill me?" Her voice rose, and the new power inside her swirled in her chest. "I've failed, I didn't protect the queen or the country, can't you leave me alone at this point?"

Ilona's face twisted, the serenity of her features morphing into a snarl. Keir spoke, "you are beyond precious to us child, we want you to survive this."

"There are plenty of people who want things they cannot have. Being divine doesn't exclude you from disappointment." Saiden tried to push her mind from the space they had brought her to.

"Just know that while you are going through this, we are doing what we can to look over you." Ilona said, her words stilted. And then they were gone, and she was back in the desert garden with Eleni.

"Where were you just now?" Eleni looked around. Saiden had never visited the gods with a witness, especially not a foreigner.

"I was visited by my gods." She said, her voice hoarse. "They do that sometimes. I am sorry to have interrupted your lesson."

Eleni reached out a soft hand and placed it on Saiden's still upturned palm. "You should not apologize for things you have no control over. Besides, you were gone only a few minutes. There is plenty of time before we are expected for lunch."

21

MOZARE

Mozare and Cassimir had been the last to leave the apartments that morning, though they were still up early. The emperor had granted Mozare his request, giving him time to look over the Taezhali guard, and hopefully time to run them through some drills. He wasn't sure what the emperor knew of his own rank in Kaizia, if he thought that Mozare would be a valuable teacher, or if he was just hoping that he would make a fool out of himself.

Cassimir loaned him the typical training clothes of Taezhali soldiers, loose linen pants and a short-sleeved tunic dyed tan. The heat was already sweltering despite the sun still rising over the desert sands. "It will be much hotter by mid-day," Cassimir spoke from behind the closed door to the room they were sharing, "you'll be glad to be free of those leathers then."

When everyone was dressed, he went to search for Loralei, unease filled his mind at leaving her alone for too long, but she had already left the apartment. Mozare couldn't imagine what she was up to, but he had to tell himself that she was able to make her own choices. If those choices turned out to be a threat, he would deal with it later.

The arena outside of the palace proper housed both the training grounds and the soldier's barracks, keeping them separate from the nobility who resided in the main rooms of the palace. They didn't seem to keep to lines and drills the way the soldiers he had trained in Kaizia did, but he tried to keep in mind that these were not his trainees.

When Cassimir walked through the gathering of men and women, all dressed in the same loose-fitting clothes, they turned and bowed to him. At the shaded side of the arena, there was a boxed suite, and he could make out the faces of two people sitting inside.

Before he had a chance to turn to Cassimir and ask who was watching them, he heard footsteps approaching from behind. He stilled, and when they were only a step behind him, he ducked, causing the assailant to sail over his head. He pulled his twin axes free, keeping the blades pointed towards the ground. He wasn't sure what was going on, but he didn't want to accidentally hurt anyone.

The man who charged him rose from the sand dusted floor of the arena, brandishing a kind of blade Mozare had never seen before, and swung at him, aiming the blade towards his head. Mozare slid back, using the film of dust on the floor to his advantage. He felt exposed in the middle of the emperor's men, unsure how many of them might decide to aid their fellow soldier.

He pulled one of his shadows, wrapping it around the man's eyes before backing up so he was protected by the wall of the arena. Two others followed the first man, standing beside him with weapons drawn. He didn't give them a chance to corner him, to have him trapped. He pushed forward, grabbing the first man that had attacked him and throwing him into the woman behind him. He did not wait for them to get back up before he attacked the first one again, the man's blade chipping the wooden handle of Mozare's ax as he blocked the assault of blows.

He waited until the attacker took a step forward, then hooked his leg behind the man's knee and sent him sprawling to the floor. He didn't understand where Cassimir was, why no one was helping him. He butted the man on the crown of his head with the handle of his axe, leaving him passed out on the ground and waited for someone else to attack him.

Across the arena he could hear the sound of clapping, the loud ring of it jarring him. He hadn't moved from his position, but as he noticed the two spectators descend from the shadowed box, he was quick to sheath his weapons, bowing deeply at the waist as the emperor and crown prince moved to stand before him.

"You may rise," the emperor said once his gold sandaled feet were in view. "That was quite the performance. I am curious to see what you can teach my soldiers with fighting skills like that." Mozare silently thanked Saiden for all the harrowing training sessions she had put them through when he was still a new recruit with the legion.

Behind the emperor, the crown prince stood, his face torn between expressions of curiosity and rage. Mozare added it to the list he was already keeping as to why they should avoid Akil. The two fighters who he had not knocked unconscious stood, causing him to stiffen, then they moved to take the third out of the arena. He didn't know what they did for healing in Taezhali without gifted healers, but he hoped they would take the man to be cared for.

The emperor spoke again before leaving. "The troops are yours to do with as you wish. I trust it will be a learning experience for everyone involved."

22

SAIDEN

A FEW DAYS LATER SAIDEN AND ELENI WERE SITTING IN THE GARDEN again. Although they had already been there for quite a few minutes, Eleni had yet to sit down or give Saiden any instructions. She worried frantically, and under the loose fabric of her sleeves she pulled at the skin around her knuckles. What if she had already pushed Eleni too far? What if Cassimir's sister, someone who she could tell had the patience of a devotee, was already fed up with her problems?

Saiden wasn't sure how she would ever have any hope of figuring this out on her own. And if Cassimir thought she had done something to his sister, whatever it was that was blooming between them, as well as the protection of his uncle, would be gone.

Eleni interrupted her spiraling thoughts with a cool hand on her shoulder. "I thought we could try something else today. I'm not very familiar with your religion, besides the perfunctory, and I think your relationship with it goes well beyond what could be written in books."

Saiden nodded. "Maybe if you could explain it to me, then I could think of something else we could do that would be helpful to you." Eleni finally took her seat across from Saiden on the moss-covered ground of her hidden garden, and smiled gently towards her.

"Where do you want me to start?" Saiden could see reason in

Eleni's thinking, but she had never talked about her relationship with her religion before, not even with Mozare, who of all the people she knew was the most likely to understand her feelings on the matter.

"My curiosity wants me to say start at the beginning, but I am sure that is more story— sorry would scripture be the right word, than we have time for right now. I think it's better if we can get into the creation of people like you, and how that relates to you and your current situation." Eleni spoke faster than most natives Saiden knew, despite the language of the middle kingdom not being her dominant tongue.

"The middle kingdom has always recognized Keir and Ilona as the creators of our world. Our people believe that they restored a balance in the universe that brought our planet into being." Saiden paused to think about the important parts of their history. There were too many details to go into it in depth, and she just wanted to give Eleni the summary.

"Because of their devotion to the gods, the people of the middle kingdom were granted powers that would protect them, should the other kingdoms one day turn on them or their religion. Over time people believe that the gifts went to those who were most loyal the gods, anyone who made religion and faith an important and honored part of their life. An early version of the legion was formed. The gifted were given purpose, at least that was the rhetoric. No one knows when we first started having gifted if that's what you were hoping to know. It's more of a military history.

"The long line of kings didn't appreciate that the people began to have more powers than they had. Not when their blood had always been all the power that they needed. They wanted that power for themselves, and for their armies. They told the people the gods had given them these gifts to serve their country.

"But the gods weren't happy that their devoted were now being forced to work in a mortal man's army, a man with no care for religion or faith. Who frequently went against their wishes. So the gods raised their own army, regained control of their gifted and that's when our country entered a civil war. The sacred war.

"At the battle of the fallen, the first King Chosen and his warriors stood against the tyranny of the blood kings. This is where it gets complicated. I was taught that the chosen kings were not gifted, because gifts would make them partial. But the rebels say that the first chosen rulers were actually gifted. They were like me."

Eleni's face was thoughtful, running over the story before she decided to reply. "That's a lot to live up to."

Saiden gave herself time, in the peaceful quiet that rested between them, to think about Eleni's response. It was a lot for her to expect to live up to a purpose she did not decide for herself. To both overcome the terror of the others in her kingdom and to rise to whatever divine purpose Keir and Ilona intended for her.

Eleni gasped, causing panic to whirl through Saiden for a second before the other girl spoke. "Look." One word, a simple command, and then Saiden understood what had made Eleni gasp. All around her in the little garden paradise, plants were perking up, stretching towards Saiden in gentle caresses, new flowers blooming at their tips.

Saiden looked down at her hands. She still couldn't control the power, but it hadn't been destructive. She had grown something, had used her powers to create new life. It might not be what her gifts were for, but in that moment, she doubted anything could have felt more right.

23
MOZARE

Mozare wasn't sure what agreement Loralei had made with the emperor, or what plans she had made for the day, but she was already long gone from their shared apartments by the time he was getting ready for his training session the next day. Again.

He planned to head to the arena without the fanfare of his arrival yesterday, more suited to observe than to be put under the prince's microscope. He wasn't a subject to be studied, and knowing that there was little he could do to deter the prince's queries made his gut wrench.

More so for Saiden and Loralei. There was very little at this point that he wouldn't endure to protect the two of them. The feeling was natural when it came to Saiden, they had spent so much of their lives looking out for the other that it was already deeply entrenched in his instincts. On the other hand, he wasn't sure what made him want to extend that protection to the fallen queen, and he didn't have the courage to explore those feelings.

Though the reminder of the prince and his habit of popping up unexpectedly did send Mozare looking for Loralei instead of heading out to the arena. He wasn't sure it was even a conscious decision, one second, he was heading outside, and the next he was walking through the tunneling hallways, searching common areas for a glimpse of her dark hair, or a flicker of pale skin.

Loralei stood out among the people of Taezhali, all of whom looked to be descended from the sun in mixed shades of umber and gold. Already dark skin deepened by long days under the desert sun.

He found her in the upper rooms of the estate, working in the kitchens with some of the palace staff. He was surprised seeing her, not only loitering in the space but working besides the other kitchen staff, flour from whatever they were preparing dotting the deep red of her newest Taezhali outfit.

The sight knocked the air out of him for a second, something he wasn't ready to admit. He was so used to her in light girly colors, and the red made it clear that she was not a girl anymore. The square in her shoulders as they complimented her for picking up a new skill, and the flush in her cheeks when she turned to find him watching her squeezed at his heart.

He hadn't even been sure his heart still worked until that moment.

"What are you doing up here?" She asked, her voice accusing yet somehow still light. He was almost entirely sure it was for the sake of the others, who looked on not so conspicuously.

She walked towards him, wiping the flour from her fingers onto the loose fabric of her pants. It took him a second to tear his eyes away from the white streaks they left behind.

Once they were in the hallway, away from the prying eyes and listening ears of the emperor's spies, Loralei's voice hardened. "Did you follow me? Am I to be under guard the entire time I am here?"

Mozare took a deep breath before answering her, giving the angry words that had jumped into his mouth time to dissipate before he replied. "The prince followed me to training yesterday and had his men attack me." Her face looked stoic, and if it weren't for the color leaching from her face, he would think her impassive. "They weren't able to hurt me, I still have my gifts thank the goddess. But it was all just a show for the prince anyway. I wanted to warn you to be careful." He said the words gently, worried that his attentions would somehow be misconstrued.

Loralei nodded, and he saw her begin to turn back towards the kitchen. He grabbed her before she had fully turned her back to him, then froze when he realized there was no logical reason for him to be touching her right now. No other warnings to issue, no threats either.

He panicked, blurting out the first question that came to mind. "What are you even doing in the kitchen anyway?" The words sounded cruel to his own ears, and he regretted them as soon as they had left his lips, even more so when he saw her flinch hearing them.

She shrugged, but he could tell from the way her voice shook that she was pretending not to care. "They don't care who I am in there. I am not a fallen queen; thrown out of her kingdom and the only home she has ever known. They do not pity me. Here, I am only another set of hands to work, and there isn't enough time to care about the rest of it."

The words fell like arrows, and he said nothing as she finally turned, setting him free to get lost in his own miserable past, as she put her hands back to work.

24

SAIDEN

Cassimir was sitting with Saiden on a canvas shielded terrace, sipping from a copper cup of sweet juice that he had brought for the two of them to share when he had suggested the diversion. She felt so unsettled here, without her routines and responsibilities, but she found she didn't mind her days being a bit more free. At least here she had choices, which was something she hadn't realized was missing from her life before.

"Would you like to learn about my country?" He asked her. She had been minutes away from drifting to sleep in the soft cushions of her lounge when Cassimir finally spoke. She forced herself to pay attention, part of her desperate for knowledge, the other part eager to learn anything about the man resting with her.

Still, she couldn't avoid teasing him a little. "Are you allowed to teach me?"

He smiled, and it was like having a sunrise only for her.

"Our history is not as sacred as our language. My family is proud of its ancestors and where we have come from. And the people here are happy too, though they are not close enough to the palace for you to encounter them on this visit." He said it like there would be other visits. Like there could be a time she was coming to Taezhali of her own will and not to seek political asylum while being driven out of her mind with power. She didn't realize until now how much she wanted a future where her life looked like that.

"I would be honored to learn your history." She meant every word.

"Taezhali was not always as grand an empire as it is now. Of course, all great empires rise, some slow and some like a desert storm that comes out of nowhere. And some day, like all great empires, Taezhali too will fall, but that time will not come for a while yet." He spoke the words like they were a great myth, a fairytale of sorts, and she wondered if to him, this was the grandest story of them all.

"In the beginning, the people of the great desert continent were made up of a series of war bands. And among the most powerful of their leaders was my four times great grandmother, Enasha. Legends say there wasn't a man who met her who didn't want to marry her or kill her, but she had refused to take a husband. Her might, she always told them, was her own. Not to be dominated or given as a gift."

"But men came anyway, and as she continued to deny them, they began to covet what she had. Without her strength, they reasoned she would be desperate to marry one of them. And they were right." Saiden felt enraptured by the way Cassimir told the story, his voice carrying like it was made of the desert wind itself.

"Eventually she did marry one of the men," Saiden gasped out loud, and then blushed when Cassimir smiled at her. "An old man the others considered wise, who many of the villages had turned to when things went rough. But she didn't marry him for the reasons they were hoping. She let them think her powerless, and because she was a woman, they believed that she truly was. When her husband was later found dead, his body mutilated nearly beyond recognition, his tribe became hers."

It was Saiden's turn to smile now. And her smile only grew as he continued the story of his grandmother. "The next man came, and she agreed to marry him as well, he who believed her to be a grieving widow in need of protection. And then, on a trip he suddenly drowned, though no one knew why he would've been near the water."

Saiden had to acknowledge that her methods were brutal, but Cassimir's grandmother had been a force to reckon with. "She had married nine men by the time they caught up to her, and she had born a son, Shen. The leaders of surrounding tribes still free from her power tried to kill her, tried to have her punished for murder, but the people she had led protected her despite her perceived crimes. And so, she passed her leadership on to the son she taught to respect the value of every person, no matter who they were."

"Shen gained even more people by going and offering his protection. He built people sturdy houses, he made sure their lands and families were safe. And so, their territory and the people who answered to him grew."

"He had three children, and of the three he chose his youngest daughter Shanor as his heir. This is the only time in history where the empire has not gone to the eldest child. But he feared that his two sons would be too much like the men his mother had despised all those years ago. Too eager to collect power, when he had been devoted to the security of his people not expanding their holdings. They already had a vast land, and he wanted to give it to a ruler who would be level-headed and just."

"And his daughter was that. My mother was named after her. But even as they strived for peace, they could not avoid the war that was coming to their lands. There were other war lords who had finally learned that strength came from the people who stood by you, and they were tired of the power my family had. They banded together and they attacked the compound she had been building."

"But there was one thing fiercer than their anger, and that was the pride and loyalty of the people who lived under my great-great grandmother's rule. They defended the compound until their last breaths, all the while, Shanor was giving birth to an heir of her own."

"He was the first true emperor, the first of my family to be recognized by other countries outside of the desert continent. And that power went to his head. We don't speak his name." Saiden didn't need to hear Cassimir's words to know what was coming next. Power had a way of corrupting even the best of intentions. But she listened anyways as Cassimir told her of his great-grandfathers exploits, of the raids and attacks that gained him the rest of the southern continent to rule.

"He died young and unmarried, though he had many sanctioned consorts, and through them, my grandmother Eleana was born."

"Eleni is named after her?"

Cassimir's smile nearly stopped her heart as he nodded. "She was a magnificent woman and an honorable empress. She set up trade routes, built foreign ties with other prominent nations, and built a system of democracy that flourished under her guidance. She gave the people of her empire a voice, and was considered a kind and just ruler."

"When she died, the entire nation mourned her. And my uncle became emperor." Cassimir's history lesson seemed to end there. It was a good place, since her own perfunctory history lessons mostly took place between the last two generations, so she was already somewhat familiar with the reign of his uncle, and even with his grandmother.

"You come from very esteemed family." She said, when she couldn't think of anything else to say.

"My family is a lot more complicated than our history, though I am grateful you think so." They both took a sip of their drinks, and together they enjoyed the sunsetting over the desert.

25

SAIDEN

They were finally all together for breakfast the next day, and Saiden felt relieved, despite the underlying tension at the table. There was clearly something going on between Mozare and Loralei, but neither of them seemed to be in the mood to talk about it, so she didn't push them.

Cassimir had actually taken the morning to sleep in, so staff came in to bring them several warm and cold dishes of food, and laid them all out on the table. The smells wafted all around her, and she sighed.

She already missed the Taezhali cuisine, and they hadn't left yet. They didn't even have a timeline for when they were going to leave, or where they were going to go.

Over the smell of spices mixing in the air, she began to smell wood burning, and flinched, when she realized that her hands were burning prints into the table.

She jerked her hands back, the force of it almost rocking her chair back off its feet. Everyone in the room froze to look at her, and the sparks at her fingertips crackled again. Panic built inside her chest and although she knew that panicking wouldn't help she couldn't force herself to keep calm.

Everything she had practiced with Eleni fled from her memory.

"Looks like the lessons are going splendidly." Loralei commented from her seat across the table, eyes roving between Saiden's hand and the fear on her face.

For the first time, she heard impatience from Eleni when she snapped back at the queen. "Your comments are not useful."

"Because your books told you everything you need to know about powers you've never seen before that are based in a religion from a kingdom that's only recently allied with yours."

Mozare joined the conversation. "Do you have anything productive to say, or are you just hoping everyone will overlook you if you're bitter enough?"

Cassimir came to stand behind her, while the arguments continued on between Loralei and Mozare, Eleni and her training completely forgotten for other animosities. He placed a gentle hand on her shoulder, and she focused on that pressure. She took her first deep breath, and then another, the only thing in her thoughts being his hand on her.

"Loralei's right." Everyone froze when Saiden finally spoke again. "Although blunt, she is right. We need more knowledge than we can get our hands on right now."

The look on Loralei's face was a mixture of shame and arrogance, which didn't sit well on her regal features. "Your idiot friend and I are probably the closest you'll get to experts on the subject matter."

Saiden turned to Eleni, but she couldn't read the other girl, and she was worried that this approach might offend her after she had tried so hard to be able to help Saiden with something none of them knew anything about.

"I suppose that the next logical step is to have someone with more first-hand knowledge help you. I know how to meditate, and how to control myself and I can teach you that, but there are a lot of intricacies I won't be able to explain."

Saiden wanted to hug Eleni, but she was far too nervous about hurting her so soon after her fingers had singed their table. Instead she shot her a small smile, and was relieved when Eleni nodded back, a smile on her face as well.

They finally dug into breakfast, and conversations around the table shifted towards more trivial things, things she was happy to just witness. She wanted to just bask in their friendship for as long as she could manage.

In the back of her mind however, she couldn't stop herself from thinking how easy it would be to lose it all.

26

MOZARE

Mozare followed Saiden and Eleni as they walked to the girls' secret garden, Loralei trailing a few steps behind the group. He tried not to worry about her, to focus all his attention on Saiden. He liked that Saiden didn't have to be the warrior she always was in Kaizia. He liked that she had found a friend in Eleni. But something inside him still felt like he was being pushed to the side. When Loralei had suggested that it wasn't enough for Saiden to learn with just Eleni, who despite her good intentions didn't know everything about god given gifts, he had jumped at the chance to be part of it.

Eleni had given them the space in her garden, while she walked around and tended to the various plants growing in the small hidden paradise. Saiden sat, crossing her legs and waited, the action looking almost routine from his point of view. Loralei sat in front of her, slanted towards Saiden's left side, so he sat closer to her right. Despite not focusing directly on balance, as Saiden said Eleni's lessons did, they were still a balanced mix of the gods' favor.

"What does it feel like," Loralei started, "when you feel your powers surging?"

Saiden looked at her hands, fisting them against the shaking he could see. "It's overwhelming." She whispered.

He took the next question, "because of the emotion attached, or because of the powers themselves?"

Saiden considered his question, as he and Loralei sat watching her. "Both I guess."

"Okay," he looked at Loralei, "it seems that your powers surface most..." he paused as he looked for the right word, "...uncontrollably when you are worried about someone being hurt. So, here where we are all safe, we can help you tap into the parts of your powers that aren't defense mechanisms."

"We'll start with something small. You could grow something." Loralei suggested.

Saiden looked at the earth beneath her, and hovered one of her hands just above it. They waited for something to happen, for a shift in the dirt to show that a new plant had sprouted in the arid desert sand, but there was no movement. She closed her eyes, focus cementing on her face, but nothing happened.

"What did it feel like, Loralei, when you used to grow all those roses in your gardens?"

Mozare waited, his eyes torn between Saiden and Loralei. She let out a wistful sigh before answering. "When I grew those flowers, when I grew anything, it felt like I was giving part of myself to the earth. And in return the earth gave me a small piece of happiness." She didn't look happy now, as she picked at the skin around her fingernails, her face crestfallen. Loralei shook her head clearing the thoughts and her throat before she continued. "Picture a seed, the way that life grows from something so small into something precious, then push it to go faster."

Saiden took another deep breath, settling so her back was straight as she sat. They waited, until the smallest part of a leaf poked through the grit, growing as if it were reaching for Saiden's hand. At the top of the smaller stem, a full red rose bloomed, the same color as the roses scattered in the palace gardens of Kaizia. The same roses Loralei had grown, and that Saiden had tattooed on her own hand.

A tear streaked down Loralei's face as she looked at the flower, the small piece of their home. Saiden reached forward, slowly so that Loralei had time to pull away, and rested her hand against her friend's cheek, wiping away the solitary tear. He realized with almost a delayed sense of time that despite everything that had happened, despite all that they had done to each other, the girls were still friends.

Loralei looked over at him. "I think it's your turn shadow boy, let's learn some dark magic." He rolled his eyes at her not-so-subtle way of moving their session along. But he didn't call her on it as he watched her fingers linger on the petals of Saiden's flower. Somewhere behind him he could hear Eleni humming absentmindedly.

"There are different kinds of darkness. That which heightens fear, that takes away the awareness of what is going on around us, and that which embraces, that soothes. Both are useful, but they take different tolls on the gifted using them." He remembered hearing the same speech when his shadows had still been out of control, his own gifts rallying against him.

"To bring comfort, is also to bring a sense of vulnerability. Whether the darkness highlights this or hides it, being in a more exposed mind space should help you call the shadows into being." He wondered how often the shadows came when she was afraid, when her new gifts forced her to be susceptible in a way that years of friendship taught him she would hate.

He watched Saiden's shoulders rise and fall with each deep breath, keeping part of his mind focused on Loralei. He didn't want this to be a moment she could take advantage of Saiden, even if their days in Taezhali had made him doubt her less and less.

She closed her eyes, and slowly but surely thin tendrils of shadows started to spin their way across her open palms, small black hurricanes held over callused skin. He didn't let his voice get above a whisper when he spoke, "you've called them."

The shadows flickered briefly as Saiden opened her eyes, a brief flash of shock passing over her features. Then the swirls grew, wrapping up her arms, and around her shoulders, coils hugging her ribcage.

Eleni clapped gently, and although small, the smile that spread across Saiden's face was genuine. He understood what that accomplishment felt like, what regaining that control felt like.

"What was it like with Rhena?" Saiden's voice was so quiet he wasn't sure if she had spoken, or if the shadows had conveyed her message for her. When he didn't answer she got louder. "You trained her in her gifts, didn't you? Was it like this for her?"

Saiden's voice pleaded with him; her eyes desperate. His stomach soured, all the optimism grown through their session burnt away at the shame he felt for leaving Rhena behind.

He was lucky that Eleni interrupted, giving him time to clear his head.

"Who's Rhena?"

He was surprised when Loralei answered. He had partially forgotten that she was even in the garden with them.

"She's a young recruit in the legion, gifted by Ilona, and quite partial to Saiden and the idiot." The old him would have bristled at being 'the idiot', but he couldn't help but agree with her. The clinical answer was helpful too, pushing his brain back to a place where he could speak again.

"We left her behind when we were trying to rescue Saiden."

He thought he heard Saiden growl, and braced himself as discretely as he could for whatever power might flare with the emotions coursing through her. Nothing came. Eleni was sitting beside Saiden, and despite being the smaller of the two, she had tucked Saiden under her arm and was gently running her fingers through the red curls of her hair.

"Have you tried writing to her?" Eleni asked.

"We would never be able to get a letter into the capital." Saiden answered, her words laced with tears.

"Maybe not if you sent it by post, but I have another way to get a letter to her. You just have to trust me."

27

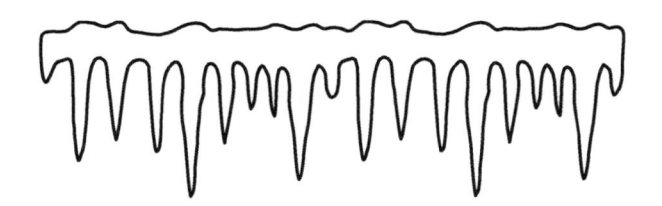

RHENA

Rhena was tucked away in her bed, doing her best to ignore the joyful sounds of the recruits in the rooms around her. The only good thing she could see from being moved to the castle was that here she got some sense of privacy, despite how thin the walls were.

At least when she cried herself to sleep she didn't have to answer to anyone in the morning.

She didn't understand how the other legionnaires in her recruitment class didn't see how Revon's rule was bad for them and for their kingdom. How could they swear loyalty to a king who had killed Maggie just to turn Saiden into a monster?

Outside her door loud voices travelled through to her. "She deserved it in my opinion." The voice was male, and she was almost certain it was Talon, a boy just two years older than her-and far stupider. "That blood cursed bitch was only ever designed for servitude."

Even as Rhena's blood boiled she could feel ice coating her fingertips. She should've stopped and thought her actions through, it's what Saiden would've wanted from her, but Saiden wasn't here now and Rhena couldn't bear to hear them talk about her that way.

She stormed out of her small room, catching Talon and the smaller boy he was talking to, Yusef, off guard. Rhena had Talon pressed against the wall, her forearm pressed to his throat and a blade at his sternum before either of them could process her appearance.

Yusef tried to reach for her, but she shot a solid wall of ice between them, ignoring the audible gasps from both boys. She knew it was dangerous to give her powers free rein when her emotions were so high, but rage and grief clouded her mind in a way that made it all seem worth it.

"What do you think you're doing?" Talon asked, trying to act brave despite the blade at his chest. There was a tremble to his lip that gave him away. She pressed the blade a little further, not caring if she drew blood.

"I think you should be careful about the vile things that come out of your mouth."

"Or what?"

"Or the only thing that will be coming out of your mouth is blood." She grabbed his chin, letting the ice at her fingertips burn into his skin. Tears gathered in the corner of his eyes, and that was what finally made her stop. This wasn't who she was.

This wasn't who she wanted to be.

She let go, pulling the ice wall down until it melted away. Rhena couldn't be sure her threats would prevent them from continuing the second they were out of ear shot, but she didn't have the energy to care.

Rhena slammed the door shut behind her, slipping down the splintery wood until her knees pressed into her chest, her sword caught between them. Tears fell freely, pinging against the hard stone floor as they turned to ice, dripping from her cheeks.

She only stopped when she heard something weird. In the corner of her room the stone of her floor began to crack, vines pushing in between every small opening. Rhena held her blade, but she was so tired, that the point began to drag. If this intruder was a threat she wasn't sure she could stop them.

Unfurling like a flower amidst the vines, Rhena was shocked to see a piece of paper, the edges worse for wear, but still whole. She didn't understand what had happened, but once she looked closer and recognized Saiden's handwriting she didn't bother with caution. She ripped the paper from its bed of vines.

> *Hello my maus,*
>
> *I'm as safe as I can be. I'm so sorry you got left behind, I never would've made that choice. Be brave, but remember to be smart. The war can't be fought in one shot, and we have to make it to the final battle. All of us.*
>
> *I will think of you every moment and pray for your safety. I only hope Keir and Ilona will heed these prayers unlike the ones that came before.*
>
> *Your big sister.*

There was a smaller note at the bottom, though she didn't recognize this handwriting. She was hoping it would come from Mozare, but it wasn't his messy scrawl.

> *You don't know me, but I pray for your safety as well, and hope that we will meet one day. These vines will grow for as long as you need them. Place any paper here and it will reach your friends.*
>
> *Princess Eleni*

Rhena held the paper to her chest for a moment before she ripped it to shreds and sent it floating down the sink drain.

28

SAIDEN

Saiden still wasn't sure she understood the magic Eleni had learned from her mother. It was so different to what she knew of the gifted, and yet it sometimes felt closer to her than her own gifts. And to know that she now had a way to reach Rhena, to know if something went wrong, it brought her more solace than she thought anything could while they were apart.

It took a few weeks for Eleni's magic to carry Saiden's letter to Kaizia and Rhena's letter to return. Saiden had been so relieved when she had gone to Eleni's garden, and seen the same piece of paper tucked into her hand. The part of her that had been terrified about Rhena calmed, giving a piece of her mind back to her. Returning to her and Loralei's room in the apartment, she tore at the seal. The others had given her space, but she imagined they were likely sitting on the other side of the light wooden door, waiting for the first sign of smoke or bright lights.

Inside, written in Rhena's tight handwriting were the words she had been waiting for. *I am safe.* She hadn't even written a name or a greeting, just those three words. Tears welled in her eyes as she read the rest of the letter.

THE BLOOD-CURSED

I'm happy the three of you made it safely out of Kaizia, and I want you to know that I am not in any danger. Revon assumed that Mozare tricked me, and whatever beliefs he had, he never even thought for a second I might have been involved. The pain I felt when I realized what he had done, not only to Mama Maggie but also to you, I couldn't believe you had gone through that. I knew it wasn't you acting like that, but it was still terrifying. I'm glad Moze went with you, even if you wanted big brother to stay and protect me, I am happy he is there to keep you safe. Write again, I will think of you all the time,

Your little sister.

Saiden held the letter up to her nose, hoping for the smell of home, but she could only smell the parchment and the wind. Her amazement at Eleni's way of sending letters only growing, and so grateful that she had brought the idea up to Saiden. She missed Rhena almost as much as she missed her mother, the two of them a hole in her heart. She wanted to go back to the time when life was peaceful, when she was happy with her family and her friends.

Someone knocked on the door, and Mozare peaked his head in. "I'm guessing the fact that the room's still here is a good sign?" Despite the tears on her cheeks, she smiled and nodded at him. He came and sat next to her, and she handed him the letter. She wasn't the only one who cared about Rhena, and she knew he was still beating himself up about leaving her behind.

He smiled when he was done reading the letter, "I miss her."

"Me too." She bumped his shoulder with hers, taking the letter and folding it so she could slip the piece of parchment under the mattress of her bed. Loralei and Cassimir were sitting in the parlor, waiting to see what was going to happen, or wanting to be somewhere else she wasn't entirely sure.

"Rhena's okay," she said, placing herself in between Cassimir and Loralei and sitting down. He placed a gentle hand over hers, squeezing briefly before letting go, and Loralei leaned over to rest her head against Saiden's shoulder. With Rhena's letter tucked away in her room, and Mozare moving to sit on the opposite side of Loralei, Saiden felt something strange bloom through her chest. She felt hope.

29
MOZARE

Mozare took Loralei with him to the training grounds this time. She wasn't his first choice as back up, though he was fairly certain she would pick his side in a fight over strangers. He hoped at least, since his first experience with the emperor's troops had not exactly been a pleasant one. He also knew she was armed, her walk suggested the added weight of multiple blades that were concealed on her person. He felt ashamed that she felt like she needed them.

When he arrived in the arena, the group of soldiers who had attacked him the first time rose to their feet, and he tensed bracing himself for a repeat, but they simply bowed and turned back to the group of soldiers semi-huddled around them. The box where the emperor and crown prince had watched them looked empty, but he couldn't be positive it actually was.

He turned to the man who had lead the attack, "what's your name?"

"I am called Noli."

"Could you run me through some of your training exercises?" He had decided the best way for him to teach was to first learn. He wanted to know how normal soldiers trained in the emperor's army so he could enhance that training, instead of being redundant and boring them.

He watched Noli pull out two long daggers, and turn towards the woman on his right, bowing before holding the weapons out in a defensive stance. She smiled, the look out of place on the training ground, a silent conversation between the two fighters. He pushed forward, and she avoided the slice of one blade aimed for her upper arm. Mozare flinched slightly holding his hand over the faint reminder of a scar from where Loralei healed the slice on his own arm. He glanced over at her and knew she was thinking the same thing. He hated it.

She hadn't taken out any weapon, and he watched as she twisted and turned around, playing Noli against himself, waiting for him to slip up. He stretched a hand towards her, and she struck at his wrist, grabbing it and pinning the arm behind his back before he had a chance to move it. She picked up the dagger he had dropped and held it to his throat.

Mozare clapped. "Excellent work."

"We focus on learning about the movement of our bodies," the woman said, "they are our greatest weapons, and sometimes the only ones we have. I am Isra by the way. I wish to apologize for our introduction, but we cannot deny the emperor a wish." Isra bowed.

"These are the fighters who you beat?" Loralei asked from behind him, her tone sharp. "It's not hard to see why. They're skilled, that's obvious, but if you used your gift, your shadows, in a land constantly covered by sunlight, there's no way they would've beat you."

He turned to face her. Whatever game she was playing, whatever score she wanted to settle, it was better if they got it over with now. Especially if she wanted to challenge him in front of a bunch of soldiers that could be a threat to their entire group.

"Don't speak when you can't back up your words."

"Who said I can't back up my words?" She reached down and pulled out a dagger from wherever it was hidden under the loose leg of her pants. And then she surprised him, because she didn't use the blade to attack him, but rather to cut a piece of fabric from the bottom of her shirt. She held the dagger in her mouth and wrapped the ripped piece of fabric around her eyes.

He waited for her to say she was joking, to laugh and pull the fabric from her eyes. But she didn't. Instead, she pulled another longer blade from behind her back, slipping her feet from the laced slippers so they rested bare on the sanded floors of the arena.

With the wrap around her eyes, he couldn't use his shadows to blind her, and as she pushed off the ground towards him, he was left with only his body to defend himself. He wished that he had more time to watch Isra and Noli fight, or any practice using the methods they used. He pulled his axe free from its sheath of his back, using the already chipped handles to block her blades. He would need to have them tended to soon if he kept fighting like this. He turned, pushing to her back, hoping for a moments reprieve, but she followed him, a vine growing from the dirt to wrap around one of his ankles.

He tripped and fell, pulling at the vines before cutting through them with his blade. He pushed back as Loralei arced the longer of her daggers down towards him, holding his breath as she hit the ground only a hairsbreadth away from the inside of his thigh. He swung, catching his blade around her elbow and knocking free one of her blades. He kicked it aside, waiting for her to strike with the other. She was relentless, causing him to keep pushing back, until there was no more space and he was sitting flush with the lowest row of seats in the arena's seating area.

She knelt down in front of him, the tip of her blade pressing against the hollow of his throat. "I like having you sweating underneath me."

A loud clapping came from the other side of the arena, as a cloaked man descended from the emperor's box. They pulled their hood back, revealing the dark curls and circlet of the crown prince Akil. Tucked under his arm was a thick book, a random assortment of papers hanging out from the edge of the pages. Loralei released him, pulling the cloth away from her eyes.

"Incredible," there was more expression in his face than Mozare had seen in the days since they had arrived in Taezhali. "I thought your powers were something to behold Mozare, but your little fallen queen," he paused, as if his mind couldn't come up with the right words to describe what he had seen, "I don't think life has ever dealt so swift a blow."

Mozare felt uncomfortable with the way he was looking at both of them. He couldn't explain it, but he felt like he was somehow under a microscope-a studied thing in the scientist's lab. He knew when they arrived in Taezhali that people would be curious about them and the gifts they had, but he hadn't been expecting this level of study, especially from a prince.

"Continue your training," the prince said, the hint of a command lacing his words. "I will be back another day to watch you again."

30

SAIDEN

SAIDEN WAS WAITING FOR CASSIMIR AND ELENI TO COME PICK HER UP IN one of the many alcoves hidden around the palace. She had thought about joining Mozare in the arena, but had decided against being around that many people when she still had so little control over her power. They were going to take her on a walk on the emperor's lands, show her all the little beauties of this place.

She had never taken the opportunity to look at a place before and just see beauty. She was always looking for threats, for hiding places and escape routes in Kaizia. But she had friends here, and she knew they were going to protect her. They were going to get her through this. She was letting her armor down, and starting to learn who she was without it.

Someone walked into the hallway, and she stood from where she sat reclining against a pillar, expecting it was Cassimir. Instead the crown prince inclined his head.

"Mistress."

"Your Imperial Highness."

"I was hoping to run into you actually. As I understand it, your" he paused, "particular situation has given you a mix of the powers that your friends have."

She nodded, but didn't speak. Something was telling her that this situation was wrong, but she wasn't sure what.

"And those powers, do you generally find them to be stronger or weaker than those of your singularly gifted counterparts?" He stared at her, his fingers twitching by his side. "Perhaps you could give me a demonstration?"

She shook her head, "your Imperial Highness, I cannot control these powers."

He stepped back, "I am sure I am far enough away that you shouldn't do any damage."

Despite her protests, she could feel the power churning through her chest, her skin itching as familiar heat burned underneath it. She felt the wind around them pick up. The crowned prince opened his book, pulling out one of the random pieces of paper and started jotting down notes. And despite his comment about distance, Akil took a step forward. Saiden matched him, taking a step back, pressing herself flat against the pillar she had been sitting in front of.

"Please," she said, but the rush of power kept her from being able to say anything else. He grabbed for one of her hands, watching as her veins lit up underneath like lightning strikes. The hallway around and above them started to darken, the air turning cold, but her skin continued to burn, small sparks shooting off her fingertips. He dropped her hand, but still he didn't back away from her.

Panic filled her lungs with cotton making it impossible for her to breathe. On the ground around her feet, small sprouts of various flowers grew, her eyes couldn't see straight enough to know what they were. They tickled her ankles where the sandal wraps weren't protecting her skin. She missed her boots, but the weather was too warm for them here. She was glad at least that the fabric was light enough for her to be fully covered, otherwise she would also have to deal with the uncomfortable vulnerability of having her tattoos on display while she was cornered and monitored.

At her shoulders light shone through the fabric, bright streaks trying to cut through the shadows she had created. The two sides of her powers warred with each other, her ears filling with the buzzing sound of chaos.

Then there was a hand on her face, a small hand with thin fingers brushing at her forehead, resting on her cheek. She was sinking, the power exhausting her as she fell to the floor. The fingers pushed through her hair, stroking calmly through the loosened curls. When she could see clearly, she realized she was sitting again, her upper body leaning resting in Eleni's lap, whose cool fingers still ran through her hair. She was singing again, whispering the words so only Saiden could hear them.

Across from them, Cassimir had pushed his cousin against the wall, his forearm pressed against the crowned prince's throat. Another shock of panic coursed through her. She didn't know if she could handle Cassimir being punished for this, for protecting her. She looked at Eleni, begging her with her eyes to stop this, trying to speak but not able to form the words.

"*Syhedi* that's enough. Let Akil go, he won't bother her again, I will talk to our uncle."

Cassimir let the prince go, who moved away as he gathered his scattered papers and rushed from his cousin. Then Cassimir was sitting next to her, his hand reaching for hers. She pulled it back, frightened that she would hurt him.

"It's alright. There are no more sparks, nothing to hurt anyone." She let him hold her hand the next time he reached for it, wrapping it in the warmth of both of his. She could hear again, the ringing from her ears quieted, pushed out by Eleni's lullabies.

"I am okay," she said, the words scratching her throat, as if her body was fighting against the lie. "I will be okay." Now that her powers had returned to their resting place inside her she felt stronger, and behind it, she felt angry. She felt abused, the prince had forced her into a place where she had no control. A place she never wanted to revisit.

"I know that face." Cassimir said, resting his hands which were still wrapped around hers over his knee. "Do not let my cousin's actions anger you. He has never been told no, never had consequences."

"You make too many excuses for him brother." Eleni said. Saiden sat up, pulling her weight from where it was, no doubt uncomfortably, resting against the slighter girl. "Besides, she doesn't need logic."

"I need a fight." She said, interrupting the siblings before they could really get into it. "I need a blade in my hand, and more control over my own life."

The two of them looked at each other, a debate going on between them that she couldn't hear. She liked watching them from this close, seeing how they bounced ideas off each other without words.

With a shrug of his shoulders, Cassimir seemed to relent, pulling her up from the floor as he stood, her hand still tightly wrapped in his.

"The smaller arena out by the Khalasta oasis is likely abandoned right now, what with the training uncle has the soldiers doing. You should be fine to go there." Eleni said, smiling up at them from the floor. "I'll see you both later for dinner. I'm cooking."

Cassimir didn't let go of her hand as they walked through the still foreign hallways, but she couldn't quite tell if he was still worried for her, or if he just wasn't ready to let go. She found that she didn't really mind either.

Saiden's first thought at they entered the small stadium was that Eleni had been right saying this space was abandoned. She just had a hard time believing it had only been abandoned for the few days since they had taken up residency in the Emperor's home. The seats that lined the wall were covered in a thin layer of dust, the same sandy coating she could feel grinding under her sandals. And theirs were the only footprints.

"They used this space when my father and uncle were training. My uncle had to know how to fight in order to earn the respect of his warriors and my father was going to be general. When they took over, they built the bigger training arena so there would be more room for sparring among the troops."

"Is that how your mother met your father? Because he was going to be the emperor's general?"

"They all grew up together. All my grandparents were close, and I think they were secretly hoping for something to happen between mama and my father. But they hated each other for a very long time."

"They did?" Saiden couldn't reconcile that image with the one she had created. Cassimir had told her so many wonderful stories of his family in the time they spent wandering the halls, and she imagined they had known they were right for each other from the moment they met.

"Oh yes, my mother wanted nothing more than to be independent. To train with the men and earn her position. She's the reason women were allowed to join the ranks of Taezhali warriors, she wouldn't let my uncle say no. I think she realized that she could be strong while still loving my father." He took a deep breath, then walked away from her, leaving her staring after him, her hand cold where he was no longer holding it.

"There should be some leftover weapons in here somewhere," he said. He was quiet, but his voice still carried in the open arena, a caress traveling on the wind.

He seemed to find what he was looking for, a small door carved into the rock wall at the other side of the arena. She hadn't seen it from where she was standing, despite the small size of the training grounds, before he had opened it.

"Swords or daggers?" he asked, "there doesn't seem to be much else."

Saiden followed him across the small space, sticking her hand out in front of her. "Daggers"

Cassimir handed her two short blades, the weight unbalanced. She missed her own kindjal blades. She had never imagined what it would feel like to be fighting without them, to not be able to rely on them.

The two handles were completely different, one thicker, the handle curved and knotted wood, while the other was sleek chiseled stone. She threw them one at a time, adjusting to their weight before taking one step back into a defensive position. Cassimir had been watching her the whole time, she felt his gaze on her. When she adjusted her stance, he moved forward, slicing one of his blades towards her knees.

She backed away, but he let the momentum carry him, turning and swiping the other blade towards her head. She could almost swear a few strands of her blood-red hair joined the layer of silt coating the floor. She blocked another strike as he aimed the shorter of his blades towards her chest, the metal sparking. She almost pulled back, afraid that somehow her fingers were the cause of the sparks, but Cassimir didn't give her time to consider it. And she was done playing defense.

She swung at him, the worry flaking away from her shoulders piece by piece. *This was her life.* She swung. *She was in control.* Cassimir ducked her blade swiping low towards her ribs. *There was no force stronger than her will.* She jumped over him, spinning her body in the air above him, landing strong, with her blade point touching the hollow of his spine. *Not even the gods.*

Cassimir put his hands up near his head and she backed off, accepting his concession. She smiled at him, swiping her blades against her pant legs. "Again?"

He nodded, but he put his blades down, which confused her. Cassimir was a strong fighter, but she knew he preferred the distance of blades. Then he was peeling the thin layer of his shirt off, throwing it into the abandoned seats with little care for where it landed.

She paused, sweat glistened on the plains of his abs, the newly healed scar a twist on the side of his body. She hadn't noticed it before, despite their swim, but on the other side of his torso he had a tattoo. Resting on his hip were the roots of a strong tree, the branches curling up his chest and behind his back. She couldn't tell how fresh the ink was, but she almost thought the leaves were colored in the exact ink Niran had mixed for her.

She couldn't think about it more, in the time she had been considering the ink, Cassimir had picked up his blade, and he renewed his attack more ferociously. She moved with him, a dance to music only they could hear, the footsteps known only now, in this time, in this space. She wanted to laugh, a bubbly feeling building in her chest. They went back and forth, switching flawlessly between offense and defense, striking and blocking and striking again.

Saiden got close to him, leaving him with less moves, and before he had time to step back, to put that space between them again, she wrapped her leg behind the back of his ankle, using the movement to knock him to the ground. She hadn't noticed that he had already released his blades, that his hands, now empty, were able to grab on to the loose hem of her Taezhali training shirt.

She threw her blades to the side as she fell on top of him, not wanting to do any serious damage by accident. Cassimir was smiling up at her, the dust streaking his hair so it looked like it was shining. They were both breathing hard, and she wasn't sure what made her do it, but she was leaning towards him, holding her body above his, and then she was kissing him.

She had never kissed anyone that she had liked before. She had never kissed anyone before. Mozare had tried as some kind of joke, but she had never felt the same bubbly feeling with him as she did when she was herself around Cassimir. He was still smiling, she could feel it where their lips met. And she knew she would remember that smile for the rest of her life.

He sat up, bringing her with him, leaning his forehead against hers as he pulled away, and she realized with a panic that maybe he had only been in shock. She tried to back away, to rebuild the distance again, but he wouldn't let go of her.

"What is it?" He asked, gentle eyes searching her face.

It took her a second to realize what it was exactly that had panic growing in her chest again. "I didn't mean to take your choice away. I'm sorry."

He tilted his head as he looked at her. And he took her hand, the one with the lily and placed it over his heart. "I have already made my choice." He kissed her again, a brief meeting of their lips. "You are my choice."

And just like that, she was smiling again.

31
MOZARE

Mozare and Loralei left the training hall a lot sweatier than they had gone in that morning. Despite the break for the midday sun, they had still spent most of the day training, and he for one was exhausted. And hungry. He secretly hoped dinner was waiting for them back in Cassimir's apartment.

Loralei walked in front of him, bare feet slapping against the stone floors. Her shoulders were still tight. Despite hours of training, anger still radiated from each of her steps. He and Saiden always took to the mats to burn off extra energy, but he guessed that wasn't the right thing for everyone.

"Hey," he said, taking a few extra steps to catch up to her. "If you ever want someone to talk to, you could always talk to me. Or Saiden."

"What so you can tell me I'm an abomination? Spout about how much better you are running my country? Except you weren't. You abandoned the country."

"To protect Saiden."

"She wouldn't be in this position at all if it weren't for your rebellion. I found that information about releasing the blood curse in my archives months earlier, and the idea to use her as a weapon never

THE BLOOD-CURSED

even crossed my mind. I killed my entire board when I realized that's why they'd imprisoned her mother."

She had killed to protect Saiden. Mozare froze a little, but his anger was too hot to be put aside. "You should have told her about that information. Then we could have protected her mother, and stopped this from happening."

"Oh, you mean the mother who was rotting away in a prison cell. Did you think about what would've happened if I had never released her."

"You used her as a hostage."

"I was left with no choice." She spit back. Their toes were touching, her bare feet touching his booted toes. Saiden had stopped wearing her boots in the heavy heat, but he couldn't bring himself to do the same.

"Wasn't it you who told me that we always have another choice. Choice is what makes us monsters. Those were your words."

"I was a monster long before I made that choice. But I didn't choose to be queen. Or to be gifted. We are all of us pawns in a game where the rules are always changing."

"You didn't choose to be queen, I didn't choose to be shadow boy," her favorite nickname for him, "Saiden didn't choose to have her mother killed in front of her, only to be consumed by powers the likes of which haven't been seen on this continent for centuries. None of us wanted to leave our homes and take refuge in this ridiculously hot country, away from everything we know."

"Who cares about this country? Why are you here anyway? Take a ship and sail far away from here. Far enough that your demons can't follow you." He didn't know if she was referring to Revon, who was no doubt still looking for them. Or if she could see the way his eyes skid back and forth whenever they were in a crowded room, how he always kept his back to the nearest wall and his ear to the door.

"We're here so Saiden can learn to control her power. So she doesn't risk hurting anyone else."

"So she gets a second chance and no one else does?" Loralei's arms were crossed tightly over her chest, a reassurance or prevention from strangling him, he couldn't be sure. He pulled at his hair, the inky locks hanging over his forehead in dire need of a cut.

He ground his teeth together. "You killed those people because you wanted blood." His face was only inches from hers.

"It never mattered what I was, or even what I thought I was. You thought I was a monster long before I ever killed anyone. You swore an oath to your country and broke it at the first test of loyalty. But I never betrayed Saiden. I wanted her and Magdalena to be safe and I did what I had to do." He tried to think of what to say. He had been so sure they were doing the right thing, he had never considered his joining the rebellion to be a breach of loyalty. And he'd never even begun to think that Loralei might have been in the right the whole time.

Before he could speak, there was a hand on his shoulder, light filled the room, and he was wrapped in a smooth bubble of air and thrown across the room. He couldn't feel his body hit anything, but he wasn't entirely sure if he had a body left at all. He couldn't feel his fingers, couldn't sense the space where his feet should've been. Then the light was fading, and he could see that despite not feeling the impact, there was a crumbling crater in the wall above his head the size of his body.

Across the space, Loralei was looking around, eyes wide despite the still receding light, weapon already in hand.

And in between them Saiden laid curled in on herself on the stone floor.

32

SAIDEN

Saiden had heard raised voices, had recognized the sound of Mozare and Loralei fighting down the hallway from where she was contentedly walking with Cassimir. Her body had reacted to the sound before her mind even had a chance to catch up. And she was sprinting, although her sandals offered her little traction on the stone floors, and hurling herself between them. Then there was light all around her, coming from inside her, from that place where her new magic flowed.

She heard the loud crashing sounds of two bodies being propelled through the space, the crumbling of wall as they inevitably made contact. She was shaking as she fell to the floor, her face resting against the cold stone as she curled in on herself. She was crying, but there was no sound. Then there were footsteps, she couldn't tell how many, walking over to check on her. She wanted to tell them that she didn't need help. That she wasn't deserving of their consideration at all.

She was every bit the monster everyone always thought she was.

People were speaking above her, and there was a hand on her wrist. "She doesn't seem injured, I can't feel anything wrong."

"Then why is she lying there. There has to be something."

No one answered that time. She didn't know what kind of silent conversation was going on around her. She just hoped that if she curled into herself, if she made herself small enough, she might just disappear. That she wouldn't have to worry about hurting anyone ever again.

Hands were touching her shoulders, too many for her to be able to count who was touching her, her senses gone haywire after the explosion of power that had surged through her.

"She just needs a warm meal, and some time for her senses to come back to normal." Eleni's voice carried over her like a song on the wind. "You don't need to crowd her either." Harsher words than Saiden had ever heard the other girl speak before, but then the hands touching her went down to just one pair.

Cassimir's warm fingers wrapped around her upper arms, helping her to stand, letting her rest her weight on him. She didn't have the energy to think about how vulnerable she was allowing herself to be. And with him, it didn't feel like a weakness.

33
MOZARE

Mozare kept finding himself looking back to where Saiden was sitting at the table by herself. They had taken over the small kitchen outside of Cassimir's apartments. Apparently, while both siblings liked to cook, Eleni was a hazard in the kitchen. After she accidentally lit one of her pots on fire, Cassimir had taken over, leaving his post at Saiden's side to make sure that they were all properly fed.

"You should go and check on her." Loralei said. He hadn't even noticed her coming up to stand next to him. "She's going to need you."

"I'm the reason we're here to begin with. What can I do now that will fix that? She needs you, someone who understands what it feels like to be isolated and worried about concealment."

"No, she doesn't. And you don't think that either." Loralei said, her low voice doing nothing to hide the attitude behind it. "You think that your guilt is more important because you already feel bad. But what you did is over, and if you can't get past that the people who need you are going to continue to suffer."

Loralei pushed her hands off the counter and went to join Saiden at her table. He didn't remember when he stopped being the only one who would dare sit with her. When he would be the first one to try and comfort her. But Cassimir had calmed her in the hallway, and it was Loralei now who was giving her the space to reach out.

Eleni was still debating with her brother about whether he should've taken over cooking duties from her, when the pot was only "slightly on fire," and he couldn't hear anything of the small conversation that was going on between Loralei and Saiden at the other end of the room. He just got up and quietly left them, leaning against the wall outside and sliding down to squat on the balls of his feet.

He didn't know how everything had gotten so mangled. He had wanted to make Kaizia into a better country, into the best country it could be. He thought fighting in Revon's rebellion had been the way to do that, but nothing had gotten better. And there hadn't been anything bad about Loralei's reign until they had started attacking her. They were the catalyst for all the bad things that had happened. He had fought for a man who had killed Saiden's mother without any remorse. Who planned to turn her into just another weapon in his arsenal.

His thoughts kept spiraling. He was running his hand through his hair, and he was fairly sure he was crying but he couldn't feel anything. He was entirely numb.

And then Saiden was sitting next to him, loose pants scraping the dusty floor, legs crossed at the ankles. She leaned her head over, and the loose curls of her hair tickled his cheek. "We really messed up huh?"

He rested his head on top of hers, not caring if he was still crying. Saiden was out here to comfort him, even when he should be the one there for her.

"Yeah, it seems like it."

"We're still together though." She reached over and threaded her fingers through his. "Since that first day, it's been you and me against the world. I didn't always know it, but I do now. And it's my turn to have your back. You can lean on me too you know."

A shaky hesitant smile broke over his face, hidden in Saiden's hair. "Besides, we can't have family dinner without you. We'd be missing something. Even if you can't bring yourself to smile and joke, we need you with us." He lifted his head from her shoulder, wiping at his face before standing up and dragging her with him.

THE BLOOD-CURSED

"When did you get in touch with your emotional side?" He asked, his attempt at teasing her to change the subject.

The voice that answered came from inside the kitchen, "that was me." Eleni poked her head through the door. "Not sure what you do in those barracks of yours that had you shelled up tighter than a kashuwan nut, but I am taking credit for cracking that one." She pointed at Saiden. "You both need to understand that you are human, and bad things are going to happen in your life. They may even be your fault, but that doesn't take away from who you are. You can only control how you react to the bad things, and who you keep by your side."

Saiden squeezed his hand as they walked back into the kitchen. He was sat between her and Loralei. He leaned over and whispered in Saiden's ear, "what did Loralei say to you?"

"She asked me to teach her how to throw people like that." He couldn't tell by her face if she was joking. "She might have also mentioned a certain shadow boy was likely pouting as she put it."

He turned to look at Loralei who was ignoring everyone in favor of the heaping serving of food on her plate. "I'm glad you came out to look for me."

"We're partners. That hasn't changed." She gave his hand a final squeeze before letting go, and then they both dug into the delicious meal Cassimir had cooked for them

34

SAIDEN

When everyone had long since finished dinner, and the sun had set outside the palace walls, Saiden finally decided it was time for bed. Her friends were all yawning and slouching in their seats, but none of them seemed willing to say goodbye to the peaceful end to the day. Even she wanted to stretch the day just a little bit longer, despite how bad the earlier parts of it had been.

She put all their used dishes in the sink, leaving them there for one of them to deal with in the morning, and watched as one by one, her small family went their separate ways to head to bed.

"I have something I want to give you, if that's alright." Cassimir was standing in the doorway between the kitchen and the rooms beyond.

"You don't owe me anything. At this point, I probably owe you." She laughed, trying to make her comment more lighthearted, but it sounded fake to her own ears.

"It isn't about debt. I got this for you because I wanted to. And in truth, you would be doing me a great favor by accepting this gift."

When she realized he was waiting for a response, she nodded, and he offered her a hand. She rested hers gently in his, letting his warmth soak into her. He pulled her close to his side as he walked out of the kitchen, their steps ringing in sync on the stone floors.

"My uncle is holding a grand feast tomorrow night, in your honor. It's traditional for prestigious guests to be welcomed in this way. I tried to convince him not to, but there was nothing I could say to get him to cancel, only to postpone." Saiden cringed. She hated the idea of attending another event with people swarming around her. She tried to swallow around the panic burning through her. "Don't worry Saiden, Eleni or I will be with you the entire time."

He led her to his bedroom, and Saiden was slightly worried that Mozare, who had left before them, was not already inside, curled up into one of the lightweight cots the staff had added to Cassimir's apartments.

He reached down to the bottom shelf of a set in the corner of his room, and pulled out a package wrapped in cream colored fabric. She had an overwhelming sense of deja vu, of remembering the new set of leathers Loralei had gifted her what now felt like a lifetime ago. She took a deep breath, and she let go of the pain of that memory, holding onto only the happy pieces of it.

Cassimir laid the bundle on the bed and watched her expectantly. Despite him tracking her as she walked the few steps to his bed, she didn't mind that he was watching her. She didn't feel judged or threatened as she would have felt in the barracks back home. She just felt seen.

She pulled at one end of a ribbon tied around the package, loosening the bow and pushing it to the side. The fabric that wrapped the package was soft, and she paused to run it though her fingertips, enjoying the feeling of not needing to rush.

She could only see a sliver of the fabric beneath, a silver blue that reminded her of the lake in Kaizia. The fabric was so light, and it looked like flowing water when she picked up a corner and let it run through her fingers. It was even softer than the packaging. She wanted to wrap herself in the fabric and sink into the cool comfort of it.

"What is it?" She was almost afraid to continue unwrapping it, to see what gift Cassimir had thought to get for her. It was something for her to wear to his uncle's festivities, but she hadn't had a lot of luck with other people picking out her clothing.

"A dress." He didn't say more. She pulled the rest of the packaging away from the dress, her hands shaking slightly. Cassimir leaned down behind her. "You should trust that I know you well enough to pick out the right dress." His words were gentle, and they tickled the back of her neck where they moved the small strands of her hair.

"It's not about trust." She said the words before she could really think about them. She trusted him, but she didn't know why she couldn't let go of this fear. Maybe because she was tired of being controlled, of being made to fit a certain image of who she was going to be.

"I know." And she had the feeling he even knew everything she wasn't telling him. The internal struggle of letting herself be vulnerable with someone who could so easily ruin her if he chose. "You will have to unwrap it at some point though."

She took another deep breath, letting the air move through her and calm the side of her that still wasn't used to being unshielded. And she pulled the dress free from its wrapping, letting it cascade down the length of her body as she held it up against her. Cassimir had made a good choice with the color. It suited both the way her already tan skin had darkened under the desert sun, and the unmistakable red of her hair.

There were no cut outs on this dress, no roses to keep her barely covered. Instead, the light fabric was wrapped so that her whole upper body would be covered, the edges finished with silver ribbons. The bodice looked almost like armor, running over her shoulders in several lines of small silver scales. The best part was that despite the normal Taezhali style, Cassimir had the dress made with sleeves. She could feel that the fabric was light enough to keep her from sweating, but yet when she stuck one of her hands into the sleeve, she couldn't get even a peak of her tattoos.

She felt relieved, and then guilty as her cheeks started to burn, embarrassment painting her face a telltale pink.

"I forgive you."

She didn't even have to explain what had made her so worried, or ask for his forgiveness. He was already there willing to give it to her, because he knew why she would be nervous about getting another dress. Why she would want to keep the tattoos on her arms hidden from large crowds of people.

"It's perfect." Her voice was quiet, but as he leaned in behind her to lay a gentle kiss on her cheek, she knew he heard her. He heard her and saw her and knew her like no one else ever had, and he was still here. And she knew without knowing how, that he wasn't going anywhere.

35

RHENA

Rhena was tired of pacing her room, waiting for the vines in the corner to spit out another letter from Saiden. She was tired of so many things these days, and none of them were getting any better while she was loafing around in her room.

On a whim, Rhena grabbed her sword, and tightened the strap of its sheath over her chest before she headed out. She wasn't sure if she should keep the plant covered or not, but she had yet to find a reason to do so. She could always blame it on some life gifted recruit overstepping their bounds.

She doubted anyone was even paying attention to what was going on in her room, though she didn't want that thought to make her complicit. It only took one wrong step for everything in her life to shatter around her. And she knew Revon was watching her, despite every fake smile he gave her, and that he still didn't trust her.

Not that he should.

Too few people waited in the training room. She wanted noise and energy and people to get lost in. And she needed a fight. Preferably with someone stronger than her, someone who would make her sweat.

Then she spotted Talon across the room, and knew that she could still get exactly what she wanted. He and Yusef were running through drills. Despite the age difference, everyone was already assuming they would become partners.

Rhena moved so she was close enough to them and started stretching, trusting that young male rage would do the rest for her. She kept an eye on the two boys out of her periphery, and noticed as Yusef pushed Talon and pointed at her. She did her best to hide her smirk when he came over to where she was stretching.

"Do you need something Talon?" She asked, not even bothering to turn and face him. Rhena needed time to hide the satisfied gleam from her face.

"I think there's a debt between us. It's time to settle it."

She knew exactly what he meant, "pick a weapon." Rhena didn't watch him stride to the wall, didn't really care what weapon he picked. She wasn't nearly as talented as her trainers, but she had been trained by the best. She wasn't afraid of a boy barely two years older than her.

He picked up the eskrima sticks, wooden staffs about two feet long, and handed her two of them. She didn't like the weapon, and she wasn't sure why he had chosen it, but she didn't care either. There was so much rage building inside her, it felt good to have a target.

She stood and got her feet spread under her, adjusting her grip as she waited for Talon to do the same. He swung first, one horizontal swing to the head, the other to her knees. She ducked the first and jumped the second, raising her own weapons so she could use them to block the inevitable third strike.

Rhena met his next strike above her head pushing back against his force. He was bigger than she was, but she hadn't listened to all Saiden's training for nothing. While he was pushing against her, she swung the other stick and struck out at his abdomen. If he were actually an enemy she would have struck much harder, but the force was still enough for him to bend forward, releasing her other arm.

She vaulted over him, enjoying the surprise on Yusef's face as she did so, and struck Talon behind the knees with just enough force to help him to the floor. She rested her stick at the back of his head, tapping him so he knew that it would have been quite the blow had she put force behind it.

Rhena backed away when she was sure he wouldn't try anything, stepping out of the way of any misguided rage. But she didn't quite understand the look that crossed his face as he dipped his head towards her.

Yusef on the other hand did not seem to accept Talon's defeat. He picked up the sticks Talon had dropped, pushing his friend out of the way and swung hard straight at her head. Outside of the circle Talon called for him to stop, but Yusef's face burned with rage, like she had personally wronged him instead of his friend. Then she remembered the wall of ice she had built to keep him from pulling her off Talon.

His reputation, no, his ego was bruised. More so even than Talon who had been at the tip of her sword. Rhena could barely keep him at bay, blocking his strikes only inches before they made contact. The kind of contact that would break her bones clean through. He didn't need a blade to hurt her.

Then she felt her gifts rising in response to his. She didn't know Yusef well enough to know how the goddess manifested in him, but she could feel the power rising nonetheless. Pieces of the marble floor cracked free, wrapping around his knuckles. One hit from that would do serious damage, and she felt her powers spike in response.

"That's enough Yusef." Rhena was shocked when Talon stepped in between them, his back to her, as if she was not the threat here. "This isn't the way."

Yusef took a single step forward, and Talon moved to match him, keeping him from getting any closer to Rhena. The two boys struggled. She had never seen partners fight like this, but most of her exposure came from Mozare and Saiden, who only ever fought in training.

Talon's next words were directed at her, though he didn't turn to face her. "It's time for you to go."

Unsure why, Rhena did what he directed, turning and getting as far away from Yusef as the barracks would allow her.

36

SAIDEN

Saiden had spent most of the day with Loralei and Eleni getting ready for the emperor's festivities. Eleni had shown up outside their door early that morning, insisting they all spent the day together, so they could get "properly ready" as Eleni had repeated time and again. She was secretly glad to spend the day relaxing, yesterday had been rough on her system, but Loralei was beyond excited to be pampered in the emperor's castle.

By the time they needed to actually start dressing, Saiden felt ready to soar. Her skin was softer than she had ever felt it, though it had taken the palace staff a while to smooth out the callouses on her feet. Eleni and Loralei had laughed, but until a few weeks ago, Saiden had worn boots daily, so she wasn't surprised that her feet were rougher than either of her friends.

Someone had even used a colorful paint to lacquer her fingernails, a shimmery silver that would match the accents of her dress. She had let Eleni choose for her, smiling as she got excited about the dress Cassimir had designed for her. She hadn't even taken it into account that the dress wasn't a normal Taezhali design, that he would have had to be involved in the decisions. Eleni thought it was super romantic.

Saiden had spent most of that conversation trying to hide her blush behind her fingers.

Loralei and Eleni picked out their own dresses, Eleni's a lighter red that shifted as she swirled the skirt around. The scarf she had chosen was dark, with small golden beads embroidered into it. Loralei had chosen a purple dress, smiling as she ran her fingers through the puffy layers of fabric. Saiden smiled at the once queen, hoping that Loralei could understand how much she regretted what had happened in the palace.

It took both girls to help her into the dress. She remembered the last night she had spent with her mom, when she had helped her through the straps of Revon's dress, helping her build her armor for wearing it in public. Now, she had friends to help her carry the armor, to carry the weight of it all.

"I can braid." She said randomly into the room, smiling when the other girls looked at her with funny faces. "I just.." She cringed. "I want to do something to help you both, the way you've helped me."

She was quick braiding Eleni's mahogany hair into a tight bun at the nape of her neck, before she wrapped her prayer scarf and pinned it into place. Loralei was more hesitant, but eventually she sat down in the small chair at the corner of the room, her back tense.

"Cara used to be the one who did my hair." Her voice sounded hollow. "But she was using me the entire time."

Saiden's heart broke. "She was wrong, to use you like that. We were wrong."

She braided the long black locks of Loralei's hair into a coronet around her head. She was the rightful Queen, and Saiden wanted to remind her that she deserved that honor.

Cassimir was wearing a suit that matched her. She was shocked at first, turning to hide behind a corner before he could even see her. The girls had decided she should leave her hair down, and they had compromised by braiding a small piece at the side to keep her hair from hanging in her face. Now she wanted nothing more than to hide behind it.

Cassimir's suit was a darker shade of blue, a stormier sky than her dress, the lapels lined in the same silver, one shoulder covered with silver scales. There was a sort of cape hanging from a chain, though she wasn't sure it spanned his whole back.

Mozare was the one who found her. His suit was completely black, though she wasn't surprised by that at all.

"You can hide back here all night, but you should know your skirts have been giving you away for like twenty minutes." She punched him and he laughed.

"I have not been back here for twenty minutes."

"I thought the sun was going to set before you came out." She glared at him. The sun was still high in the sky, and during the warm months, Taezhali was bathed in sunlight for most of the night. "What are you worried about anyway?"

She didn't have an answer. She had just seen the boys, and had the overwhelming feeling of being a fraud. Of not belonging in this group of people who had already sacrificed so much for her. Who had already bled for her.

She took a few calming deep breaths before stepping around the corner, Mozare laughing slightly behind her where he followed, careful not to step on the edges of her dress. She watched Cassimir take her in for the first time, and felt everything slow around them. Mozare was still laughing, the sound louder now, yet somehow farther away.

He bowed to her, and she did her best to curtsy the way Loralei always had, an elegant twist of her body and her skirts. She was sure she looked like a fool, but she wasn't bothered by it. He offered her an arm, and they walked in behind the rest of their friends.

He leaned over to whisper, "as stunning as I thought it would be."

"And how long were you planning this dress?" She teased him. He smiled sheepishly as he looked down at her.

"Probably too long. Since I saw you at that dinner." Cassimir answered after a moment. "I knew you deserved to be dressed in clothing that suited you better. That showed who you are."

She didn't understand what he meant, but she didn't mind it either.

She was happy. Loralei was sitting next to Mozare, the purple a bright contrast against the backdrop of his black. Still, they looked like they belonged, and she wondered how she hadn't seen it earlier.

Saiden sat across the low table from them, resting in a pile of soft cushions in between Eleni and Cassimir. And she felt formidable.

Saiden hadn't been expecting so much food. Though, with the way Cassimir cooked, she probably should have. She had anticipated this evening to be a lot like the balls that Loralei used to host in Kaizia. Ones she had reluctantly participated in, between her shifts standing guard at Loralei's side. There were still people dancing, a beautiful more rhythmic dancing. She sat watching them move, the bright swirls of color swaying about the room as couples twirled around each other.

She was more than happy to spend the entire evening eating. There was nothing that matched the rich flavors of Taezhali cooking. And while the music and dancing were tempting, her friends were seated with her at the table, and she was content to stay with them.

Her friends, it turned out, were not. Eleni was the first to stand, dragging Mozare and then Loralei with her into the crowds, spinning and moving in and out of the rows of couples. When Eleni sat down for a break, the two Kaizians remained, dancing together as Saiden watched how they responded to each other. They were completely out of step with everyone around them, and yet they still flowed together.

She smiled behind her napkin, and sent a prayer to whoever was listening for them to both find the happiness they deserved. Even if they only needed each other in order to heal. Cassimir kept leaning over, whispering one thing or another about the different guests in attendance. He was careful when introducing her to different members of the royal council or to his own extended family, making sure she was never pushed too far out of her own comfort zone.

She didn't even have to ask. One moment they were greeting one of his father's closest friends, and then they were eating fried dumplings, the inside bursting with juicy flavor. She moaned as she bit into another one, savoring the way the spices danced across her taste buds. Then Cassimir was offering her his hand. She stood from her cushions, making sure she wiped her fingers on one of the silk napkins before resting her hand in his.

She figured they were going to be meeting another dignitary or politician, but then he was leading her into the crowd of dancing people. She pulled her hand out of his, freezing on the edge of the swarm of people. She didn't see the beautiful swashes of color anymore, just too many people. Cassimir rested a hand on her face.

The overwhelming sound around her quieted a bit. "We don't have to do anything you aren't comfortable with. When you are able, if you wish it, I would like to share this with you." He didn't pull her into the crowd, or move for her to sit down, he just waited. And he watched her, reading her face for any sign that he should get her out of there.

She knew she could do this. She had been practicing control, how to regulate her emotion, and squash her powers into a box where they were contained. Now, here with Cassimir, she would be able to have this happiness without anything ruining it. She placed her hand back in his and he pulled her closer to him.

Dancing here was like nothing she had experienced before, though that wasn't surprising considering her limited exposure to parties. Even at Loralei's ball she hadn't danced more than once or twice, and she and Mozare hadn't been paying attention to the steps. Now, she was focusing on the back and forth. The way Cassimir would push her away, only to pull her closer.

She tried to learn, but every time she looked down at her feet she would trip on something. The people around them had cleared enough space so she wouldn't keep bumping into them. Normally she would've been embarrassed, would've found someplace to stand where no one would notice her. But she didn't mind sharing this space with Cassimir.

She tried to look at her feet again, but his finger on her chin stopped her. "Just lean into it. Trust the movements and flow." Cassimir smiled at her, using that same finger to push a stray piece of her hair back behind her ear. She realized that despite her best efforts, her armor was still up. She looked at Cassimir, the way he was smiling across from her, and then she closed her eyes, letting the music flow through her, trusting him to lead the way.

It was invigorating, letting go of the control. When she felt her powers swirling within she subdued them, turning with Cassimir, his leg bent between hers. She would've thought the skirts would get in the way, but he moved around them, never once stepping on them.

She smiled, letting her head fall back as he twirled her, both hands holding tightly to her waist as she sank into the feeling. He pulled her up, one of his hands pressing in between her shoulder blades, removing the space between them. She was breathing hard and she opened her eyes, looking up at him.

There was a gentle smile on his face, as he leaned down over her. She was sure he was going to kiss her. She wanted him to kiss her. But then she felt a tap on her shoulder, and Cassimir pulled her to his side.

"May I cut in?"

37

MOZARE

MOZARE WAS HAVING A TERRIBLE NIGHT. HE WAS TRYING TO ENJOY THE evening, trying to smile and dance the way everyone around him was, but he couldn't control his reactions. Every time he bumped into someone on the dance floor, he felt his hand reaching for the spot on his back where his axes should have been. He had danced with Eleni and Loralei, ignoring the other girls who tried to get his attention.

And he was doing his best to keep breathing. To remember that he wasn't in danger here, that they could relax and enjoy the evening. But there were too many people for his senses to stop kicking into overdrive. He wanted to grab each of his friends and bring them somewhere safe. He went to get something to drink and was surrounded by different council members, each of them trying to ask him a different question.

He couldn't find anyone to get him out of this. He stuck his hands in his pockets, hiding the way they were shaking. Hiding the way his hands were eager for a blade. Battle would've been preferable to this mess. He would even take fighting with Loralei over standing here and trying to diplomatically answer the questions of a bunch of strangers who were all too self-important to let him finish answering before jumping onto the next question.

He excused himself after the fourth one, claiming that he needed to go find a bathroom. He couldn't care less if any of them had actually believed it, but as the room spun around him, the walls pulling in closer, he knew he had to get out of there before everyone got a front row seat to his panic attack.

He found an abandoned hallway, crouching down in a corner where he could lean on both sides of the hallway. Even here, the space was still closing around him, despite the open frames of the windows. He put his head in his hands and lowered it so that he was breathing from in between his knees.

He felt the shadows curl around him. The way they had all those years ago when he had first developed the gift. Trying to comfort him, or just banish the outside room from making it worse, he couldn't tell but he was grateful all the same. He had no control over his own thoughts, but maybe this would buy him enough time to get through the tightness in his chest. To be able to take a full deep breath before rejoining his friends.

He wanted to scream. Wanted to push all of this horribleness out of himself. Let the world deal with the darkness it had forced on him. All the shadows he'd had to hide behind. He was crying again, sobs pouring out of his chest. He didn't care if anyone could hear him, and the shadows around him were so thick that he knew even if they did, they couldn't find him here.

In the distance he could hear the sound of bare feet slapping on the cool floor. He focused on it, a steadier beat than his own heart, a rhythm that helped to pull him away from the edge.

She must have turned the corner, because he heard a gasp, and then he felt his shadows bending to let another person in. He had never felt that happen with his powers before. Especially considering Loralei was not gifted by the goddess of death. There was no way for her to be controlling the shadows, but in protecting him they seem to have taken on a sentience, and they decided to let her through.

She didn't speak at first, just wrapped her arms around him and let him fall into her. She smelled like flowers and fresh sunshine. Like everything warm and good in the world. His hands were clenched, wrapped in the scratchy fabric that made the layers of her skirts. Her long fingernails brushed through the tangled strands of his hair where he had been pulling at chunks of it.

Gradually, he felt the tightness of his chest loosen just enough that he pulled back from her, and worried about the stains his tears left on the front of her gown. She couldn't go back to the party now, not without being the object of everyone's attention.

"I should go get Saiden." She said, pushing her weight back to the heels of her feet as if she was going to get up from the floor. To leave the little safe haven here in the comfort of his shadows. He grabbed for her wrist before his brain even had time to process what he was doing.

"No." He shook his head, trying to get his thoughts in order. "No. Please stay." He felt selfish asking that of her. Asking anything of her, but she stayed anyway, leaning her bare back against the stone wall next to him.

"Why?" She asked the question without looking at him. He couldn't tell what she was asking for, and he knew there was so much he owed her an explanation for. So much he should beg her forgiveness for.

"I need someone who's been in the shadows, to show me the way back to the light." He didn't look at her either, but when she didn't repeat her question, he figured he had answered the right one. "I don't know how to fix all the bad things I've done, and it's tearing me apart."

"You can't." It wasn't the answer he had been hoping for. "You can't go back and fix things. Don't you think I would've done that already. We were given shitty cards and we played them the best way we could. Now we have to focus on being better. On learning from the pain we've caused. Otherwise, it really was for nothing."

He looked at her now, really looked at her. Without their titles, without any kind of uniform or armor to hide behind, he could see her more clearly. She was still just a girl, and they had made her into a monster by trying to force her to fit a mold. But she wasn't meant to be contained. She was meant to grow wild and free like the flowers she loved so much.

"Maybe we will figure it out, and maybe we won't" she continued. "But as long as we try, that has to count for something." It came out more like a question.

"It counts." He needed it to. They both did.

38

SAIDEN

The Crown Prince of Taezhali was waiting behind Saiden, a gold embroidered tunic hanging from his shoulders and a mischievous grin on his face.

"Even you cannot disobey the crown prince dear cousin. Especially in front of all of these witnesses. I think it's best you do as I wish before I cause a scene." Cassimir was stiff beside her, not yet letting go of her hips, where he held her tightly to his side. She stepped away. Whatever scene the prince was thinking of causing, she was sure it would do no good for anyone. And she didn't want the evening ruined by that. She could survive one dance.

She curtsied, doing her best to make this one truly formal. "It would be an honor your Imperial Highness."

"At least your new toy knows how to respect the chain of command." She could swear Cassimir growled at the prince's words. She stepped into Akil's open arms, letting him sweep her back into the dancing crowd before Cassimir had a chance to do something reckless, like knock his cousin out in a room full of people.

"You've impressed a lot of people Mistress." He leaned in when he spoke to her, like he was trying to share a secret. Saiden forced herself not to flinch at the proximity. "Even my little brother Khari couldn't stop talking about how magnificent you are. Not that I could blame him, you are an admirable specimen."

She couldn't stop her shiver that time, though if the prince noticed he simply continued his conversation without caring about her reaction.

"But none of them saw what I saw you do in that hallway." She felt her power surge at the memory, but she pushed against it. There were too many people in the hall for her to explode. "None of them understand the raw potential that exists inside you."

He ran a finger down her arm. She had never in her life been more grateful for sleeves. She caught Cassimir's glaring face at the edge of the crowd, ready to step in if she gave any sign that she needed him. That she wanted his interference. She gave a slight shake to her head.

"I am honored your majesty." She inclined her head, despite everything in her body, everything she had been trained to know since childhood telling her she should not let this man out of her sight.

When the song ended she quickly excused herself, not caring that it was rude, or against etiquette. She needed to get out of there before she killed him with just the scales of her dress. Cassimir met her by the door, opening his arms so that she could step into the warmth of him, surrounded by his smell of spices and citrus. She could feel the prince's eyes still lingering on her back.

"Come on we'll go." He said, tucking her under his arm as he made his way through the thinning crowd and outside. The sun had barely dipped past the horizon painting the sky in a thousand shades of blue and red and orange. Cassimir removed his jacket, laying it on the sand so that they could sit.

"Your cousin is…." She searched for the right word. "Eclectic."

Cassimir laughed, but there was still a hardness to his features. She grabbed for his hand, holding it between hers in her lap. "That's certainly one way to put it." He took a deep breath. "My father worries that he is not exactly fit to be the next emperor. It's why my uncle has refused to pass the throne on to him. But without concrete proof of wrong doing, there is nothing they can actually do."

Saiden grimaced. In her kingdom, they had taken the throne from one person they thought didn't deserve it and gave it to someone who was not able to run their country. Here, Cassimir had to face that the person who would someday inherit responsibility for the country he loved was not fit to be its ruler.

She leaned over and rested her head against his shoulder, watching as more of the sunlight faded, and the first stars began to shine in the darkening night sky.

"If we could run away somewhere, do you think we could find someplace better?" She asked. She had wondered about that a lot as she was growing up, if there was somewhere she could go, where no one would recognize her hair as the curse marking that it was. Where people wouldn't see her and avoid her without even knowing her first.

"I think, we have a responsibility to make these places the best we can. To not give up on these places we love, because they are our homes. And if we don't take care of them, who will?"

"Why did Taezhali send its ambassador to fight in a Kaizian rebellion?" She had been wondering that for a while, and was using it now to move the conversation somewhere she was more comfortable. Facing their responsibility seemed too much, too big of a weight for her to pick up right now.

"My uncle said that the people have a right to be free of rulers that do not suit them. Though I am sure that he had something else to gain from it." Cassimir smiled, standing up. "Whatever it was, I am glad it led me to you."

He pulled her up too fast for her to keep her balance, resulting in her slamming into his chest. He laughed as she rubbed at a spot on her forehead she was almost certain was going to bruise.

He bowed, offering her another hand. In the distance she could still hear the music playing from inside the palace. She smiled as she took his hand and he pulled her into him, not caring about form or style. They just swayed back and forth, content together.

Cassimir walked her back to their room after their dance, both of them smiling brightly. Her feet ached slightly from the dancing, but no worse than a long day of training in her heavy boots. She pulled the wrapped sandals off in one of the hallways and made the rest of the way to Cassimir's apartment barefoot. The cool touch of the floor against her feet helped to keep her face from heating too much.

He grabbed her arm gently before she could reach the handle of her door, stopping her, and slowly spinning her around.

"I think we might have been interrupted before." He spoke, his voice low. She wasn't sure if he was worried about people hearing them, or if he just wanted to keep the words between them. She looked up at him. She had never minded that the other soldiers seemed to pair off, that Mozare used to disappear at night to meet up with different members of the legion. It was like her heart knew that there was someone waiting for her, and hadn't allowed her to feel this way until she met him.

She smiled shyly. This was completely new territory for her, the back and forth flirtations, the vulnerability of allowing another person to truly know you. But she liked that it was Cassimir who was taking the time to know her. "Were we?"

He took a step forward, and she took a matching step back, watching as the smile on his face grew. She had to force herself not to laugh. She gasped slightly when her back touched the wall, the warmth seeping through the fabric of her dress. Cassimir pressed a hand to her cheek, running his fingers through her hair.

"You'll tell me if you want me to stop?" He kept his eyes level on hers, and she nodded.

"I promise."

He leaned his head down slowly, giving her time to change her mind, to pull away from him. She tilted her chin up, into his kiss. And then his warm lips were on hers. He tasted like the citrus that always came through in the smell of him. She gave him control, letting him lead the same way he had while they were dancing, his hand moving to grip her around the waist again. She smiled into the kiss, loved that she could feel him doing the same.

She stood on the balls of her feet, pressing herself into the kiss, wrapping herself in the feeling of him. What felt like hours later, they pulled apart, and he rested his forehead on hers, both of them breathing heavily.

"How was that?" He asked her. She smiled at him, blush coloring her cheeks.

THE BLOOD-CURSED

"It was perfect." She set herself back on her feet, hiding slightly behind her hair. "I'll see you in the morning?"

"And every morning after." He smiled, using one hand to dramatically flip the half of his jacket with a cape, bowing before turning and heading for his room.

Loralei wasn't in their room, but Saiden figured she was still at the party, dancing with different lords and ladies. Saiden hoped she would consider Mozare, but she also knew that there was some pain you couldn't forgive. She would just continue to pray that they both found the happiness she knew they deserved.

Saiden was awake with the sun the next morning, her face bright and yesterday's smile still lingering. She slipped into loose pants, the front layered so that when she moved certain ways her bare knees could slip through. She tugged a white long sleeved shirt over her head, tucking the material into her pants. She had an early session with Eleni this morning, to which she would probably still be late, despite waking up so early.

Eleni was a morning person, waking even before the sun to conduct her rituals and tend to her garden. It was the same kind of dedication Saiden had had to her training when she was first starting, and she admired Eleni for it.

She opened the door to her room and was surprised to find Loralei and Mozare lounging in the common room. Mozare laid across her lap, tie loosened, wrapped in the layers of Loralei's purple gown. Loralei looked up as Saiden entered her room, pressing a finger over her mouth for Saiden to keep quiet. Whatever was going on, she had lots of questions, but for now Mozare was actually sleeping, so she carefully snuck through the room, leaving the door open a crack in case the click of it closing would wake him.

She went into the kitchen. Someone had come after their family dinner to clean and put away all the dishes they had left scattered around. On the middle of one of the counters they had left two bowls. The larger one was filled with various fruits. She grabbed an orange slice and took a big bite wiping at the juices that dripped down her throat with a piece of cloth from the counter. Then she grabbed a handful of kashuwan from the smaller bowl to share with Eleni.

She traced the path back to Eleni's garden, knocking at the secret door hidden in the wall. She waited, but no one came to answer. She felt worry start to pool in her belly. Eleni had never missed a session, never arrived later than Saiden. Her handful of nuts was forgotten as they tumbled from her fingers and she dropped to her knees in front of the small hole she had seen Eleni use to unlock the room.

She didn't have a key, only Eleni and the Emperor did, but she wouldn't let that stop her. She needed to find her friend. She could have fallen and hurt herself, she could be stuck in there in pain. She pressed her hand to wall, and let the panic push at her powers. She couldn't control it, and she couldn't push it down, she just let the raw force of it explode through the lock.

The door opened next to her, and she stood, racing to push through it. She made her way through the maze, calling out Eleni's name, looking for her mentor, her friend, among the rows of growing plants. Saiden's voice broke on her name, and then she heard someone calling her own.

She pushed her way back out of the secret garden, not paying attention to the different plants she was likely stepping on. Cassimir was standing in the hallway, his smile dropping when he saw her.

"What happened?"

"I can't find your sister. Eleni, she isn't in the garden."

"Maybe she just slept too late." She could see on his face that he didn't believe himself even as he spoke the words.

She grabbed his hand, pulling back through the hallways moving to find the small room outside of Cassimir's apartment where Eleni slept. They knocked on the door, and when no one answered, Saiden stepped back and kicked the door in. She didn't even check to see if it was unlocked, her brain was racing far too fast, her heart beating a thunderous rhythm against her rib cage.

"She's not here." Cassimir's voice was small, the words broken. He turned to look at her, mouth opened, words missing. Someone behind her interrupted.

"Your grace, mistress, the emperor has summoned you both to his chambers." The servant bowed, turning and retreating back into the hallway before either of them could ask what the emperor needed this early in the morning. They shared a look before he grabbed her hand, leading the way through the winding tunnels. She never could have found it on her own.

The palace was built like a labyrinth on purpose, the emperor and his sons buried at the heart, protected by the rest of his house. A clever design, though she couldn't bear to admire it now when she was frustrated with how far they had to go just to get there. Not when Eleni might still be hurt somewhere. Although maybe she had already been summoned. Maybe she would be waiting with her uncle, having morning tea with an excuse as to why she hadn't thought to send word to Saiden before they were supposed to meet at the garden.

They pushed through the door, and were shocked. The emperor stood in only his night clothes, a loose tunic hanging on thinning shoulders. Without the regalia she had always seen him wearing, he looked small. Utterly human. And frail, a man past the prime of his life who had born the weight of ruling a vast empire.

Cassimir's father was kneeling on the ground next to him, head in his hands

"You should both sit," the emperor said, motioning to some cushions scattered on the floor. "You aren't going to like what I have to say."

39
MOZARE

MOZARE WOKE WITH HIS FACE WRAPPED IN THE FLUFF OF LORALEI'S GOWN. He froze, his whole body tense as last night came flooding back to him. In the hallway he had told her everything. It was as if a well inside him had burst, the words flowing out like water. He picked his head up, letting their conversation run through his head, rubbing at his temples.

"I haven't slept properly in weeks." He had told her. "I keep dreaming that Revon has a hold of Saiden, or of Rhena. That he kills them the same way he killed you."

She had responded with a vulnerability of her own. "I feel that pain every time I close my eyes. I remember what it felt like to be hanging on the brink of life, to let a guard drag my body from my own palace."

They had been holding hands, but he couldn't remember who had grabbed for the other. "I can keep your nightmare away. Fight them off." He laughed at his own joke, trying to lighten the darkness in both of their lives.

"We can protect each other from the horrors nightfall brings." She had answered, completely serious. That was how they had ended up on the floor tangled around each other, his head in her lap. How they had fallen asleep in their evening dress, their clothes now wrinkled from sleep. He couldn't bring himself to look at her. To see pity on her face.

She ran a fingernail down his arm. "You are going to have to face me eventually." She said. And he knew she was right, but he didn't want to agree with her. He stood up from the floor, leaving the room and getting them both a glass of water. He heard an indignant huff as he left, though she gratefully accept the water he returned with. She drank so fast that some of the water dripped down her chin, soaking into the neckline of her dress. He couldn't bring himself to stop staring at it.

She caught him, and he felt his cheeks burn red. He turned away from her, finishing off his glass and setting it on one of the low tables. Saiden's door was already open, as was Cassimir's so he figured they were both off taking care of their morning routines. Loralei must have assumed the same thing, because when he turned, she was leaning towards him.

There was hunger on her face, and he was sure his expression matched. She gathered her skirts, crawling towards him on the floor, and sat with her legs straddled over his. He looked at her, waiting for her to make fun of him, for this to be another joke.

When she didn't move, he asked her, "What do you want?" His voice was hoarse around the words.

"Stress relief. A break from hating you maybe." She leaned in and kissed along his jaw, her long fingernails running through his hair again. He sat up straighter, wrapping his arms around her, holding her as he turned his head and met her lips with his. She made a small sound at the back of her throat, reaching one hand to the back of his neck and pushing his head closer to hers. He ran his fingers over the soft skin of her back, running one finger over the raised scar just inches from her spine.

She shivered at his touch, arching into his fingers. He grinned, removing his lips from hers, sucking at the skin below her ear. She moaned, pressing herself against his chest. He hadn't felt like this, like he deserved any happiness however brief, in a long time. She made him feel alive again.

There was a knock at the door, and they sprang apart, straightening their clothing as they turned to look at who was seeking their attention. He pulled his shirt to hang loose around him.

"The emperor requests your presence in his chambers. Training for the day has been canceled, and your friends are waiting for you. I am here to guide you, should you need the assistance." Mozare nodded at the man, then looked at Loralei.

"We're going to need a few minutes." There was no way they were going to meet the emperor in last night's wrinkled party clothes. Not to mention, he needed to cool down after what the servant's message had just interrupted. "Then you can take us to his majesty."

40

SAIDEN

Saiden saw Loralei and Mozare enter the room a few minutes after them. The tension in the room was already thick enough to press against her, but something between them was definitely different, strained but not with the same anger. She couldn't bring herself to think about it long when she was still waiting for the emperor to share his news. He had been worrying at the same sheet of paper since they got there, but he waited, not wanting to have to share the news more than once.

They sat on opposite sides of her, Cassimir still pacing a path on the rich carpet behind them. She knew she was going to need both of her friends to get through whatever news had brought Cassimir's father to his knees, sobbing without a care for who saw him.

The Emperor held up the paper and started to read. "For far too long, we have lived in the shadows of your rule." Saiden's heart dropped into her stomach. "While you reveled in opulence and waste, we snuck into your maze, and we have taken a treasure for ourselves. Your beloved niece will make a nice addition to my crew, if I do say so myself."

Saiden's face paled, her skin pulling tight, her fingers cold. She pulled the sleeves of her shirt down to cover them as the emperor continued. "Of course, I would be happy to return your niece unharmed, if in return, you free the Island of the Severed Key and grant authority for its trade and rule of its people to me. You have until nightfall to make your decision. Yifa will wait until then to receive your letter."

She only then noticed the large bird hovering in the opened window, talons scratching the ledge. She had grabbed both Loralei's and Mozare's hands, squeezing so hard her knuckles were white. It was a surprise that neither of them had shown any signs of pain. Perhaps, in their own shock, they had barely noticed.

Behind them, Cassimir had stopped pacing. She was afraid to turn around, to face him, but she owed him that much. He had saved her from a horrible fate, and now it was her turn to see him out of the darkness. She let go of her friends, standing as Cassimir yelled out.

"Give them the damned island, uncle." His face burned with rage and he did nothing to hide the hostility in his words. "They haven't wanted to be part of the empire for decades. They have Eleni, they have my sister, your niece. Surely, she is worth more than some floating piece of rock."

"It is not about the island nephew." Saiden didn't understand how the emperor continued to be so calm. How his sister's husband and his own nephew could be basically begging him to do something, and yet not a single hint of emotion showed on his face. "If we give in to their demands, my people will see that as a weakness. Who else will continue to exploit it?"

The emperor crumpled the piece of paper in his hand, throwing it into a pile of similarly crumpled papers. Cassimir dove towards it, sorting through the papers on his knees, looking for it.

"You are forbidden from going after her." The emperor didn't even look at him as he spoke the words that ripped through the room like a blade. Cassimir didn't look up from the ground either, didn't give her any hint of what was going on in his mind, the devastation he must be feeling. Saiden felt her spine stiffen. The emperor was a coward, she could see that now. Why he hid behind the jewelry and clothing and ceremony. Why he refused to do something about his son.

But she was no coward. And she had seen enough battle to know

THE BLOOD-CURSED

what was worth fighting for. She wasn't going to let another family be broken.

Saiden went straight back to her room after the emperor had dismissed them from his suite. She knew she should have stayed to comfort Cassimir, to give him someone to vent his feelings to, or just to hold him, but she had a limited window of time to get out of the palace before someone figured out what she was doing. That she was disobeying a direct order from their emperor.

Mozare came into her room a few minutes later, watching her turn and dance through the small room, grabbing all the things she had borrowed, the only things that were hers now, and stuffing them into a bag she had found in the closet. It wasn't the best thing for a pack, but she couldn't ask for provisions, so it would have to do.

"When are we leaving?"

"You have to stay. I need you to stay Moze."

He looked incredulous, like his brain could not even comprehend the idea of her going without him. "What, no. We're a team, we go together."

"I need you here in case Rhena needs help." If she sent them a letter because she was in danger, someone needed to be here to receive it. She saw him deflate, but there was understanding on his face. It would be hard for both of them, but this was the best way. "Try to stay out of trouble. The emperor won't be happy that I've disobeyed him, even if he didn't give me the order. He wouldn't want anyone questioning his authority. Just be careful around him, and that nasty prince. I don't trust him." The words rushed from her mouth, every warning she could think of, everything she could say to keep Mozare the safest he could be after she abandoned him.

She slipped into the kitchen, Mozare directly behind her, and realized that Loralei was subtly guarding the door, picking at her fingernails while she leaned against the frame. Giving her time to get out of there. She felt a wave of gratitude run through her, but she couldn't take the time to properly thank her. She looked at Mozare and he nodded, and she knew he understood her silent request to take care of Loralei as well, to have her back the same way he had always had Saiden's.

In the kitchen she packed the rest of the fruit and the full bowl of nuts, dumping them into wax wrappers before sticking them into her bag. She would have to be careful, make sure to spread them out. She didn't know if she could hunt in the desert, if her skills would be of any use trying to track whatever kinds of animals made their home in the Taezhali sands.

She went to move out of the kitchen and bumped into someone, pulling back and rubbing at her forehead. Cassimir was outside their kitchen, a pack over each of his shoulders.

"I was looking for you." She froze, unsure of where the conversation was going. If she should admit to going behind his uncle's back. "I'm coming."

She looked at him, tilting her head to the side slightly. "You knew I was going after her?"

"I know you aren't the kind of person to leave a friend to suffer. And you have no loyalty to my uncle." His eyes told her what his words didn't, that he was starting to doubt his own loyalty to the man. "Besides, you won't last long with what you've packed. I know the desert, you'll need me with you."

She nodded, and he reached into one of the packs to pull out a new sheath. He handed it to her, almost reverently. "I was hoping to give you these on a happier occasion, but there's no way you should be going into this unarmed."

She pulled one of the blades from its sheath. They were the brighter versions of the kindjal blades she had carried, the ones Nakti had given her. "I knew nothing could replace the ones you've lost, so I wanted to give you something different." They were exquisite, the blades both perfectly balanced. She strapped into the harness, feeling the weight like a long-lost comfort finally returned.

She reached over and hugged Mozare, squeezing him tight before letting go. She gave a small bow as they ran past Loralei, and she sent a prayer to the gods, hoping she would see them both again soon.

Cassimir led her through hallways she had never been down

before, the layout of the palace still confusing to her. They were careful in their booted feet not to make too much sound, not to alert anyone to their presence or where they were going. When they were free of the palace they ran, their feet digging into the sandy hills slowing them down, but they couldn't afford to walk, to be spotted by a rotation of guards.

When they were far enough away, she sunk to her knees, her chest and legs burning with the effort of running. She had taken too much time off from her exercise routine, preferring to train with Eleni on control and balance. And the desert terrain was so different from Kaizia's mountains. She wasn't prepared for this run. Her thoughts spiked her powers, and she shoved against them, pushing them back into the small cage she had built for them in the inside of her mind. She didn't have time to deal with them right now.

Cassimir gave her a canteen of water, instructing her to take small sips. He had obviously packed with more thought. She hadn't even considered water, used to being able to find lakes and streams whenever she was sent on emergency missions.

"The island of the severed key is due east, if we head that way, we should come to a small port village within a few days. Hopefully they will still be there, waiting for word from my uncle. If he hasn't sent that awful bird away yet, it might give us more time to get to her before they manage to get to a ship." Saiden nodded, agreeing with his plan, glad to have his knowledge and experience.

"We'll walk as far as we can today, and then we'll rest." She added, "push ourselves as hard as we can today to stop them from gaining too much of an advantage."

41
RHENA

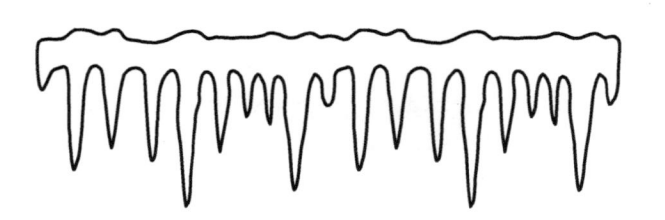

Rhena was being smart, laying low, but she wasn't going to be useless. Every day that went by without word from Saiden, either from the plant or through the official briefings from Revon, fostered more anguish in her chest. And their king was growing frantic, his madness more and more evident in the frequencies of his executions.

There had not been a day in recent weeks when the floors had not been soaked with blood.

Personally, she had seen enough bloodshed to last her quite a few lifetimes. Especially when Revon's idea of a trial consisted of him reading a list of perceived crimes as the ax swung. She wasn't going to sit by anymore, not when she knew these deaths weren't just.

Rhena might not have Mozare's talents for shadow bending, but she was good at sneaking around. And she knew the castle well because of Saiden and Mozare. She crept through the halls, listening for the footsteps of other soldiers, keeping her breath steady so that the cold in her veins wouldn't chill the air around her.

She'd stolen one of Mozare's cloaks, and his scent wrapped around her as she pulled his hood tighter to obscure her face. It wouldn't do for her to get caught. Not when there were people in the dungeon relying on her to get them out.

There was no way Revon knew about this entrance, and she was grateful he hadn't taken the time to explore the hidden passageways or seal them off. The stone groaned as she pulled it free, it wasn't used that often. But Rhena had planned the moment for the change of shifts, and when no one came running, she sent a quick thank you to her goddess for getting it right.

There were three young men caged together in the back cell. Rhena didn't know them. They were part of the old queen's guard, the non-gifted soldiers who had protected the dead queen before she had enlisted Saiden's service. Revon's men had found them holed up in the woods, but she didn't believe that they were plotting. Only that they represented an influence he wanted to snuff out.

They were set to be executed first thing in the morning. It was mandatory for all legionnaires to attend. Except these prisoners wouldn't make their appointment.

Rhena stepped to their cell, pressing a finger over her mouth when one of them began to speak. She focused all her will-power and control, and used it to form the ice in her veins into a key. This way, when the water melted there would be no trace that she had even been there.

She motioned for the men to follow her as she led them back to the tunnel. She didn't know any of them, and while she didn't believe they were traitors, she couldn't trust them either.

"Are you our rescuer or our doom?" She thought it was the silliest question she'd ever heard.

"I let you out didn't I?" She couldn't see them in the tunnels to know if he nodded or not. The other men didn't speak, and a dark thought made her wonder if they even could. She wouldn't have been surprised to find Revon had made it permanently impossible for them to plead their case.

"Then let us kill him. It may not set things right, but at least the cycle will begin again."

"I can't. This is one battle, not the war. You can't win here." He stepped closer to her, and despite the fact that he was bigger than she was, Rhena didn't step back. She was right, and she knew her conviction would prove it, if she only had the courage to stand for it.

This was what Saiden had meant. Small acts of bravery, small victories. This was what would set them free.

The sound that woke Rhena the next morning had her half convinced she was dying. It was a shrill noise that sank into her depths and wrapped around her bones. Rhena didn't even know what it meant, and all she wanted was to turn it off.

Someone came to her room, hands over their ears as they tried to speak over the sound. Rhena couldn't hear them, but she strapped her boots on, and threw a shirt over the tank top she had been sleeping in and followed them from her room.

A rush of people were all heading to the same place, and then Rhena finally realized what the alarm was for. *Revon had finally noticed the missing captives.* She had escorted them all the way to the woods, and then made them swear to never return. She couldn't know if they would keep their oath, but she hoped they would. For their own sake. Revon wouldn't wait for an execution next time.

He would kill them on sight.

Revon was pacing, his clothes wrinkled, the shadows at his feet fully formed into a small black cat. She hadn't seen that power before, but given no one else seemed to notice, she imagined Revon wouldn't appreciate her drawing attention to it.

And she didn't need to bring his focus to her. She couldn't give Revon any reason to hate her, any reason to suspect her more than he already did.

42

MOZARE

Mozare and Loralei were dragged from Cassimir's apartments by a group of eight guards a few hours after Saiden and Cassimir had left. Mozare kept his fingers crossed that since they were being brought to the emperor, their friends had managed to get far enough away to avoid capture.

He couldn't keep the smirk off his face as they cuffed him, and one of the guards punched him in the face when he askedabout keeping the cuffs for later and winked at him. He didn't care, as long as they kept their attention away from Loralei. Let him be the rebel they want to punish, if that helped to keep her safe.

He saw Loralei glare at him from the corner of her eye, but he couldn't tell what it was she was angry about. Him, for flirting with the guard, or if she could tell that he was only doing it for her benefit. Mozare stood tall as they were led to the imperial throne room, their escorts huddled around them despite the fact that they were in chains. He smirked again, it was smart to overestimate them, they could likely both escape their chains easily if they tried.

The guards forced them to their knees, pulling on Loralei's hair when she growled at them for handling her like that. She looked at them with enough venom to kill a man, though they only smiled back, winking and making comments about how good she looked on her knees. He burned each of their faces into his memory, prepared to kill them all as soon as he was freed from his chains. No man who would take advantage of a chained person deserved their life anyway.

The emperor had donned all the formal clothing and jewelry he had been wearing the day they had arrived, and then again at his party. But now that Mozare had seen him without it, he could point out all the places where the jewelry hung loose, where his tunic had been adjusted to hide the slightness of his frame.

He pulled his face into the mask of perfect stillness. He knew the emperor would wait, would try to get them to confess by simply maintaining silence. But he had used that tactic himself enough to know that he could wait out even the most stubborn of people.

The emperor did not turn out to be very stubborn. "My nephew, it seems, has been tainted by that girl you brought here. They've escaped together, likely to go after my niece. You were given this information only because of your closeness to Eleni, and now they have disobeyed orders."

Mozare let his face betray nothing of his feeling regarding the emperor's orders. Or the fact that while they were staying in his palace, they still weren't his subjects and had no reason to obey bullshit orders that made no sense.

The emperor banged his fist against the arm rest on his throne, the resounding clang of his jeweled wrist echoing through the cavernous throne room. There were no cushions on the floor this time, only empty space. And the two of them stuck in the middle of it.

"There will have to be a punishment for such corruption." He turned to look at Cassimir's father, tucked behind the right side of the throne. "Since it is your son who has disobeyed me, you will pick the punishment, and who will receive it in his absence."

Mozare turned the full brunt of his gaze towards Rami, letting the tiniest bit of himself slip through the mask he had put on. Begging Cassimir's father to bestow his punishment on Mozare, to let him take the blame, to leave Loralei out of it. When the emperor turned back around to face them, Mozare sealed away the emotion again. He knew the emperor would use it against them, hurt Loralei to make them both suffer if he saw how much Mozare was trying to avoid that outcome. But he saw Cassimir's father give the subtlest nod behind the emperor, and relief flooded through him.

"Your Imperial Highness," he spoke loud enough that all the room could hear him. "Because the girl can heal herself," an oversimplification of her gifts that Mozare couldn't tell if he understood or not, "the punishment should be bestowed on the boy. I think lashes would be a fitting punishment."

The emperor nodded, "50 lashes, to be served immediately." He saw Cassimir's father flinch, but there was nothing he could do that wouldn't make it worse.

Loralei on the other hand, had no problem sharing her outrage. "You'll kill him."

"Would you like to serve the sentence instead?" The emperor asked. He looked back at her, pleading with his eyes that she just let him do this. "Besides, if you are as talented a healer as my brother-in-law suspects, then you can make sure he doesn't die."

They made him face Loralei as they stripped him of the light Taezhali fabric. As they lowered the band of his pants just enough that the entirety of his back was exposed to the warm dry air. He tried to get her to look away, to look anywhere but at him as he heard the first swing heading towards his back.

"Count them girl." The emperor commanded from his throne. The snarl that ripped across her face was the only thing that made Mozare glad she hadn't turned away from him, there was no way the emperor would have let her get away with that.

He flinched as the strip of leather connected, arching his back away from the sting. Loralei started counting. There was another swing, then another. Three more and the lower section of his back was numb. His head was sagging. He lost count as they continued to pull back and slap the leather strip against his back. Loralei's voice barely broke through the fuzziness in his head. He felt it when they finally broke his skin, the warm blood running down his back.

"Look at me." Loralei's voice broke through the ringing in his ears. "Look up right now." She was blurry, but through his own tears he could see hers streaming down her cheeks. "There's only a few left."

His breathing was ragged, his chest tight as his body tried to separate from the pain. He saw a guard come behind Loralei, and he pulled against the men holding him. The guard smirked, but only bent over to unlock her chains. She pushed herself off the blood-soaked floor, catching him as the guards released his arms and he fell forward. His blood was soaking into the bottom of her skirt, dying the tan fabric a color that matched Saiden's hair.

She lifted him, and he could feel the muscles in her arms flexing as she supported his full weight. His feet dragged on the floor and he willed himself to put them to use, to help her, but his muscles wouldn't respond. She didn't even turn to look at the emperor, still sitting on the high dais of his throne room, before she pulled him free.

43

SAIDEN

Saiden was surprised by how exhausted she was when Cassimir finally said they would make camp for the night. He pulled two tightly wrapped sleeping rolls and a canvas tent out from the bag he had been carrying around all day. She watched as he silently unfolded them, getting to work setting up the tent without asking her for any help.

She felt completely out of her element, both in setting up a desert campsite, and in easing the tension that was clear between Cassimir's shoulders. She bit at the dry skin around her thumbnail as she watched him tie the last knots to keep their tent up. She set her backpack down, kneeling in the fine sand to pull out a small serving of fruits and nuts for them to eat tonight. They hadn't taken a break all day, and her stomach was reminding her of that fact now.

"You are going to have to sit at some point." She did her best to keep her voice gentle, to remind him that she was here if he needed it without using those words. She patted the spot next to her on one of the sleeping mats. He took a deep breath, running a shaking hand through his hair before he folded into a seat next to her.

She smiled slightly, and offered him a handful of the nuts she had stolen from the kitchen, splitting them between them. They ate in silence, watching the sun sink lower on the horizon. She hadn't expected to watch another sunset with Cassimir so soon, especially not so far away from the palace. She hoped that her friends would stay where they were safe, but she couldn't deny that she was grateful he had come along despite his uncle's orders.

When he was finished, he bent at the waist resting his head in his hands. Hesitantly she reached over, running her fingers up and down his back in slow circles, waiting for him to tell her how she could help him. Waiting to feel like she knew what she should do to make this better.

"Tell me that we'll get my sister back." He whispered between the cage of his fingers. "Tell me that I won't have to lose another piece of my family." He was crying, his back shaking slightly with ragged breaths.

"I promise you, if it is within my power, I will return Eleni to you hale and whole." She added the words of her own vow in her mind. *And if I can't, I will destroy everyone who took her from you.* Cassimir looked up at her, not trying to hide that he was worried and terrified. Not trying to hide the piece of him she could see was proud.

"My sister was twelve when our mother died, I was fourteen. She looks just like my mother, the same wild spirit in both of them too." He laughed, despite the unshed tears in his eyes. "The night we sent her spirit back into the universe I barricaded myself in my room, told myself it was better to keep my grief hidden, to cry my tears and be done with it."

"I'm still not sure how she did it, but somehow my sister found a way through all the furniture I had used to cover my doors, to keep people out, and she stayed with me. I am the big brother, yet she sat there comforting me, tears in her eyes. And then she started to sing. I'd barely remembered the lullabies our mother used to sing us, but Eleni knew every word. She sat with me until the sun rose in the sky, and the pain, the hole that loss had carved inside me, she had filled it with memories and love. I keep thinking that there won't be enough to fill the hole if I lose her too."

Saiden reached over and grabbed his hand, holding it tight to her chest with both of her own. His skin was warmer than hers despite the sun they had both been under all day. "You won't lose her." The words were out of her mouth before she realized what she was promising, but they felt true as she spoke them. "Your sister is strong and resourceful, she will give us the time we need to get her back."

He smiled at her, wiping the tears from his cheeks. "We should sleep." His words were accented by a yawn. He stretched up, revealing a band of golden brown skin at his waist that made her look away and blush. She had already seen him shirtless twice, yet this felt suddenly more intimate.

She pulled her sleeping mat away, grabbing a thin cotton blanket from her bag, not for warmth, but for the comfort of wrapping it around herself.

"You should lie closer to me," she heard the hint of a tease in Cassimir's words. "It can get very cold at night."

She turned to look at him, shaking her head. "It's not safe. If I have a nightmare I could char you where you lay." She folded her hands together in her lap, fear making her pull away from him. "I can suppress it during the day, but at night it's out of my control. I am a danger to everyone close to me, you've seen what I become."

"When you were unconscious and those men attacked us-" Cassimir began.

"I could've killed you. And Moze.

"But you didn't." He reached across the space she had made between them, pulling her hands free from each other so he could hold them both. "Your power was all around us, but it didn't touch either of us. You were death personified," she flinched, but he shook his head at her, "glorious justice as you stopped them from hurting us. Something inside you, the special thing that makes you who you are, protected us even when you were overwhelmed with power."

She shook her head again, "Moze and Loralei," she hadn't stopped having the scene in the hallway on repeat in her head.

"You wrapped them in cocoons of light. The only thing that sustained any damage was the architecture, which is doubtless already fixed by now. You didn't hurt them then, and you won't hurt me now. You aren't capable of it."

He pulled on her hand giving her time to pull back as he stood, and then rearranged their sleeping mats so they were side by side under the cover of the tent. And he waited. For her to decide if this is what she wanted. Despite everything that must be going on inside his mind, he still gave her the choice. She laid down on one of the mats, fluffing out her blanket and lifting the other side for him to lay under.

He smiled, the same gentle smile she had been sharing with him all evening, and laid down to watch the stars until they were both sleeping soundly.

44
MOZARE

When Mozare could finally open his eyes again, he saw the cream colored sheets of the big bed in Cassimir's room. The ambassador had originally offered to let the girls share this room, but they had chosen the smaller one Mozare assumed Cassimir usually put guests in. He could hear the soft echo of snores next to him, but turning caused pain to flare back through him. The snoring stopped, and then Loralei was hovering next to him.

"You idiot. You ripped open another of the wounds." He moved so he was laid flat against the bed again, and then Loralei's face was suddenly level with his. "Did you not think I had enough work trying to make sure you'll be able to feel your back again? Thought it would be helpful to pull at my hard work while I tried to get a few minutes of sleep?" She was angry, but the words lacked their usual bite.

"It's good to see you too." His words slurred, and he looked at her for an explanation.

"The chef brought me some sedatives. Gave me time to get the worst of your back fixed without you wiggling and making it difficult. I'll need a bit more time before I am able to do any more, I've never exhausted my gifts like this. It's harder, being so far away from a temple, and I've never had much practice working on others to begin with-" she was rambling, her voice shaking.

"Come lie down." He sat, lifting his arm only high enough to pat the warm spot where she had been sleeping. "You need your strength too. I can handle some time like this." To be honest, he couldn't even feel enough of his back to know how bad it had been, or how much she had already healed him. But he knew what that exhaustion felt like when you had run through your power, and he didn't want her to burn out.

He felt her reluctantly return to her side of the bed they were sharing, her eyes still trained on his back. She ran a single finger near his shoulder, her skin cool against his. Fever was sure to be setting in now if it hadn't already, and the dry desert heat didn't help.

"Do you have water?"

She reached around him, grabbing a small cup and gingerly lifting his head to help him drink. What little water spilled on the bed felt soothing as he laid back down. He wanted to talk to her, wanted to hear Loralei's voice, but he didn't know what he could say, what he should say. He had never had an injury that wasn't quickly dealt with, and now he was stuck here with a healer that shouldn't be here anyway.

"Why did you stay?" He turned his head to the side to watch her face shift, surprise flitting across it before her brow furrowed in thought. "You could've left as soon as we got here, went somewhere else and made a new band." Now he was rambling.

"This is not the first time I stayed where others did not want me," He tried to interrupt her, but she didn't stop. "This is the first time I've felt I should stay, that I had purpose. And that I owed it to myself to figure out if I could forgive you both." Her words got quieter as she spoke them.

"Did you figure it out?" He felt sleep pulling at him, the sedatives still strong in his system, pure exhaustion or a mix of both he couldn't tell.

She leaned forward and kissed him gently before turning her back to him and going back to sleep. He watched her, curled tight around herself, until sleep pulled him back under.

THE BLOOD-CURSED

He slept for what felt like weeks before waking again, Loralei's hands hovering over the wounds on his back. "How long have I been asleep?"

"Long enough for me to get another chunk of flesh healed. You'll have some horrid scars though. He turned his head to look at her behind him, the broken look on her face as she stared at his back. She didn't look at his face even as she asked him "why did you make Cassimir's father punish you?"

He closed his eyes, remembering the desperation that had flooded him when he needed Cassimir's father to recognize the question on his face. "I want to earn your forgiveness."

"In blood?"

"If I have to."

Loralei picked up a cloth, wrung the water into the clay bowl under it and gently dabbed it on a spot at his side. He hissed, residual pain lingering, but he didn't mind that he could finally feel again, even if it was pain. The cloth's water was cool, and he focused on that feeling instead, as Loralei continued to rinse the rag and clean spots on his back, gradually turning both the cloth and the water red.

45
SAIDEN

Loud sounds woke her from her sleep, and she shook Cassimir awake as the first cart in a long line seemed to fly past the small dune where they had camped for the night. She put a hand over his mouth, putting a finger over her own to show him they needed to be quiet. When he nodded, she rose to the balls of her feet, moving quietly to where she could get a better view of the travelers.

Heavy carts wove tracks in the sand that were quickly covered after they had passed through. Merchants, if she had to guess, the backs of their wagons lumpy and covered in brightly woven fabrics. Cassimir had packed up most of their camp while she watched as cart after cart passed in front of them.

"Wherever they are going, we need to follow them." She helped break down the rest of the camp, shoving things haphazardly into her pack, not wanting the last of the carts to pass before they had the opportunity to follow after them. Even if they had to run the whole way, a trail of merchant carts was a good way to find a town. They could ask questions, see if anyone had seen Eleni, if they knew where her uncle's enemies had taken her.

Cassimir followed her lead, likely coming to the same conclusion, and then they were running, pushing their already exhausted muscles even harder than they had the day before, skipping breakfast entirely in favor of keeping up with the caravan. She tightened the straps on her pack so it rested snug against her back, content when she felt her new kindjal sheath press into the base of her spine.

Her boots did little to help prevent her from slipping on the sandy hills, but she pushed herself to step lighter, to be more careful where she placed her weight down. She wished again that she had taken the time to get used to the terrain, to prepare herself for this kind of thing, but she hadn't imagined something like this would happen.

How could she have thought they would need to escape this way? They were all supposed to be safe here, Eleni most of all. Saiden didn't understand why the emperor wouldn't have gone for his niece.

Saiden should have never stopped looking for the possibility of danger. There was nothing she could've done, she hadn't even known about the threat these men posed. But she still couldn't stop herself from thinking that she should have done more.

Now, she was going to fight until she made things right. Even as the muscles in her legs burned and the sand clogged her lungs. She owed Cassimir and Eleni that much.

46

MOZARE

Once Mozare's back was healed enough that he thought he could train without having to deal with Loralei's disappointment that he had injured himself again, he went back to attending training sessions with the emperor's soldiers. He couldn't let anyone think he was more vulnerable than he absolutely had to be in order to heal.

The fact that Loralei's healing abilities, along with her other gifts, just seemed to keep getting stronger wasn't harmful to his expedited recovery either. She had nursed him for a few days while he was in and out of consciousness and he was surprisingly grateful that she was the one who had been stuck with him. He wasn't sure what that said about him.

And they still hadn't talked about their kiss. He couldn't stop thinking about it. Couldn't stop thinking about what might have happened if they hadn't been interrupted with the bad news about Eleni's capture. He wanted to know if she was trapped replaying it too, or if she had blown it off as the stress relief she had originally claimed it to be.

It wasn't like Mozare hadn't had lovers before. There had been women and men for him at the legion. He was used to a tussle in the sheets purely to burn off energy. But his kiss with her had felt like more than that.

He was clearly spending too much time thinking about it, and was rewarded with a punch to his jaw that knocked his feet out from under him. The young soldier he had been sparring with looked shocked, as if they were about to be punished for landing an excellent blow. Mozare had deserved it, considering the lack of discipline he seemed to have over his own thoughts.

Finally, the soldier reached a hand down to help Mozare back to his feet. "That was a good hit." Mozare told them, and some of the fear seemed to be replaced with pride. "Just make sure you turn your fist all the way, so there's less risk of breaking a knuckle." Mozare gestured, asking them for permission before gently guiding their hand back and forth in proper form.

After that lesson, it was time for Nori to teach his fighting techniques to Mozare. He would come and show him some of the moves the Taezhali soldiers had used to jump him, the first day he had come to the arena. He had no idea when Saiden would be back, and where they were going next, so he figured it was a good use of his time to build his repertoire with southern techniques.

While the fighting style they learned in the middle kingdom was reliant on sturdiness and frequently accompanied by weapons, the southern styles his teacher was pulling from were more about movement and momentum. He spent more time learning about the way his body moved, than actually fighting, but he could feel the difference in his muscles whenever they spent a few hours running through the motions.

He was curious to see what Saiden would think, and if these techniques might finally be enough to surprise her. Not that he thought the surprise would last long. Saiden was a fast learner, and she would no doubt have the techniques down in half the time it took him to learn them. He smiled fondly, until he saw Loralei in the crowd.

She hadn't been there when he arrived, not that he had looked for her of course. But as she caught his eye now, she gave the smallest nod of her head towards the box he now knew was meant for the emperor and his sons. The elder prince had been watching the whole training session, Mozare could practically feel the prince's eyes following him across the arena. It was why he had chosen not to use his gifts again, at least until he could determine why the crowned prince was so interested in them.

He nodded back, not stopping the motions until his instructor called it time for a rest. Because of the relentless sun and the fact that all their training arenas were outside, the commanding officers of the emperor's army required the men to take midday breaks. They were forced inside, where they either napped or found some other task to keep them occupied until the evening session.

He casually strolled towards Loralei, slipping his hands in his pocket, and keeping his attention on the emperor's box. He had already fought one ruler, though his relationship with her was drastically different now, and he had no problem fighting another if he was a threat to them. But Akil didn't come down from his box, didn't try to approach them as they left or corner them in the hallway like he had with Saiden.

Which he was extremely grateful for when Loralei grabbed his hand, led him to a darkened corner and pressed him against the wall. She had a look in her eye that was somewhere between anger and desire, and then she was kissing him, stretching up on her toes and into his chest so that she could reach without him needing to lean down. She tasted sweet, so sweet he sighed, and Loralei instantly stepped away from him.

He felt the absence of her body like a missing limb. "Is your back alright?" She asked him. He breathed out, trying not to let relief tint his face. It wasn't that she was regretting kissing him that made her pull away, she was just worried about his back.

"Come here and I can show you." His voice was rough, like he hadn't spoken a word in days. And he was slightly amazed when she listened to him, closing the space between them again and sticking her hands up the back of his shirt.

She didn't seem to mind the sweat as she lightly dragged her fingers across the stripes of newly acquired scars on his back. Without her, he wasn't sure he'd even be able to feel her fingertips where they dragged against him, which would have been a damned shame. Something in his gift reached out to her, and he knew she was using her own power to search for damage, for any lingering hurt she had been unable to heal the previous times she had agonized over the skin, draining her power until she too had to sleep for hours.

He leaned into her, breathing in the floral scent of her hair, peppering gentle kisses to the soft skin of her neck. Loralei leaned into him, the fabric flowers of her top crushing against his chest. He hoped she didn't mind the flowers getting damaged, because he couldn't stand for there to be any space between them.

"As much as I would love to continue this," Loralei started, and hope bloomed in his chest. "You stink."

He hated to agree with her, especially when it meant he had to stop kissing her, but he knew that he was sweating quite a bit, far past the point where it could possibly be attractive.

Mozare and Loralei were sent an invitation that night to join the emperor and his nobles for dinner. Considering the outfits that accompanied their invitation, it seemed to be more of an order than a request, although he and Loralei weren't really in a position to ignore an invitation in the first place.

Since Saiden and Cassimir weren't here, they both had rooms to themselves, and their respective outfits had been delivered to the separate rooms, tied with twine. He didn't like thinking about there being other people in what he considered to be his space, but they had brought so little with them when they escaped Kaizia that he doubted they could find anything informative in the room. Still, it felt too similar to what they had dealt with at Revon's command.

After showering off his training sweat he was unable to find Loralei until it was time for them to actually start getting ready for dinner, at which point it was far too late to continue what they had started in the hallway earlier. And, judging by the smirk on Loralei's face as she floated into Cassimir's suite, flour dusting her clothing, she knew exactly what she was doing by coming back this late.

He was fine with her games. He was playing to win.

He wondered how Loralei felt about that. Too often recently his brain has been trying to think about how she would see things. If she would feel the same way or if they were still opposed on so many things.

He hoped they would have time to figure it out.

He was dressed far before Loralei. The outfit they gave him would never pass for formal in the north, but it was elegant nonetheless. His pants were loose down until his calves, which he thought would look sloppy, but the fabric was a shiny black that caught the light as he paced through the room.

The jacket they had given him was lightweight, black threaded with gold details. The shoulders were beaded in a way he was almost sure was meant to look like armor plating, but reminded him of the light Saiden had cast around them in the hallway what felt like months ago.

His feet felt light in the fabric slippers, but for the first time since arriving in the southern kingdom they weren't sweating, which he could admit was quite a reprieve. Even if he preferred the sturdiness of his boots.

Mozare was still pacing when Loralei came out of her room, so he didn't see her before she started talking.

"This stupid dress has far too many buttons. I think maybe I should just go naked."

Mozare's chest stopped moving, and for a second he felt incapable of taking a single breath. He steeled his spine, unsure what to expect as he slowly turned around and faced her room.

Despite having neglected his lungs, there seemed to be enough air for him to exhale when he saw her. Even without having the back done up properly, Loralei was stunning. She would have been stunning in the plainest clothing, but this dress accentuated everything about her beauty that he already adored.

Since being in the desert, Loralei skin had taken on a golden glow, and the lavender silk of her dress complimented it. And as he took the whole look in, he noticed how the fabric got darker as his eyes went down her legs, until the bottom was as dark as his own outfit, covered in gold embroidered constellations. Whoever had picked their outfits had an extremely cruel sense of humor.

Mozare almost choked when Loralei moved, and he finally noticed that the skirt had a slit that reached almost all the way up to her hip. He could feel his face warm, and Loralei was most certainly laughing at him, as she held the open pieces of her top against her chest.

He tried to clear his throat, but his first words still cracked, his voice rough and grumbling. "I can probably help you with that."

The first few steps towards her were a conscious effort, and required Mozare's dedicated will. The closer he got to her, the stronger the smell of flowers surrounding her grew. And when he noticed the flowers resting gently in her loose curls, he assumed that was why.

Loralei's skin was nearly flawless. The only thing marring it was the scar Revon had left her, the reminder of her dance with death. Without realizing it, he was touching her, just the gentlest scrape of his fingers against her back. And she was gasping, neither of them moving closer to the other, but neither of them pulling away.

He took the two sides of the fabric, and looking at the row of clasps there, he also wondered if it might be better for Loralei to just be naked. Though if she was, he knew they would never actually make it to dinner.

Deftly he clipped the first set of clasps together, noticing how Loralei had let go of the top resting her fisted hands in the fabric at her thighs. He clipped another, and then another before pausing. He felt Loralei's ragged breathing as he leaned down to kiss along her spine as he continued to secure the top for her.

He took his time, partly because he did not understand how women's clothing could be so complicated and partly because he knew Loralei was being vulnerable with him right now, and he wanted to show her that she could trust him with these moments.

When they were finished he was fairly certain they were both out of breath, but he gave her his elbow, and she tucked herself close to him as they made their way to the banquet hall.

Everyone stared at them as they entered, and he sincerely doubted it was because of their outfits. Everyone in the hall was dressed similarly to them, their outfits lightweight, although brighter than his black ensemble. And even though none of them were as stunning as Loralei, he doubted even her beauty could cause the silence that now spread through the hall of nobles.

Of all the attention they were receiving, there was only one set of eyes that truly bothered him. And as the crown prince stood and made his way towards them in the crowded hall, the only thing he wanted more than to take Loralei away from there was the feeling of a weapon in his hand.

But he pushed those feelings down and bowed next to Loralei, still keeping himself between the two of them. Between Saiden's warning and his own intuition he was thoroughly suspicious of Akil.

"I'm glad you took my invitation." Mozare's skin crawled. They had only made this effort because they believed the emperor had been the one to send them the invitation. "I've saved you seats in the position of honor, although it is quite rude that you are late. But I will forgive this, since our customs are still so new to you."

Mozare honestly couldn't tell if he thought they needed this information, or if the prince just liked the sound of his own voice that much. Mozare was quick to tune him out as he brought them to their spots.

Unlike last time, they had actual seats and raised tables in the hall. Prince Akil pulled out a chair, which Mozare was sure he was going to offer to Loralei, so that she would be seated at his side. A quick assessment of the table, and Mozare decided the old man on the other side was a safer choice for her. He took the proffered chair for himself, a gracious smile on his face as Loralei was forced to sit one seat further from the prince.

Whatever he had to do to protect her, he owed her that much. Even if it meant tolerating a night of the prince droning on about whatever boring policies were spilling from his mouth.

Loralei placed a gentle hand on his thigh under the table. Whether she knew what he had done for her, or was just reassuring them both that they would get through this, Mozare couldn't tell, but he appreciated her gesture all the same.

The old man next to them seemed like a true gem, despite the fact that he spent a large part of their conversation convinced that they had to be married, which was embarrassing and somewhat wonderful at the same time.

And despite the tension, the food was delicious as normal. Cassimir had been so right when he said that the spices available to them in the middle kingdom were nothing when compared to what they used here. He couldn't identify a single one of the flavors in the many dishes served through the night, but the lack of knowledge did nothing to dull the euphoria as the flavors danced across his tongue.

He found an even greater appreciation for the slit in Loralei's dress, which gave him the perfect access to touch Loralei. There was an intimacy in the way he touched her now, that had nothing to do with the heat he felt when he was with her. He felt calmer when he touched her, and somehow stronger too, like they were enough together to face this problem. To wait out the turmoil until Saiden and Cassimir returned with Eleni, and then to figure out what they were going to do next.

And the few times the prince turned to him and actually expected an answer, or wanted them to weigh in on a conversation it didn't seem as hard to do. Loralei was brilliant; he was awed at the ease with which she could answer the multitude of political questions. Despite their ideological differences, she was extraordinary, and it only attracted him to her more.

Dinner took multiple courses, including a desert that was so sweet he pretended not to notice when Loralei switched her empty plate with his and ate his serving as well. There was no dancing this time, which might have been a good thing, because he wasn't sure he would have ever been able to let her go.

47

SAIDEN

SAIDEN AND CASSIMIR ARRIVED IN THE TOWN NOT LONG AFTER THE merchants, taking a moment to breathe behind the line of carts being set up for the market. Cassimir stepped towards one of the merchants, leaning in to speak to him in a language Saiden didn't recognize. She hadn't ever heard him switch to his native language, to the revered language of the Taezhali people and she yearned to lean closer and here it clearer.

"They've heard of the men," Cassimir said, clutching the worn paper of Eleni's ransom letter. "They've seen them travel through port here. You are brilliant." He leaned in to kiss her forehead, running his hand through the tangles in her hair. She smiled at him.

"We are going to need a little more information than that." She said gently, watching his face drop. "We can't find them just because we know they've been here before. Can you ask them to show you to a bar? Thats where I've always found the best gossip on patrol." Her chest tightened as she thought about Mozare, and what he and Loralei must have gone through when the emperor realized they were gone.

Cassimir walked back to the merchant, who gruffly pointed him into town, speaking with his back still turned as he continued to pull small wooden statues free from his packed storage. Saiden came up next to Cassimir, admiring the figures before digging into her pack to take out a single hramam to give the man in exchange for a small statue that looked like a butterfly. The man bowed to them both as Cassimir grabbed her hand and walked them through town.

She could smell the bar before she could see it, the stench of alcohol permeating the air from inside as people moved between outdoor and indoor seating. She squeezed Cassimir's hand, nervous about being inside with so many people when she was already having to fight to keep her powers at bay. He squeezed back, pushing through the door, and asking someone to find them a seat.

Patrons glared at them as they walked past, being shown to a small table at the back of the crowded room. Saiden didn't care, if they were curious she could work with that. Get them to share information they might not want to, especially after a few drinks.

"You know it's interesting that you chose a butterfly," Cassimir said, leaning over to whisper in her ear. She didn't turn to look at him as she distractedly asked why. "Because they are the animal of new beginnings, of fresh starts."

She turned and smiled, leaning in to kiss him briefly before turning back to the crowd. She surveyed the patrons, quickly dismissing anyone who was already too drunk to be useful, or too paranoid to talk to them. She pointed to one pair of men at the other corner of the bar, "that's who we want to talk to. Go offer them a drink, make sure you flash your coin."

Cassimir didn't ask her to explain as he left her at the table and went to invite the two men to drink with them. From the corner alone, Saiden was careful not to make eye contact with any of the men too far into their drinks, not wanting to start a fight that would hurt their questioning of the bar patrons or get them kicked out.

Cassimir came back a few minutes later, two tall glasses in his hands, one of which he set down in front of her. She took a sip as the other men sat down across from her.

"What's a pretty lass like you doing in a place like this?" One of them asked, reaching across the table to grab for one of her hands. She pulled back, keeping both of her hands under the table and away from sticky fingers. "A private one then, that's fine. You won't be like that by the time we're done." He winked at her, "I'm Finlay."

His friend smiled at her, "I'm Mason."

"Your friend said he'd buy us a drink or two, but by the looks of his pockets I'm sure he could buy us quite a few drinks." Finlay spoke, leaning back and taking a deep drink from his mug. Saiden left hers untouched on the table.

"We'd be happy too, in return for some information."

"I knew you had a game going on. Not as shy and demure as you'd like us to believe then." Finlay laughed, a deep belly laugh that shook the table. "I like it." Mason didn't speak, his eyes going back and forth between her and Cassimir. She leveled him a stare, waiting for him to break his gaze.

"What do you want to know?" Mason's tone was straight, not the same lilting flirt that laced Finlay's words.

She nudged Cassimir, and he told them everything about his sister while she watched their reaction. Around the room people were quieting down, doing their best to listen in to the conversation that had so much coin exchanging hands.

"I'm sorry to say, but we ain't never heard of pirates. We've only just arrived from far away shores, we're not yet familiar with the town's folk." Finlay looked at Saiden, "though I'd like to get familiar with you dear."

Cassimir put an arm around her shoulders, a clear sign that he wasn't interested in having Finlay continue to flirt with her. She let it slide, despite knowing that she could handle herself, she knew that his protection let her push her senses around the rest of the room. Across from them, two other patrons were whispering to each other, far enough away that she couldn't hear, but she could see them speaking.

Cassimir threw them another coin as they parted ways, leaving the small corner table to get more drinks at the bar. Saiden grabbed for her things, reaching for Cassimir's pack and handing it to him.

"Come on."

Cassimir looked at her hesitantly, pulling on her arm as she started to leave. "We don't have any more information. You said we needed more to find her."

She looked at him, but didn't answer pulling on his hand and leading him outside of the bar.

"Those men across the way," Saiden pointed to another table of men drinking away. The one's she had actually been listening to. "They work for that thief. They called him a pirate, said they knew he was keeping the princess somewhere called bow cove." Cassimir's face grew pale and he ran both of his hands through the lock of his hair, pulling on the ends of it. "I take it you know where that is."

"It's a smaller island off the coast of the severed key. It's barricaded on all sides by rocky seas."

Saiden said, "We'll find someone to get us close," even though her chest tightened with every word. "Someone has to know how to get there, otherwise no one ever would." She put a hand against Cassimir's cheek, fighting against her own dread of setting foot on a ship, of being forced to leave land for the first time in her life.

But Cassimir's breathing steadied, and his hope, his reassurance, was enough to make it worth it. She would risk everything to get Eleni back for him.

48
MOZARE

Mozare was waiting for Loralei in the alcove they had been using to spend time together. He had just had lunch with the emperor's soldiers, and they were supposed to meet now to spend the afternoon rest time together. She met him in a flurry of skirts and fingers running over his cheeks and through his hair. He smiled at her before she was kissing him.

He felt her smiling into the kiss, and he pulled her into him, lifting her so he knew her feet were barely touching the floor. Her hands tugged at the hair at the nape of his neck.

He pulled away, keeping her close to him. "How was your morning?"

"It's better now." She leaned in to kiss him again. "But I can't stay long. The chef is going to teach me how to make their sugar globes and I have to meet her in the kitchen in just a few minutes."

He frowned, but he couldn't keep it there as he saw the excitement on her face. He kissed her forehead, and smiled, watching as she walked back down the hallway, the long strands of her ponytail swinging with her steps. He smiled behind his hands as he watched her dramatically swing her hips down the hallway until she turned the corner.

"Romantic, truly." Mozare pulled a dagger from his belt, turning to face the intruder. "What a lovely pair you make."

Mozare pulled the shadows out of the hallway, revealing the face of the person speaking. Prince Akil was watching him, hidden inside another one of the secret alcoves like the one that lead to Eleni's garden. He flipped the blade in his hand, flashing it in the light to warn the prince. Behind him, he could feel Loralei coming back towards them, and his brain raced.

"You won't be needing that." The prince stuck his hand out, as if he actually expected Mozare to willingly hand him his weapon after being stalked and stared at. The prince had no idea who he was dealing with if he thought that was how things were going to go.

He stepped past Loralei, whispering in her ear as he did, so quietly he couldn't even be sure she had heard him, until he saw the way her shoulders tightened.

He wrapped the prince in shadows, listening to the padded thumps of Loralei's feet run through the hallway. They had no allies left in the palace, no one to protect them besides each other, but he was hoping the kitchen staff would hide Loralei away until it was safer. He couldn't believe they could spend so much time with her without starting to love her.

Guards grabbed him from behind, and he wrapped them in shadows too. He didn't need his hands to be free in order to use his gifts, though they were too unstudied to know that.

"That's enough." Akil, stepped forward, hands in front of him, searching until they landed on Mozare's chest. Then, quicker than Mozare would've expected from the prince, something sharp pierced his neck.

He lost control over his shadows, couldn't reach the part of him inside that connected to his power. Panic flooded his system to the point that he couldn't tell if it was Akil's potion or his own crippling anxiety that made his vision blur. The guards told him to move, but his brain wasn't speaking to his feet, and then they were dragging him.

He wasn't sure how they managed their way through the labyrinth without getting caught, couldn't remember any of the turns they had made. He would be of no use getting himself back out of this hell.

Then the guards were throwing him down, his hands barely registering the scrape as he reached out to catch himself.

And then he was alone again.

49

SAIDEN

SAIDEN THOUGHT SHE HAD BEEN PREPARED TO GET ON BOARD A SHIP, TO put aside her anxiety about traveling on open seas to find Eleni, but staring up the entrance ramp, she couldn't help feeling nauseous already. She shook out her hands, trying to ignore the sweat gathering in her palms, and the sense of dread building in her gut. She had done much harder things in her life, but yet she couldn't force herself to take the first step onto the wobbling planks of wood.

Above her, men traveled back and forth on the decks of the ship, most of them carrying trunks, barrels or other large objects, likely storing them below deck for trade or supplies for their journey. Their captain had been reluctant to take on two more mouths to feed. That was until Cassimir had supplied enough coin to keep his crew fed for a year, and the captain had agreed to let them stowaway, not asking questions about their reasons.

Cassimir waited patiently beside her as she fought her inner battle, struggling against the anxiety that spiked her powers, pushing against the fear that spiraled in her mind. She was stronger than this, and she was wasting time. Every minute she waited here safe on land, Eleni could be suffering for it. She took a deep breath, then took her first step onto the shaky wood. Not giving herself time to look back, to return to solid land, she raced up the plank, almost barreling into two men carrying large planks of wood between them. She apologized, her face burning.

Cassimir came up behind her, hands full with more food he had bought in town, and both of their packs, since she had almost broken the straps on hers while she had been desperately trying to stop her hands from shaking. From the corner of her eye she saw the captain walking towards them, reprimanding a handful of men who had stopped their work to stare at her.

The captain tipped his hat at them, stepping up onto one of the drains in the middle of the ship and leaning over his leg as he spoke to Cassimir. "You might want to stake your claim now mate, otherwise the men might think she's up for grabs. We don't often have ladies on board the ship with us, and the men get lonely."

Cassimir turned to her. "I'd like to see one of the men try to claim her." He said, turning back to the captain. "They should only risk touching her if they're willing to lose a hand, those blades she carries aren't just for show." He smiled charmingly at the captain, a hint of a threat in his voice. His blades were less concealed than hers, and she knew they weren't for show either. He might look like proper nobility, but under the charm he was a trained warrior.

She smiled at him, letting the captain take her measure, letting him wonder if she was as much of a threat as Cassimir made her out to be. She didn't do anything but let him look, let him make up his own mind. If he underestimated her, that would be his problem, and she couldn't worry about it now.

The captain smiled at her, then turned to his men. "The girl's off limits by my orders. Touch her and you'll be on night shifts the entire journey, understood?" A chorus of disgruntled agreements rang over the ship deck, the captain's message likely to be shared with those below deck later. Saiden hid her smile, wondering what it was the captain saw in her that made him choose to warn his men off. Either way it suited her, she didn't want to spend this harrowing journey fighting off drunken pirates.

"I ain't got any suites for ya, ship ain't meant to be carrying nobility." The captain smiled at Cassimir, letting him know he saw him for who he truly was, "or their guests, but I've had the crew set up some hammocks for you at the far end of the bunker."

"You have my immense gratitude captain, both for your service and your discretion." Cassimir's own warning that he knew exactly the kind of man he was dealing with. "We shouldn't be a burden to you or your crew."

The captain called over one of his men by the name of Nico, who led them into the bowels of the ship to show them to their hammocks. Her anxiety spiked again as they left the sunlight of the decks, sparks popping at her fingertips. She hid her hands behind her back when the crew member turned to look at her, to look for the source of that sound. She just smiled, internally wrestling her power back into its cage.

The hammocks were barely that, they looked more like recycled pieces of a sail, tied haphazardly with leftover rope. She'd slept in worse places, though she had hoped her first sea journey would be slightly more comfortable. Still, at least the captain had managed to place them together, away from the rest of his crew.

She inclined her head to the crew member and he left, she assumed to return to his normal duties. He seemed young to be aboard such a ship, but then again she was young to be as skilled as she was, so she couldn't really judge him. Cassimir took the outer of the two hammocks, keeping her between him and the wall of the ship. She ran a hand lightly over the damp wood, feeling all the knicks and dents from years of use.

"I can't believe you've never been on a ship before." Cassimir turned to her, a smile in his voice. "The almighty warrior, afraid of sea travel."

"I am human you know." She said, teasing him right back. "I was bound to be afraid of something." She turned back to her hammock, checking the knots to make sure they would hold her. She felt Cassimir's arms slip around her waist, his chin resting on her shoulder.

"Of course," he whispered, "but I was starting to think that perhaps there was nothing that would frighten you."

She didn't answer him. There were a lot of things in the world that frightened her. Loosing Mozare, letting her friends get hurt. She was afraid of what was happening to Eleni, whether she would be okay when they found her. She didn't need to tell him that, she could feel his own apprehension in the tightness of his arms around her, in the way he sought solid comfort amid the tossing waves of uncertainty. She wrapped her arms around his, letting him stay there as long as he needed.

Saiden looked over at Cassimir, perched gently in his hammock. She had felt him watching her as she went through the rest of her things, reorganizing everything she had crammed in her pack in an effort to chase after the merchant's caravan. There was sand in most of her things now, and she tried to get rid of the worst of it without shaking too much into her hammock.

"What is it?" She asked him.

"I just wanted to say that you were absolutely brilliant in the pub." She looked at him funny. There was no reason for him to be saying that now, she was just doing what she had been trained to do. "Don't look at me like that. You're amazing. I don't think you realize that enough."

She shrugged her shoulders. She wasn't used to this kind of attention, and below deck there was nothing she could do to diffuse the way this conversation was making her feel. "I just went with my instincts. You followed me without questioning it, why?" She wanted to turn the conversation towards him, to move back into space where she was comfortable.

"Because I trust you with this. I trust that you will do everything in your power to make this right. I trust you." He emphasized the last words, making her skin start to itch. This wasn't the diversion she had been hoping for.

"You shouldn't."

"Why not?"

"Because I'm a curse. Bad things follow me. My parents, and Mozare and Loralei, and now you and Eleni. You shouldn't trust me, you should want to be far away from me."

He sat and looked at her for a moment, and the space between them seemed to grow. "I don't think so. I think you had a curse, and that made your life difficult. But you are good, and light follows you. You make people feel safe and inspired, and others are bound to fear that influence. But I am not afraid of you and I don't want to be any farther from you than we are now." He leaned forward. "Bad things happened to good people Saiden, but none of them were your fault."

He reached for her and she stepped into his embrace, set off balance by the swing of his hammock. She was shaking, a combination of the sway of the ship and the jitters that ravaged her body. Cassimir pulled her up, slipping back into the hammock, laughing when they both almost fell out the other side.

"You need rest, and I'll sleep better knowing you're here." She laughed at the pouty look on his face before giving up and snuggling up next to him. It wasn't like they hadn't spent last night together, and she doubted that she would have slept well alone with her thoughts in the other hammock.

With the sway of the ship around her and the warmth of Cassimir's body next to her, she slowly drifted off to sleep.

50
MOZARE

Mozare was in a cold dank prison cell. He didn't mind the darkness, he had always been at home in the shadows, but he couldn't sit without cold seeping in through his pants, and shivers coursing through him. At this rate he might die before the prince was able to do anything, which seemed a blessing compared to the gleam in the prince's gaze as he had his men throw him in a cell.

He hoped Loralei realized he was gone and left, hoped she ran as fast as she could and never looked back. The thought played in his head on repeat, a silent prayer or a dying wish he wasn't certain. He couldn't tell how much time had passed without a window, but no one had come to bring him food, and they had left him only a bucket in the corner to relieve himself.

He heard the rattle of keys shortly after, and stood, sinking into the corner of his cell where the shadows were the thickest. He wouldn't trust anyone with a key to this place, wouldn't let any of them close enough to touch him. They had stripped him of his weapons, but he was a fighter, and he would fight tooth and nail before he gave in to them.

There was a loud groan, and he tensed at the sound of a body being dragged, and then keys were rattling again, exchanging hands or being

THE BLOOD-CURSED

thrown he couldn't tell. But someone had definitely been knocked out, which made the hair on the back of his neck rise.

From inside the darkness of his cell he saw a small bubble of light traveling through the halls, searching for something as if it could see. He stepped forward from the wall, his heart dropping in his chest as he saw her pale skin hidden under the hood of a cloak. She saw him a moment later, and rushed to the bars, ruffling through the keys and trying to find the right one to fit the door.

"What are you doing here?" There were tears on his face, panic in his bones. He had imagined seeing her again, but he never thought he would. He didn't want to see her again in this place if it meant she would be relegated to the same shadows.

"Obviously I'm pulling off the daring rescue." She tried another key and cursed when it didn't fit. She dropped the keys, fumbling with them as she tried to get him out of the cell. Then, instead of using they key, she just held her hand an inch above the ground and closed her eyes. Cracking through the cement floors a vine of ivy leaves and thorns grew, growing until it was tall enough to reach inside the lock.

He heard the door click and pushed it open, drawing Loralei into him, relishing the feel of her and the smell of her hair. "You shouldn't have come."

"I knew something was wrong when you didn't come back for dinner. You've never missed a meal before ever." She patted his stomach, despite the fact that training kept him in good shape. "I waited until nightfall to start looking for you, though the emperor does hide his prison well in his stupid labyrinth."

He smiled in her hair, "we need to get out of here now."

"It's too late for that." Mozare pulled Loralei behind him as once again a voice spoke from the shadows. He cursed himself for waiting, for not taking the first chance he had and running. For not getting Loralei far away from here. "You think I would just let him sit here with only one guard? How foolish you truly are. No wonder they were able to take your throne from you so easily."

Behind him Loralei growled, her light growing between them and the prince where he sat on a carved wooden seat at the end of the prisons' hallway. She was trembling against his back, and he wondered briefly if her feet were still bare. "I thought it would be obvious that I wanted to study you both, though Mozare was much easier to kidnap than you young queenling. You spend too much time in my kitchens for someone of your status. Or is it former status? The politics of your country have always been too confusing."

The prince clapped his hands, and a line of armed guards poured into the hallway from both directions. They pulled Loralei away from him, and he struck, hitting the first guard that got close to him, not waiting to see the thin man hit the ground, before he was facing a second guard. One of them grabbed him from behind, holding down his arms as the guard in front of him rammed a fist into his stomach. He braced himself, then used the man holding his arms as leverage to kick the guard who hit him in chest with both legs.

The guard behind him dropped him, and he bounced back from the ground, only to be grabbed by two more guards, a third wrapping an arm around his neck and pressing down. Loralei's light had already started to fade, and now dark spots filled his vision, until he lost sight of the prison all together.

51

SAIDEN

Saiden had to admit, as the sun set on their first day aboard the ship, that she didn't hate traveling by sea as much as she had thought she would. She and Cassimir had stayed confined to the space between their hammocks, and the men had left them alone. Cassimir had packed extra food from the market before they had boarded, so they didn't even leave to eat meals with the crew. They only left their sanctuary to relieve themselves, and Saiden made sure to do that as infrequently as possible given the number of men using the same bathrooms.

Cassimir was teaching her a card game, the rules of which she still hadn't grasped, but his face lit up every time she got one of them, and that made the game more than worth learning. And they shared stories, small things about them that no one else knew. She mostly talked about training and her life in the barracks, while Cassimir went on about his family. She loved hearing about it, even as it made her heart ache for her parents. For the life she could have had with them.

She sat up as the feeling of dread raced down her spine, just before the ship rocked to the side, a loud noise echoing throughout. She looked at Cassimir, panic in her eyes. He just grabbed her hand, rushing above deck with the rest of the crew who had been sleeping.

From the right side of the ship, Saiden could see the dark sails of another ship, passing far too close for her comfort.

"Get back below deck you two," one of the crew members yelled, fighting to get a cannon ball loaded. "This is pirate business."

Another large explosion surged from the opposite ship, causing them to rock unsteadily back and forth. Saiden didn't know how much damage the ship could sustain before sinking, and her heart dropped as she noticed some of the people aboard the other ship swing heavy ropes across the space between them. She ran to the first one she could see, disobeying the crew's suggestions to hide below deck, and sending three pirates into the water by releasing their hook.

Even she could tell the other ship had more crew members than they did. There was no way they would be fast enough to remove all the hooks, to keep their crew from taking over, while keeping the ship intact enough for them to still sail to the island of Severed Key to rescue Eleni. She looked at Cassimir and saw that he had come to the same realization.

She had never been more grateful for a gift, than she was for the new blades Cassimir had given her. She had hoped, as she did when she gave Rhena her sword, that the blades wouldn't have to be used, but her life didn't grant such peace. She pulled them free from their sheaths, and moved across the ship so she and Cassimir each defended one half. Some of these men were bound to be fighters, but others, like the skinny boy who had led them to their beds, likely weren't.

She'd fought on ice before, but the rocking of the ship, made worse by the continuing stream of cannon fodder, was something foreign to her. There was no good purchase, no strong defense line that she could take advantage of. She saw the first of the men reach the ship, grabbing the side of railing to pull himself overboard.

She pulled her leg up, stomping her heal against his fingers and letting him fall into the sea below. Next to her, men were pulling their bodies over the railing, reaching for weapons in their boots and strapped to their belts. She moved to the man closest to her, swinging low so he would lose traction before she pushed him over board.

The next man came at her, fist raised with a short sword. She ducked under his first swing, stepping in close to him to slice the shorter of her kindjal blades at the inside of his arm. She didn't wait for him to switch hands, grabbing him by the elbow the throwing him towards another group of men approaching her. All around her was chaos, and she could barely catch glimpses of Cassimir at the opposite end of the ship.

She stabbed the next man in the gut, hating the loud suction sound when she pulled her blade free covered in his blood. Two men came at her from opposite sides, and she jumped out of the way when they were seconds from grabbing her, letting them collide with each other before a swift kick sent them over the side to join the rest of their crew.

The men were clearing out, running or being thrown overboard, giving her space to move through them. She was careful, she didn't know enough of the crew members to tell who was on her side. She backed any man she had seen in the brief time they had been on deck, stabbing or cutting any man who charged her.

The chaos around her slowed when she caught a glimpse of Cassimir, who moved to stand in front of the skinny boy the captain had called Nico, raising his blade too slowly to stop himself from being impaled on the spikes of one of the pirate's three pronged spears.

52

MOZARE

THE PRINCE'S FACE WAS ONLY A FEW INCHES AWAY FROM MOZARE'S WHEN he woke up in another room. His first instinct was to stretch up and bite him, but when he tried, he found himself strapped to the table he had first thought was a very uncomfortable bed.

Panic flared in his chest, but he tried not to let it show on his face, tried not to let the prince see any kind of weakness despite the fact that they both knew he was completely at Akil's mercy. He stretched his peripheral vision to its limits, but he couldn't turn his head enough to tell if Loralei was in the room with him.

He had never wished for a different blessing before, but right now he would give anything to just feel her heartbeat and know that she was okay, even if she was stuck in this hell with him. He knew that together they had the best chance of actually getting out of here.

"It's good to see that my guards didn't do too much damage," Akil finally said, leaning back and grabbing a notepad. He scribbled vigorously, occasionally peering back at Mozare or one of the machines he could see on the walls beside him.

He tried to speak, but his voice wouldn't work, and his mouth tasted like metal. Whatever the prince was doing to him, or his guards had already done, it wasn't good. Dread moved in beside panic in his chest. He needed a clear head, needed to avoid giving in to the terror he was feeling, but that had never been his strong suit. And most of the time, it worked for him. Saiden had always balanced his jittery need for action with her calm determination. Together they could get through anything.

But Saiden wasn't here, and for all he could tell neither was Loralei. He was alone for the first time in so long. He tried to take a deep breath, but his chest quivered, and his vision began to blacken at the edges. He could feel his powers responding, shadows pooling in his palms where they were strapped to the table.

Akil's eyes widened and his writing picked up. The sound of his pencil scratching against his paper was the only thing Mozare could hear over the pumping of blood in his ears. Then he remembered the way Loralei had sat with him in the hallway during the party, how she had held him and whispered good things and she had made him feel calm. He focused on that.

Akil started speaking just as soon as Mozare had finally calmed down, threatening to send him spiraling again. "I really appreciated your friend showing up to save you. A true time saver, having her present herself like that. I would have preferred that Saiden be here to study, since she is so much more magnificent than either of you, but she followed my cousin across the desert to rescue that brat Eleni."

"But you both seem to be adept specimens of your respective gifts, so lacking her excellence, you will have to do." Mozare felt something poke into his arm, and then heard Akil scratching his pencil across the paper again.

"You prick." Mozare finally managed to push out of his mouth. His brain had so many other things it wanted to say, but his mouth was back to not following directions.

"Save your energy. The drugs will wear off soon, and that's when the real fun begins."

A light poured into the room from the wall opposite the beeping machines, powered by something Mozare did not understand. The technology here in this weird dungeon far surpassed what they had in the middle kingdom, and that was even more terrifying.

There was a pounding, but he couldn't tell if it was a sound happening in the room or something happening in his head. The wall between this room and wherever the light was coming from must have been made of glass because he could hear it crack. So the pounding was outside, and it was something powerful enough to break glass. He filed the facts away despite the likelihood that it would not be useful to him while he was strapped to the table.

"She may not be as extraordinary as your friend, but she is a rare creature indeed." The strap on Mozare's head loosened, and he sat up before Akil had even stepped back.

Loralei was on the other side of that glass, watching them. She was the one pounding. The one who had cracked the glass with her bloody knuckles trying to get to him.

"What do you want with us?"

Mozare didn't think the prince would answer, but apparently he had been right when he assumed that the prince liked the sound of his own voice. "Scientific theory suggests that your power must come from somewhere. In your backwards country you think it has something to do with devotion to your religion. It's foolish. Inside you there has to be some provable, tangible reason for your powers and I am going to find it. And then, I am going to replicate it. My father is a weak man who allows himself to be ruled by weak men. And he refused to take power even when it was right in front of him. I will not be that kind of man."

Mozare's head was finally clearing, "you are weaker." He wished he could put more strength behind the words, but by the change in the prince's face he was sure he understood his meaning anyway.

"Perhaps, but I will not be weak for much longer." His face was blank of all emotion. "My father did not want to harness the priestesses power, despite his sister having the gift. And my cousin refused to learn, to be initiated, so she was useless to me. But you have power beyond any prayer, anything their rituals could offer them. And it will be mine, even if I have to drag it from your corpses piece by piece."

53
SAIDEN

Saiden was shoving through men, not caring whose side they were on as long as they moved out of her way. Any man who tried to swing at her was brutally put down, no thought in her mind for being careful, only for getting to Cassimir. The man pulled his weapon from Cassimir's body as he sank against the wooden steps that led to the captain's station.

She was in between them before the man was able to move another inch, swinging one blade into the man's shoulder, removing his weaponed arm at the joint, before she sliced the shorter of her blades across his throat.

She dropped her blades next to her, kneeling down in the growing pool of blood, not caring that her clothes were already stained red, that her hands were growing sticky with it. She cradled him in her arms, focusing on the powers deep inside her, the well that she had been fighting against for weeks now.

There was nothing. No sparks at her fingertips, no itching burning sensation just under her skin. She felt hollow. Useless.

Tears were streaming down her face, falling to land on Cassimir's forehead. "I can't do it. I can't heal you."

She brushed the tears away, a trail of red left behind on his brow.

Another mark of the terrible things that she brought to the people closest to her. She kept trying, kept searching inside herself for some kernel of power, for the goodness Cassimir saw in her. Something to fix this so she didn't have to say goodbye to another person she loved.

Cassimir lifted a weak hand and cupped her face gently. Blood still gushed from his stomach despite the pressure. Behind her someone handed her more fabric, but the blood was spilling too fast for her to control it.

"I won't mind *preeyapet*," he coughed, and blood trickled from the corner of his mouth "going to the next life, if yours is the last face I get to see." She moved her hand so she could hold his head.

"No." She whispered, but she saw it in his eyes, saw that he only had a few moments left. "I love you."

She leaned in, despite the number of people's blood that coated her skin, despite the blood still trickling from his mouth and she kissed him gently. She wished she had more time, more than the too few kisses she had shared with him. She wanted more than what they had been given.

She closed her eyes, her mouth still touching his and she looked inside herself once more. Now everywhere she looked she was overwhelmed with peace. With memories of cooking with Cassimir in the kitchen, and training in the yard with him and Mozare. She remembered the sunset they had shared, and she knew that she couldn't let him miss the next one.

And there she found it. The small piece of her powers that came from Keir, that spoke of healing and time and goodness. She reached out to it, not pulling or forcing, but hoping beyond hope to be able to touch it.

She heard the crew gathered around her gasp before she even felt the power start to flow through her. She opened her eyes, willing Cassimir to keep his gaze on her, to hold on just long enough for her to fix this.

He put his hand back in her hair and she focused on the feeling of him, alive and whole again. There was a burning feeling in her hands, and for a second she wanted to pull away. Until she remembered the light that had shone under Loralei's skin the first time she had healed

THE BLOOD-CURSED

Saiden. And she watched through the hole in his shirt as his skin slowly knit itself back together. She doubted that there was anything she could do at this point to help with the blood loss. She already felt her grip on her powers loosening, but at least he wasn't bleeding anymore.

"That's enough of a show for you folks, get back to your duties, and start swabbing this deck. I don't want no bloodstains on my ship." The captain pushed through the crowd, a deep cut on his cheek that he ignored as he bent on to one knee in front of her and Cassimir. "I owe you both a great debt of gratitude, for protecting my ship," he looked straight at Cassimir, "and saving my son."

Saiden finally collapsed against the wooden door behind her, her muscles giving out. "I'll get someone on the crew to help you to my quarters, and send something to clean yourselves up." He gave Saiden a long glance without directly looking at her. "What you did today was a miracle you know. Ain't many of us get that close to death and live to tell the tale."

54
RHENA

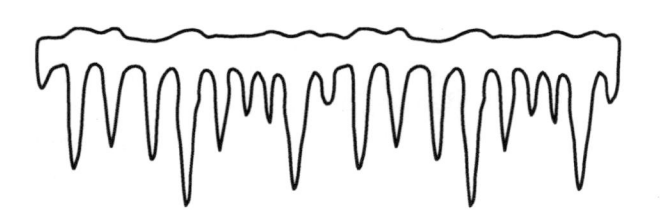

Being called from bed at all hours of the night was beginning to be an ordinary occurrence for the recruits in Revon's army. Rhena was used to it, but she would never grow used to the nerves that ran through her- wondering if this time would be her last as ice coated her veins and chilled the room around her.

It always took her a moment to get her powers back in check after hearing the alarm ring through the barracks, and she was grateful that she was still a recruit and could pass the spikes off as lack of control. If she had spent a few more years training in the legion it would have been much harder to pass under Revon's notice.

She slipped on her boots. She had already begun to sleep in her uniform pants despite the heat, and was buttoning up her jacket as she joined the stream of her sleepy-eyed companions all marching towards the main hall.

As usual, Revon was pacing on the hastily-constructed stage at the front of the hall, three men bound and kneeling in front of him. He did nothing to hide the shadowy creature weaving its way through his legs at every step. This scared Rhena more than anything, that Revon was so lost he was no longer maintaining appearances.

Rhena pressed herself into the crowd and did her best to make herself smaller. Even still, she could feel his eyes when he finally found her, his suspicion never truly satisfied. She hoped he mistook her fear for something other than it was, or she would soon be joining those poor men at the front of the hall.

She didn't let herself feel relieved when he finally turned away from her. Any perceived difference in her behavior could be enough for Revon to have her locked up. Plenty of men had died in the recent weeks on much smaller charges.

When the room seemed full to bursting Revon finally paused his pacing, turning to face his captive audience and straightening the lapels of his jacket. He never came to them in gear, as an equal. There were always subtle reminders that he was superior to them. She couldn't remember Nakti or Loralei acting like that, but now wasn't a time to remember the dead.

It was a time to mourn the living.

Revon started this execution like he had all the others. By calling them to prayer. Rhena closed her eyes and recited the words with the others, but just like all the times before, she couldn't feel Ilona's caress press against her mind. Their gods weren't here with them.

She wasn't entirely convinced they hadn't abandoned the people altogether.

When Revon's near blasphemous words were over, he went one by one and pulled the hoods off the men at the front of the room. She managed to keep her face neutral at the sight of the first two bloody faces, but the third one sent another wave of ice through her.

The third hood lifted to reveal Talon. She hadn't even noticed that the boy had been missing from their training. She tried to search the room, to find Yusef, but there were too many people around her for her to make any progress, not without drawing too much attention to herself.

She didn't understand, after the terrible things she had heard from him about Saiden, her brain couldn't wrap itself around the idea of him being brought on charges of counter-revolutionary actions. It didn't make any sense to her.

And she doubted she would ever know the truth. Not now that he was on Revon's stage, his cruel idea of justice just minutes from being carried out. She wasn't naive enough to believe Revon brought them here on correct charges. Rhena sent her own prayer into the universe, not letting the words move her lips. Even still, she finally felt Ilona press against her mind, and knew her prayers were being heard.

She hoped his death at least would be swift.

Someone Rhena didn't personally recognize strode on to the stage, all the bravado of an actor in his steps, executioner's hood in his hand. Even if she had been loyal, she would never have understood the joy Revon's executioner got from these deaths.

He stood poised behind the first man, blade at the ready as Revon listed off the crimes he believed this man had committed. No one even bothered with a trial anymore. Revon was king, and in his eyes that also made him judge and jury. No one went before him without being convicted, and there was never a chance at defense.

The blade swung, and the first man's head fell to the floor with a sickening wet thump. The second man's head followed soon after, leaving only poor Talon kneeling on the stage. Revon stepped towards him, a low hand halting the executioners process.

"Now you are more difficult to handle dear boy." Revon gripped the hair at the back of Talon's head and pulled backwards so he would be forced to face Revon. Even from her distance, Rhena could see him shivering, a telling puddle growing under him.

"The gods bless us every day, and yet their own child turns against them. Gifted by Keir himself, yet you turn from his teachings, and mine. But death does not call for you yet." Rhena almost felt relieved, before Revon continued. "Even if your name is not on Ilona's list you cannot go unpunished. The gods may see fit to spare your life, but they are not the only ones wronged. For your crimes against the kingdom of Kaizia, I will have my pound of flesh. May it serve as a reminder to you and your peers the cost of straying."

Tears streamed down Talon's face, and Rhena could feel her own gathering, but she would not let them fall. Not here where so many eyes watched her.

But she let Talon see the fear in her own face, and she hoped that was enough for him to survive. Because she had questions he was going to answer.

THE BLOOD-CURSED

It was hours before Talon was finally left alone in the infirmary, and only because the healers mending him were so close to burning out that they needed to rest. Rhena knew she wouldn't have time, not much of it anyway, but she cared more about answers than she did about being caught. It was quite foolish after what she had just witnessed, but she wasn't thinking rationally at that moment.

She had caught Talon just a few days ago running his mouth in the hallway in support of Revon and his actions. How had he landed himself a privileged spot among his special guests? She intended to find out.

"You might as well come out. I could feel you coming. Gave the whole room a chill." Talon's voice was weak, but there was still a teasing note to it that made Rhena think he had miraculously managed to make it out with his spirit intact, even as his skin hung in ribbons from his body.

Rhena crept into the room, even if he already knew she was there. He was laying on one of the hospital cots, all the blankets around him stained red. There were fresh bandages on his skin, but she could already see the stains gathering. She had known just from watching his punishment that he was in bad shape, but seeing it up close, and seeing how bad it still was after hours of healing had her breakfast threatening to make a sudden appearance.

He must've been watching for her reaction, but his quiet voice filled the space again. "It's not as bad as it looks. They gave me some meds that made it so I can barely feel my body at all."

"Can't you heal some of it yourself?"

"I'm gifted by Keir, but not in the healing arts unfortunately. Probably part of why the king himself chose this punishment for me."

"Did you deserve it?"

He eyed her quizzically, until turning his head made him flinch and he looked forward again. Rhena moved, crouching low against the wall so they could speak eye to eye without causing him any more pain. "Probably depends on who you ask. You don't like me much, what do you think?"

Rhena took a moment to think about it, although her answer didn't change no matter how she ran the problem over in her head. She was risking a lot by voicing it, but it didn't seem fair to be anything less than honest in this moment. "No one deserves that."

He chuckled, or at least Rhena thought he tried to chuckle, before the action devolved into a moan of pain. She pressed her hand palm up on the bed and let him squeeze until the pain had gone once more.

She tried to think of something to say, but he beat her to it. "You should be careful. You're at the top of quite a few dangerous lists. A few days and you might be in the same state as me." She cringed at the thought, but tried to hide it from Talon. He didn't need to see his fear mirrored in her face.

"I can look after myself."

"The whole reason I'm here is because you can't."

The words shocked and angered Rhena. "What do you mean?"

"I caught you." He paused to breathe. "Sneaking prisoners out of the dungeons."

Ice cracked over her knuckles, and she tried to pull her hand back from his before she could do damage; but he didn't let her go. Her brain started to race, trying to figure out the game and get herself one step ahead of Revon. There was no way he didn't know by now. He must be waiting for her to slip, to put her on that stage and do far worse than what he did to Talon.

"I didn't tell anyone."

Her brain slammed to a halt, and she just stared at him. "You were braver than I ever hoped to be. I wanted to help you. And when I tried to go back, I missed the guard rotation and they caught me, just as the prisoners slipped into the forest."

"But all those terrible things you said about-" she stuttered over the words before finding them again, "about Saiden. I heard you praising Revon."

"Yusef is a stout supporter. It really was his neck you should've risked cutting."

Rhena slumped back against the wall, fingers still wrapped in Talon's sweaty hand. "You saved my life." She couldn't even doubt the statement. It felt like the puzzle inside her head finally began to form a picture, and Talon was in every shadowy piece. "I don't understand why."

It wasn't necessarily a question, but Talon answered her anyway. "We have to be the hope for a people without any. We keep the flame alive so that others can keep fighting."

The words sounded like a prayer, and as she felt the press of her goddess against her mind, she figured someone must've been listening.

55

MOZARE

Someone had come and replaced the glass between Mozare and Loralei. All he could do from his side was watch her trapped in her own mind, her body curling in on itself. They had removed the table and the beeping machines, and silence echoed through the new prison. They didn't leave him free though, and the chains on his wrists kept him from being able to reach the glass and show her she wasn't alone. There was no power under his control strong enough to get through to her despite how close they were. Nothing he threw at the window was strong enough to break it.

Loralei's knuckles were a rusty brown now, though underneath he was sure the skin had already healed, whether she wanted it to or not. And with a matching set of chains on her own wrists, she had no choice but to use her gifts to try and break through from her side. A small pile of quickly rotting plants sat at the bottom of the wall, the only sign she had tried at all. Tears slipped down her cheeks, leaving trails in the dirt that he could still see through the curtain of her hair. Through the walls she was already trying to build around herself.

He prayed. He hadn't asked for anything from Ilona in so long, but his skin trembled, and he needed her to give him strength. To get them both through whatever hell was coming for them next, and out of this prison alive and intact. To get Loralei through whatever the prince had in store for them.

Ilona's voice filled his cell, and surprise shuddered through Mozare. He had not been sure she would even be able to hear him locked away down here so far from her. "Do not fear my child." Her voice flowed through the cell like wind sailing through chimes. Each word gave him a little more strength.

He felt a phantom hand trace its fingers down his cheek. "We do not choose our warriors lightly. I have given you everything you need to survive this, you must only find it inside yourself."

"I need to protect her."

"Do you not think that she was in your path for a reason my child? That perhaps she is not your duty but your destiny?" Mozare didn't have time to think of all the implications of that sentence. He could only focus on the now, on getting them both freed. On getting out of this hell blasted kingdom and away from wicked princes.

"Trust in me and in yourself, and freedom is never out of your reach." He felt it when she left, felt her absence like a chill.

He filled his room with shadows. To him there were different kinds of darkness. Darkness that was fear, that hid things meant to do harm. Or darkness that comforted, that soothed old hurts and smoothed broken edges. He sent his powers searching for cracks in the wall, even the smallest hole where he could push his darkness next door to Loralei.

He wasn't sure how she noticed it, but he saw her shoulders relax as he wrapped her in a cocoon of darkness, imagining he was there to wrap his arms around her. Imagining they were together somewhere where neither of them ever had to be in danger again.

In his cocoon of shadows, Loralei lit a small light, just wide enough to illuminate her palm as she stretched out as far as her chains would allow, shining for him just like she had that night when darkness had threatened to consume him entirely. He pulled himself past the safe limit of his chains, not caring about the cuts they dug into his skin as he reached towards her. They tried to touch through the glass wall, forgetting where they were, forgetting that they were in grave danger.

"How fascinating." The prince's voice began to automatically trigger panic inside of him. He pulled his shadows back at the same time Loralei extinguished her light, backing into the farthest corner of her room away from both of them. "I was told those chains would be impervious to your gifts."

Mozare wasn't entirely sure the chains weren't impervious. He had tried breaking through them, and had seen Loralei try the same, with no success. But it didn't stop them from accessing that power. He didn't comment. Loralei didn't even look at the prince.

She didn't even look up until someone stepped into the room with her, and then her face shifted to violence, and he was sure if he could hear her she would be growling. He was standing too, pulling at his own chains as hers were unlatched and the man shoved her from the room, one hand raised to stop himself from being blinded.

Another guard came into his room, and Mozare didn't fight when they removed his chains from the wall, leaving the lengths of them trailing behind him as they forced him into the hallway. They were following the prince and the guards with Loralei, so he didn't fight back as they shoved at him, didn't flinch or call his shadows or threaten them in any way. He just followed after her.

There were so many rooms down here, and they were so different from the palace that he couldn't be sure they were even still in the palace dungeons, or if the prince had moved them elsewhere.

It wasn't as important where they were as long as they were together. They would have to find their way out, and then if they weren't at the palace they would have to find a way to intercept Saiden and warn her.

His brain was running in circles again, but he didn't feel as panicked as before. He felt like he could pull all the strings of this situation together and come up with a plan. He was going to find them a way out of there.

56

SAIDEN

It took Saiden and three crew members a while to help to get Cassimir down the steps into the captain's quarters. Someone else had already collected their belongings and deposited them beside the captain's own things. Everything important they had with them left in a small pile.

Two other men had brought in bowls of clean water and a large pile of rags, the best they would be able to do to get the blood off their skin. Saiden already noticed pieces flaking from her fingers as she flexed them open and closed. Still she waited for them to leave before she looked at Cassimir. His skin was pale and sweat beaded on his forehead, but every inhale of his chest eased the pain in hers.

He didn't have nearly as much blood on him as she did. She took one of the bowls and set it carefully on the bed next to Cassimir, ripping his shirt to get the blood stains underneath it.

"Already trying to undress me are you?" Cassimir's voice was quiet, but she could still hear the gentle tease.

"You know I'm trying to clean you up. Don't be silly." She laid the fabric pieces to the side so the healed scars of his injury were on display. She ran one finger over the longest of the scars, he sucked in a breath and she froze.

"Your fingers," he said, reaching for her hand "are awfully cold." Detached, she watched him pick up one of the rags and run it over her fingers, cleaning the flaking blood from her knuckles and under her fingernails. He turned her hands to clean her palms, running a finger over the bruises she had given herself from holding her blades too tight. She didn't feel any of it.

"You almost died."

"And you saved me." She pulled her hand out of his reach, grabbing for one of the towels and dabbing at the blood on his abdomen. Her brain was still trying to comprehend everything that had happened in the past hour. How she had seen his life fading. How she had controlled her gift and used it to heal him.

He didn't try to speak as she cleaned the last of the blood from his chest, and fetched him a clean shirt from their bags. She let him lean on her as he slipped out of the bloodstained shirt, replacing it with the fresh one.

He didn't move back to rest against the cushions, taking a handful of water and letting it drip into her hair. She would need a good bath and scrub to get all of the bloodstains out of it later, but she was grateful. She let him take care of her, let him scrub the rest of the blood from her hands, realizing that maybe he needed that contact as much as she did.

She changed on the other side of the room, not caring that he was there, that he could be watching her. She doubted he would without her permission anyway. Besides, she had changed gear in front of people so often that the thought never crossed her mind to be shy.

When she finally brought herself to look at his face, she realized there was still blood on his forehead and the thin line of blood trailing from his mouth down his neck. She grabbed a clean cloth, soaking it in water and sat down in front of him to clean it off. She started with his forehead, eyes skipping between the blood and his constant gaze.

Then the bottom of the trail of blood at his throat, turning his head up with a finger and cleaning gently. She saw him swallow and wondered if he was still in pain. Then he was looking at her again, but her gaze was still stuck on his lips, on the last bit of blood, evidence of how close to death he had been. Then she cleaned that away too.

When she put the last rag in the bowl, setting them both outside the captain's room to be taken away by other members of the crew, she didn't know what to do with her hands. Cassimir was still staring at her, watching her every step across the small floor of the cabin. When she was close to him, he reached out, faster than she thought he could after being so close to death and pulled her into the bed with him.

"Don't shut me out." His eyes were pleading with her. "You can't, I can't take it."

"I'm not." The words sounded wrong, her voice out of place in this conversation. He leaned forward and kissed her, and she remembered so clearly how his kiss had centered her, how he was able to give her peace amid so much chaos.

He rested his forehead against hers. "You told me you love me."

She pulled away. "You were dying." Suddenly the fear in her chest had a different name.

"I love you too." He smiled at her, a gentle smile like he was worried she would retreat back into herself, would run from him. "Besides, if you kiss a man while he's dying, I'm pretty sure you mean it."

Saiden looked at her lap, blush burning her cheeks. He turned her to look at him, "I love you, but I also love sleep, and I think I am fairly close to passing out." She moved to untangle herself from him, giving him space to sleep on the soft bed and let his body heal what she hadn't been able to. But he grabbed her wrist, and she knew that he wanted her to stay there with him. To remind him he was whole, or that she was still there, she wasn't sure.

She lay down next to him, letting him get comfortable in the pile of pillows the captain had left on his bed. She tried to give him space, but the bed was barely big enough for Cassimir to sleep, much less the two of them. So he slept wrapped up in her, as she carefully kept a hand over his heart, making sure it continued its beautiful rhythm.

57

MOZARE

Mozare sat down in the seat next to Loralei, despite the way he knew the guards wanted to keep them apart. And he pulled his chair closer to hers just because he doubted they could stop him. Not when the prince was staring at them in bewilderment and would not give his guards any orders.

He rested his leg against hers, taking in the warmth of her skin through the thin fabric of his pants, relishing in the feeling of her hands as she laced her fingers through his underneath the table.

Neither of them spoke.

The room wasn't silent. He was aware of each of them men around them, his body intent on listening to the sound of them breathing and keeping track of where they stood guard around them. Loralei squeezed his hand, and then he felt the strand of divinity inside him react to the flare of her power.

Something sharp and jagged stabbed into his shoulder. He couldn't help the sound that came out of him as warm blood soaked his shirt, warming the skin on his back.

The prince tsked. "If you try in any way to harm my guards, there will have to be punishments of course. And since you, highness, can heal so easily, it seems only right that they are inflicted on him." The prince didn't even turn his gaze away from Loralei. "Because I do not think physical harm to your own body would be enough to sway you otherwise, now would it?"

Mozare swore he could see every one of Loralei's teeth as she snarled at the prince, but she didn't deny what he was saying either. The prince made another note in his pad of papers. "The same applies to you boy. Step out of line and the punishment will fall on your disgraced queen." Mozare kept his mask carefully blank, though anger writhed under the surface.

"I have questions." The prince did not give them the courtesy of deciding if they wanted to answer these questions or not. "I suggest you comply," he started, as if he had read Mozare's thoughts, "or this will become very uncomfortable for both of you."

Loralei's fingers were white where she was holding tight to him. Of the two of them, he knew there was so much more she wanted to keep secret. He also knew that she wouldn't put him in danger for those secrets, no matter how painful it might be for her to share them.

Mozare focused on the healing sensation in his shoulder as Loralei slowly unleashed tendrils of her power into him, healing his shoulder in such a way that it sent the blade clattering to the floor. The prince flinched at the sound, interrupting the steady flow of questions that had started pouring out of his mouth with no end in sight.

"Let's start with the basics. For the record state your name, age and gift- be specific on this one, no skimping on details to try and keep things secret. If I find out later that you hid things from me, it will not be pleasant."

Mozare started, only because his fear that he might get Loralei hurt was so rampant the words couldn't be held back. "I'm Mozare, 18. My gifts come from Ilona, the goddess of death. My talents include shadow summoning, and detecting pregnancies."

Akil watched them, letting the others with him take notes. It was like he was hoping for Mozare to disobey him, like he wanted to find some reason to punish them.

"And you queenling?"

Loralei hissed, baring her teeth. When they pressed another blade into his other shoulder, he watched her shrink, the fight in her eyes dying out as fast as it had come. She had finally been freed of the constraints of her rule, only to find herself in another set of chains.

"I'm Loralei. I'm probably 17? And my gifts come from Keir, god of life. He gave me the ability to heal and to create. I can grow flowers and I have a small talent for light."

"What do you mean probably?"

"It's hard to know how old you are when you live on the streets. We just guessed for a while. They don't give urchins calendars or birthday parties do they."

"How quaint. And what about that light show your friend pulled off. That's a gift from your god is it not?"

"Not one I have an affinity for." Loralei answered. Mozare wasn't sure that was true anymore, though it originally had been. He didn't fault her for lying, not when he had a feeling the lie would protect her in the long run.

He hadn't been lying about earning his forgiveness in blood if he had too.

"A pity. It really is a shame your friend decided to leave when she did. Though my cousins would have made this so much more difficult. Perhaps it is a worthy exchange."

"Next question. Explain what it's like when you reach for your power. I want to know about specific triggers. If there's a location in the body that you harness the power from."

Loralei squeezed Mozare's hand, and she answered first this time. "The thing about life gifts is that life is everywhere. Even here in this decrepit hellhole I can feel each of your hearts beating. I know every time one of you feels fear. Every time your heartbeat picks up, every twitch as you wonder what we might actually do."

The guard put the blade through his leg this time. He didn't wait for Loralei's healing to push the blade back out, he ripped it free on his own. In his peripheral vision he could see a feral smile split Loralei's face.

"Didn't think about the fact that you just gave a trainerdkiller a weapon when you decided that was the way to punish me did you?"

He heard them step closer to them, and threw the blade away, avoiding the disappointment on Loralei's face. He couldn't risk her getting hurt.

"For me, it's different. There's darkness everywhere sure, but my shadows come from inside me more than from the environment. I don't need darkness to make shadows."

"And the pregnancy part?"

"I can tell when a woman is pregnant. That one seems self-explanatory."

A guard stepped towards Loralei, but he didn't have the spine to get close to her with the look on her face right now. Mozare got the message all the same.

"Babies exist between life and death. Before they are born, they are cared for by Ilona, and protected by her power."

"How do you use that power?"

"In the legion it wasn't a power often used. I know that it was used by legionnaires assigned to more remote villages in the kingdom. It helped to tell what the sex of the baby was. And also to deal with complication that might endanger the mother or child during labor."

"Where does this knowledge come from in the body."

"I think it's more instinct. Unfortunately, I don't have a lot of experience in the matter."

"Do you know what happens when someone with your gifts gets pregnant themselves?"

Mozare didn't want to leave the prince without an answer, but there wasn't anything he could say. Very few soldiers spent time in the barracks if they were going to be starting a family, and he never would have thought to ask.

"We can switch to a new topic. What was it like for you to learn about your gifts." Mozare would have tensed, except he had long ago healed the wound his parents had given him by turning him over to the legion.

Loralei on the other hand froze completely, fear breeding behind her eyes. He didn't know if the prince could see what his question was doing to her or not, and he prayed that he couldn't.

She wouldn't want him to be able to feed on it.

He decided to go first. If only to give her more time to breathe through the fear. He knew the prince wouldn't let her get by without answering.

While he was talking, the hole in his leg knit back together, Loralei's power pulsing through him. He called a thin trail of shadows, and ran it through her fingers, all the comfort he could offer her while they were being observed.

"I trapped myself in the dark for a whole week straight. I almost died. My parents were elated." The two sentences feel wrong together, but they were the truth. "They knew their prayers had finally been rewarded. They dropped me off at the legion as soon as they could find me."

"Did you eat or drink during that time?"

"I couldn't find my own toes, much less food."

"How did you manage to go a whole week without eating?"

"Divine intervention? I don't know." He had theories, but he was absolutely not going to share them right now.

The prince turned to Loralei "And you?"

Her face was pale, her hand in his was frozen.

"I was living in the palace. I started growing flowers on my balconies."

"Should I remind you what happens when you keep things to yourself?"

One of the guards stepped behind him and pressed a blade to his throat. "Do you still think you could save him if I have my men cut open an artery? Or would he bleed out so fast that even your power would be useless? I'm happy to test it."

"You might not know about this, but Kaizian law doesn't allow for gifted monarchs. They had already had to remove the child before me. They couldn't deal with the backlash and instability a second time. But they didn't want me to have power either.

"They locked me somewhere they thought I would be unable to use my powers, away from life and light, but it didn't matter. I was still alive, and so my powers were still alive. They left me in there until I denied my gifts just so I could see the sun again.

"They killed my lover Jeremiah when he found out about my gifts."

When Akil finally seemed satisfied with her answer, he moved on, but he didn't let them out of that room for a long time.

58

SAIDEN

SAIDEN WATCHED CASSIMIR SLEEP, TURNING TO LOOK OUT THE SMALL window to watch the way the sun reflected on the waves. She watched his chest rise and fall, to be sure he was still breathing. The ship rocked back and forth, a personal lullaby hanging between it and the sea. And she pulled at her power. At the growing pieces that were come back to her.

Cassimir stirred in front of her, stretching and pulling her closer to him. Then he smiled, the last traces of sleep still holding onto his face. He blinked and looked up at her.

"Why does it smell like oranges?"

She laughed, and held out her hand to him, showing him the small orange she had grown while he was sleeping. "They make me think of you." She said keeping her face tight against his chest.

"You grew this while I was sleeping?" He took the orange from her hand, lifting it to his face and smelling it before he started peeling it open.

"I realized something, after I healed you." Saiden started, "that peace is stronger than fear. That love is stronger."

He smiled at her again, then he grabbed her waist, flipping her over so she was lying underneath him in the small bed. "Say it again." He leaned down and kissed her softly.

"I love you."

He leaned down to kiss her again, lingering over her and smiling into the kiss. She pushed him back, "You're injured, you need rest."

He lifted his shirt, running a hand over the trio of scars across from the tattoo at his hip. "I am not injured anymore," he kissed her again, "thanks to you." She still pulled away from him, sitting crossed legged at the other end of the bed, her knee still pressed against his. He moved the pillows so he could lean against them, a small strain in his eye as he turned to get comfortable.

"Niran let you use my ink didn't she?" Saiden asked, forcing herself to push the words out. She had wanted to ask him the question ever since they had fought in the arena, but so much had happened since then.

"I was wondering when you were going to pick up on that."

"So it was a test?"

"What? No." He reached forward, and she saw true pain on his face this time. Pain that he didn't try to conceal as he reached for her hand. "I wanted to show you that you didn't have to carry the weight alone. All vines need something to hold onto."

Her head spun, trying to understand what Cassimir was thinking. "These deaths are my weight to bear."

"You are not responsible for every bad thing in the world."

"These are people who died on my blade." She stood, pacing the room. "And how many more people have died because Revon took the binding off my powers." She hadn't spoken his name in weeks, hadn't acknowledged the hand he had in all of this. "Their blood, their deaths, they're my fault."

Cassimir opened his mouth to speak, but nothing came out. Whatever he had meant with his actions, whatever he was trying to do, she couldn't imagine this was how he had seen it playing out.

She pushed through the wooden door, needing to get out of the captain's quarters, needing space and fresh air to get her thoughts organized again. She was spiraling, and there was no reason for her to take it out on him, to be angry or upset with Cassimir for trying to help her.

Her mother's words came back to her, the force of it almost knocking her off her feet. *There are times when you need to take your armor off, to be vulnerable with your friends.* She wasn't letting herself do that with Cassimir because she was afraid again. And she was building walls so she wouldn't have to face him when he saw all of her, so she wouldn't have to risk letting him see her and him choosing to leave her.

She took another deep breath of the ocean air, letting the salt sink into her skin, letting the waves wash away the last pieces of her wall.

Cassimir was leaning on the wall next to the door when she came back to the room. "Apparently, loosing that much blood can make you very dizzy." He tried to laugh, but she saw how he forced it for her.

"I'm sorry. I just need time."

"We have no shortage of that. Not now."

Not now. Now they could stay in this room and not worry about anything, and they would deal with the rest of it together. She helped Cassimir back into bed, teasing him about thinking he was indestructible instead of resting like she told him too.

They sat and answered questions, and she let herself sit in the uncomfortable feeling of being vulnerable, because she wanted to be close. To be known and to know him.

Saiden was pulling beads of water from the ship's wood, which splashed in Cassimir's face when the captain surprised her by opening the door. Cassimir laughed, wiping away the worst of the droplets with the edge of the blanket.

"Just wanted to check you were still in the land of the living. Seeing your lady up on deck startled a few of my crew members." Saiden lowered her head, smiling slightly. She might have been a bit scary, storming out of their quarters like that, but she hadn't meant to be. "Also just want to let you know the ship will be arriving in the outer limits of the island at nightfall. We'll do our best to give you cover, and we'll be waiting for you as close as we can."

She looked back up at the captain, surprise plain on her face. They had paid him only to take them to the island. They figured once they had safely retrieved Eleni, they would need to hide somewhere on the island until they could book safe travel back to the mainland.

"You have our gratitude captain," Cassimir answered, bowing as much as he could considering they hadn't stood from the bed.

"And you have mine."

59

MOZARE

THE DARKNESS AROUND MOZARE WAS A KIND SO ABSOLUTE, NOT EVEN HIS shadows could find their way through it. He wasn't sure how the prince had managed it, considering the southern kingdom had nothing of their gifts, but he couldn't bother himself with trying to figure out the mechanics of his new cell.

The room was too quiet. Wherever he was, Loralei was not with him. Part of him was relieved, that her light wouldn't be subject to this dampening, but the other half of him was terrified about what could be happening to her in his absence. What similar hell was the prince putting her through while he was unable to defend her?

He forced himself to regulate his breathing. He hadn't been afraid of the dark in a long time, not since he had learned to control the darkness he could weave, but panic over Loralei and their shared imprisonment, was keeping him from being level headed.

Mozare didn't know what the prince expected him to do, what he was hoping to learn from putting him in a room so dark even his highness's gaze might not reach him.

If he listened carefully he could hear machines ticking in the room around him. He didn't know enough about technology to have any idea what the prince might have set up in here while he was sleeping.

THE BLOOD-CURSED

It didn't make him feel any better. Above his head, the prince's voice came into being, crackling through the room until it surrounded him. He wrapped his own arms around himself, not caring if the prince could see him after all. Anything to keep the terror from settling into his bones.

"Sorry if the darkness is unsettling. It seems even with your gifts there is a threshold for how much darkness the human psyche can take without crumbling. Interesting."

Anger burned away some of his terror. The gifts his goddess granted him didn't make him less or more human. Of course he was still afraid. He was tired and cold and had no idea what was going to happen to them. The darkness was only the beginning of it.

Mozare could picture the prince's pencil scratching across his notepad, and that helped to focus him. There was an enemy here, and that meant there was something he could fight.

He couldn't fight the sharp sting in his side as something attacked him from the darkness, cutting through the fabric on his shirt and leaving a thin slice under his rib cage. He pressed his hands against it, but without extra bandages, with nothing more than the shirt on his back he had no hope of stopping the blood.

He certainly couldn't manage it when another blade sliced into his bicep.

He gave up entirely when a third blade cut the top of his thigh, a fourth striking near his ankle. He couldn't find the prince, but he let his words fill the darkness. "You can make me bleed all you like, my gift isn't in my blood. It isn't anywhere you can reach it."

His voice was stronger than he thought it would be, and he sat on his hands to keep the prince from somehow seeing them shake. If this was his last stand, he wasn't going out afraid.

"We shall see, shadow boy."

The blood pooled on his skin began to dry, and as time passed he could feel himself start to sleep, even against his own wishes. He tried to find a corner, but the room felt impossibly huge with everything shrouded in darkness. Instead, he curled in on himself, trying to keep himself safe.

Just as he began to fall asleep, something pressed into his back, power shocking through his body. "You sleep when I say you can demon."

He didn't know how the prince himself wasn't drowsy, but now every bit of sleep had been chased from his body. He pulled at his own shadows, and even though he couldn't see them, he pushed them through his fingers, playing with the tendrils of power until his brain stopped racing, his heartbeat returning to his normal pattern.

A second time he started to sleep and a second time Akil's machines shocked him awake. He didn't need to see the prince to know that he was disappointed, and at the same time, writing some note down about Mozare's "condition".

The longer he waited in this room, the more comfort he felt. This darkness might not be his, but it was shadow all the same. From deep inside its cocoon Mozare started to tug at his own darkness. And inside him, his powers started to answer.

He built walls around himself, pulled the shadows until they were solid, pushing them together the way an architect would start the foundation of a new building. He tested it once by leaning his body weight against the material, amazed when it held him without sagging. This time when the prince's machines tried to reach him, they couldn't get past his barriers.

"Fascinating."

One word, and cracks started forming along his walls. He was still Akil's subject, something he was surprised he had managed to forget in all this darkness. He was tired, he had lost a lot of blood and the sting still reverberated through his body. He couldn't take much more of this.

Then he realized, the darkness was no longer foreign. He had been able to control it.

Which meant he could get out of here.

He stood, balancing his weight between his injuries. And then he called the darkness back to him. There was nothing Akil could do, nothing to prevent his goddess given gifts from getting him out of here.

He was Ilona's weapon, and it was time to fight back.

With the darkness snaked around him, he could finally see Akil

THE BLOOD-CURSED

behind another one of his glass walls, rushing to pull a weird set of glasses from his face as light once again filled the space. His face screamed anger for a brief moment before he started clapping.

Something pinched Mozare's neck, and then he was falling back into the darkness.

60

SAIDEN

The captain's men brought Saiden and Cassimir bowls of warm stew, letting them eat their fill of the ship's food so they were prepared for the swim they would need to get from the boat to the island where they had overheard the men in the tavern say Eleni was being held captive.

She stripped out of her baggy clothing, choosing the tightest of her long sleeve shirts, and a pair of training pants she adjusted at the ankles so they hugged her calves and kept the pant legs closer to her body. They needed the least amount of weight on their bodies so that they could make the swim. Especially if they might need to carry Eleni between them on the way back. She left her boots paired neatly at the foot of the captain's bed, the only thing she brought with her were the blades Cassimir had given her.

He did the same, although he opted to skip a shirt altogether. She had a feeling it had less to do with the swim, and more as a reminder that the weight wasn't hers to bear alone, something he felt was so important he had it permanently inked into his skin.

Two of the crew members extended a rope ladder down the side of the ship, offering them both a hand over the railing and into the water. It felt like ice on her skin, but beneath it, she felt her powers calling to her. She reached into that well, and pulled on the flames that had terrorized her, using them not for fire, but to warm her body.

She reached for Cassimir as he lowered himself into the water, his sigh rippling in the blue around him when she passed the warmth to him.

They were still drenched and cold when they finally reached the island, both of them having swam into or kicked multiple sharp rocks that jutted beneath the water out of sight. She had the distinct urge to curse, something she hadn't felt before, but suppressed it; the need for surprise overweighting everything else.

They shook themselves out, ringing water from their hair and the thin layers of their clothing. She didn't dare try to dry their clothes with her powers, too worried she might light them on fire and alert the pirates they were here. Cassimir leaned in close and whispered a plan, and she listened, trusting his instincts the same way he had relied on her in the pub.

She stayed behind on the beach, counting her breaths until she was sure she had left enough time to follow Cassimir without anyone seeing her behind him. She tracked his footsteps through the wet beach sand, glad the waves were calm enough they hadn't yet been washed away. She stood a distance away as she watched him walked into the makeshift camp of tents, broken bottles littering the ground where some of the men and women were passed out from the night before.

On the other side of the camp was an overhang, a rock that had stood against the ocean's erosion. She knew that was the best high ground for her, for Cassimir's plan. She pulled on the shadows inside her, the part of her powers that connected her to Mozare even with the distance between them, and wrapped herself in them. After lurking around the edge of the camp she began her climb up the side of the overhang.

Her fingers felt strong as she flipped herself over the edge, keeping her body close to the ground, hoping there wasn't anyone stationed there to sound an alarm.

She wasn't sure why she was even worried when she noticed the one guard, a woman passed out on the ground with a bottle still in her hand. She crept to the edge, watching as those sober and conscious enough to notice the intruder started to stir, grabbing for weapons and surrounding Cassimir in the middle of the camp.

Her heart fluttered, imagining another scenario where she couldn't get to him in time, where he bled to death on board the ship. She pushed the thoughts from her mind, focusing on Cassimir, trusting that he knew what he was doing. That she would be able to pull off her part in his crazy plan.

"My name is Cassimir, son of Rami, Prince ambassador of Taezhali and nephew of the emperor." Cassimir had explained on the ship his title, though she still had a hard time understanding the patterns of succession in the Taezhali monarchy. He stood tall despite his wet clothes and the growing number of weapons being pointed at him.

She held tighter to the rock, resisting the instinct to pull her own weapon, to run to Cassimir's side and fight her way out of it. But she waited, her breathing tight through her chest. "I am here for my sister, you will return her to my care, or you will face the might of those who follow me."

She giggled. Truly giggled despite the danger they were in. If they knew what the might that followed Cassimir was they would kill him where he stood, yet he sounded like armies had followed him to the island.

"You expect us to just give up the emperor's favorite niece because you've come to us, soaking wet and asked for her." One man step forward from the crowd, leaning on the handle of his axe. "These royals get crazier and crazier. We want freedom. Unless the emperor gives us that, unless he sent you to bargain, which I doubt, then your sister is dead."

Cassimir looked to the cliff top, somehow finding her even though she had been wrapped in shadows, and she knew that was her sign. She stood from her hiding place, digging into the well of power that now rested freely inside her, pulling at it, and lighting up the night sky.

She sent her consciousness out to Cassimir, wrapping him in a protective bubble the same way she had so instinctually done with Mozare and Loralei. Now that her powers were somewhat under her control, they did what she asked of them. She sent a small piece of her light to look for Eleni.

Relief coursed through her when her powers recognized her friend, wrapping her in the light like the tightest of hugs. Something crashed into the back of her head, slicing pain radiating from her scalp. The woman, who had been passed out behind her, stood, the broken neck of a bottle clutched in her hand. Saiden unsheathed her blade, keeping her focus on the light as she swung out at the woman dodging away from her. The woman slipped gauntlets on her hands, bladed spikes at the knuckles and on the sides.

She evaded the first swing, careful to keep the blades away from her skin, careful not to move too fast and make herself dizzy. When the fighter made a careless step towards Saiden, she jumped, using the woman's bent knee to propel herself over her, kicking the handle of her blade against the soft spot on her skull and watching her collapse to the ground, truly knocked out this time.

She couldn't care what happened to the fallen fighter, too worried because she could feel the power fading already. She jumped from the cliff, falling down on one knee, and flipping her wet hair back before charging into the camp to find Eleni. The light dimmed, the stars beginning to be visible again as darkness regained its territory.

She pushed harder, fighting the first woman who attacked her, disarming her and swinging her into the nearest tent. The light she wrapped around Eleni acted like a beacon, and she focused on keeping that strong as the rest of the light through the camp faded, replaced by the loud sounds of men fighting. She sent a prayer out for Cassimir, that he had taken the time in her protection to get out of the middle of the ring they had created around him.

She found Eleni in the back of a tent towards the middle of the camp, gagged with her arms and legs tied together. They had taken her scarf. She let the light fade, dropping to her knees to pull at the fabric in the other girl's mouth, cutting through the ropes at her feet and hands.

Eleni was crying as she reached forward and grabbed Saiden. Saiden held her, doing her best to give the support that Eleni needed, just like she had done for Saiden. She pulled off her shirt, the fabric mostly dry after her light show, and helped Eleni wrap it around her hair.

"It is so good to see you again." Saiden said, carefully running her hands over Eleni and checking for injuries. She tried to send her power through her, but with so little training, she had already exhausted its strength. "But we need to get out of here."

She sheathed the longer of her blades grabbing for Eleni, wrapping her small hand with Saiden's own. And she pushed aside the tent's flap, looking around before she pulled at Eleni and started running. Her own feet were sore, the ground covered in broken glass and other careless debris, and she hoped that Eleni still had her slippers, and that they were enough to give her some protection.

Digging into the last dregs of her power, she reached her consciousness towards Cassimir, using it to guide them through the camp. They were almost clear when she heard someone's heavy footsteps charging after them. She pulled Eleni behind her, throwing the smaller blade with all her strength across the space between them and her pursuer.

Then she was running again, pushing Eleni toward Cassimir, keeping her ears open for others following them. "Go. Take your sister back to the ship, run as fast as you can. I'll be right behind you."

Cassimir placed one of his chakram in her hand, and then took off behind his sister, using his frame to keep her hidden from sight, from being targeted. She waited a moment, and raced after them, keeping their path clear. Giving them time to get to the ship. Two people attacked her, reaching for her arms. She pulled back, swinging for the first one's face, cutting their cheek with Cassimir's weapon.

The second warrior had long braids down the side of his head, and he looked at her for a long time before aiming a fist at her face. She ducked, spinning around him and kicking at the back of his knees.

Saiden left them on the ground, hoping they didn't follow as she raced towards the beach where they had arrived, wanting to get away from the camp as fast as possible. She heard one, then both of them following after her, and she pushed her already exhausted body harder.

The water came into view, Cassimir and Eleni already past the reach of the beach. She dove in the water hands first to keep her from hitting one of the rock spikes they had kicked on their way to the island.

She surfaced and heard the others jump into the water after her. She was overwhelmingly grateful for all the afternoons she had spent swimming in the river, pushing herself harder in her training. Everything that gave her an advantage now, with two pirates on her tail. Cassimir was on the ladder of the ship, his sister being pulled over the railing by Nico. She smiled, pushing herself to swim faster. They were too close, and the ship was too far, and then she heard a loud noise, and the water splashed over her head.

"That woman is under my protection." The captain was aiming his cannon, smoke still spiraling out of the barrel. When the ringing in her ears ceased she realized no one was following her anymore.

She swam the rest of the way, her friends and other crew members pulling her up by her armpits, orders already being shouted to pull up the anchor and get away from the island.

61
MOZARE

Mozare woke up stuck in his room on the other side of the glass wall as Loralei was strapped to a table just like the one he had been on just a few days ago when they had first been moved to these cells. And no matter how much he pulled on his chains, they still didn't have any more give than they had any other day since they had been stuck down here.

Loralei pulled against her straps, fighting harder than he had when those same straps had secured him to the table. He felt his stomach sink to the floor as he watched, helpless from the other side of the glass as the prince walked into the room, a guard and a man in a weird jacket following closely behind him.

"I'd like to test some theories. It will involve minor physical pain, and a forced distressful environment." The words sounded muffled to Mozare from his room, but to him it almost sounded as if the prince was asking for her permission instead of forcefully torturing political refugees. The thought almost made Mozare laugh. He might have even laughed if he had been the one strapped to the table instead of Loralei.

"I've already been dead once, there's nothing here that you can do to me that would be worse than that." She spat at the prince, writhing against the table even as they secured the strap on her forehead, pinning her completely to the metal slab. His heart went out to her.

The prince perched near her arm, adjusting himself as if he were conscious of Mozare watching through the window, as if he desperately wanted Mozare to see what he was doing so that he could run two experiments at once. He wasn't sure if he would be able to control himself enough to prevent the prince from getting what he wanted.

Akil drew a small metal object down the pale skin of her arm, blood tracing her skin where it touched. Loralei didn't even flinch, though Mozare's whole body shuddered. He knew what Akil had done to him in that dark room, but he didn't have the same gift for healing, he couldn't be pushed as far as Loralei without doing irreparable damage.

The cut on her arm started to heal, and the prince measured it, touching the skin around it, dictating notes to the man in the jacket that Mozare was unable to hear. He repeated the steps, tracing that same line until Mozare was sure he would be able to see it there for the rest of his life no matter how well Loralei managed to heal it.

Loralei had many talents, and as she had been freed to explore her powers since being dethroned, he had seen those talents grow more powerful than any other life gifted he had met before. Not only could she heal extensive damage like what had been done to his back, but she had brought herself back from the brink of death. Her flowers bloomed brighter and lived longer, and she had even managed to learn Saiden's light bending ability despite not being born with it.

Despite his control over his gifts, he was nothing special, but Loralei, she was magnificent. And now the prince would exploit that to the fullest of his ability. Anger swirled in his gut, at their situation, at himself for not keeping her safe, at the prince for deciding he had a right to their god gifted abilities.

He felt his shadows gathering inside him, but he didn't let them out. Not as Akil used a long pair of tweezers to rip one of Loralei's fingernails off, not when he began to cut the guard in the room to see how far Loralei's healing range went, not when he left longer and deeper cuts on her legs.

Then, with all his power inside he remembered another gift of his, one that he rarely ever used because it didn't serve well in combat. Mozare could commune with the dead. Now that he recalled this facet of his gifts, he understood the hint his goddess had given him. He also knew the prince had been responsible for the deaths of many within these prison walls. He pushed out his senses and started calling on the dead, offering them something he knew they wouldn't be able to resist.

He offered them a chance at vengeance.

62
SAIDEN

Cassimir's arms were around her before she had even gotten both feet over the railing, his head in her hair. Eleni's hands grabbed her arm, pulling her away from her brother and hugging her again. Beside them, Cassimir wrapped his arms around them both. She couldn't tell if she felt like laughing or crying.

Eleni had a hand on her face, "it is so good to see you sahadi." She watched Eleni as the adrenaline left her body, and then she was sagging in Saiden's grip. She had her hands around her before she dropped, holding her body tight so Eleni didn't fall to the ship deck. Cassimir came behind her, picking her up and carrying her into the captain's quarters, apparently still claiming it as theirs for now.

He sat with her in the bed, cradling his sister in his arms, tears in his eyes. Saiden pressed two fingers against her throat, checking that her pulse was regular, and focused on Cassimir. "She's only sleeping. A side effect of so much adrenaline, we see it a lot when new recruits go on their first missions. She'll be okay in a few hours." She didn't mention the cuts or bruises. Didn't draw his notice to the fact that Eleni was still wearing Saiden's shirt as a head scarf, leaving Saiden in only her pants and chest wrap.

She kissed his forehead, running a hand through the wet tangles of his hair. With just two fingers on her shoulder, Saiden started pushing small pieces of her reserve of power into Eleni, hunting out her injuries and taking away the pain. There was very little she could do with her strength so spent, but she wanted to give her friend peace.

She slumped next to Cassimir, leaning her head on his shoulder, and for the first time in what felt like days, she slipped off to sleep.

The room was warm when she woke, sun spilling through the small circular window she faced. Three of them were all wrapped up in each other on the bed, Cassimir likely having fallen asleep after her. She reached into herself and tested her powers. She felt her strength coming back, and she used it to check on the siblings, healing their injuries as she searched through their bodies with Keir's healing talent.

Cassimir stirred first, smiling that sleepy smile of his as he turned to check on his sister. Eleni woke as they were both looking at her, which caused them to both look away quickly, making her laugh as she pushed herself up in the bed, leaning back against the captain's headboard.

Saiden tried to take control of the situation. "Cassimir, go find Nico, ask if he can bring us some more of that stew," she paused to think, "and come back with some clean rags and a bowl of water."

She waited until the door was closed before focusing on Eleni, taking time to watch her before speaking. "I need to ask you something that might be uncomfortable." She reached for her hand, the skin soft between Saiden's calloused fingers. "Did any of those men try to... touch you?" She hated the words, hated that she had to ask them, but most men were not courteous with their prisoners.

Eleni shivered, and moved closer to Saiden. "They spent most of the time ignoring me besides a few bruises." Her voice was shallow, the happiness leaching out of it with every word. "One of them tried to touch me when he was drunk, but I punched him." She held out her hand the knuckles still bruised despite Saiden's healing efforts. "He's the one who stole my scarf."

THE BLOOD-CURSED

Saiden stood from the bed and retrieved the wrap she had bought in the market, a colorful replacement for the shirt that was still lumpily tied around Eleni's hair.

"Thank you." Saiden nodded in response, gratitude and relief overwhelming her as she watched Eleni, and the idea that she was here safe with them finally settled into her bones.

Eleni settled into the sheets, excitement lighting in her eyes. "So you and my brother huh?"

Saiden's cheeks began to burn, and she grabbed for the knotted ends of her hair, anything to give her something to do with her hands. "I told him I love him." She whispered.

Eleni squealed from the bed, tripping over herself trying to get up. Saiden stepped forward to catch her before she completely face planted against the wooden slats of the floor. Eleni got her feet under her, bouncing as she held onto Saiden's forearms.

She stopped, looking at her face, at whatever she could see that Saiden hadn't managed to hide. "He said he loved you too, right?" She nodded. "Then what's wrong?"

"It's just, I think it must be an awful thing to love me."

"Not for me," Saiden hadn't noticed Cassimir had opened the door, and she jumped at the sound of his voice from where he leaned in the doorway. He didn't look away as she stared at him. "Never for me."

She felt her blush travel down her neck, coloring the skin still on display. She moved, pulling a new shirt from her pack and sliding it over her head while the siblings had a silent conversation behind her back.

"It will be nice, I think, to finally have a sister." Eleni kissed Saiden on the cheek and then slipped outside the door.

"She does use that word quite often, whether in Taezhali's sacred language or in mine." Saiden joked.

Cassimir took a step forward, setting the bowl of water near the bed. "She's thought that about you since the first moment she heard about you." He took another step, "she must have seen everything in you that I hadn't seen yet."

He took another step up to her, their still bare feet toe to toe. He reached his hands up to cup her face, fingers tangling in the hair at the nape of her neck, and leaned down. "I'm going to keep reminding you of all the good I see in you, until you finally see it too." Then he was kissing her. She leaned into it, craving the warmth, the security and peace that she had when she was with him.

He moved his hands to her hips, pulling her flush against him and deepening his kiss, tilting her head back with his. Then he was kissing the skin just under her ear, his hands circling her back and he devoured her. She sighed, then she remembered that they were still on a ship full of people, that Cassimir's own sister was still likely outside the door, and she calmed down.

"There's plenty of time," she reminded him, the same words he had given her. "We have all the time we need."

She walked past him, swaying her hips just a bit more than she normally would, as she invited Eleni back into the room. The rags were meant for her anyway, to clean the small traces of blood from her cheeks and her fingers. To clean away the horrid memories of the past few days. She sat with her as Eleni insisted she could do it herself, knowing from experience that having someone there made it easier, even if they weren't doing anything.

Eleni leaned into her when she was done and Saiden wrapped her arms around her. Her heart was conflicted. She realized how much she truly did feel like they were sisters, but at the same time she missed the relationship she had developed with Rhena. She was tired of having to choose which family to stand with, to protect. She just wanted her little family to be together again.

63

MOZARE

When he had summoned enough of the corpses beneath his feet, his focus returned to the power swirling inside his chest. If Loralei had managed to learn an entirely new ability in their time here, Mozare figured there was no reason he couldn't push himself to expand his own gift. He imagined his darkness taking form, solidifying into weapons sharp enough to cut skin, hard enough to break through glass.

When the prince stepped away from Loralei to confer with the man in the jacket, Mozare tried to get her attention, flashing shadows above her face where she could see them without having to turn her head. He thought he saw light flash briefly at her fingertips, but even if he hadn't, he needed to take advantage of the fact that the prince was occupied, and wouldn't notice as his ghouls came for their revenge.

He broke through his chains with a swing of a shadow axe. He wished he had thought of the idea earlier, had tried harder to get free before the prince had started to cut them both open, but he didn't have time to dwell on regrets. He only had focus enough to get Loralei out and safe, to get the hell away from the prince as fast as they could.

The glass shattered with one strike of his new weapons, causing all three men in the room beyond it to jump, and the guard to reach for weapons of his own. He didn't care about his life as he threw one of his shadow blades into the guards chest, not even waiting to see his body hit the floor.

The creatures he had summoned occupied Akil and the man in the jacket, and Mozare used the small tendrils of his shadows to free Loralei from her bonds. He didn't want to underestimate the prince's strength, or his ability to call in reinforcements. Doing so was what got them in this trouble in the first place.

Based on the way Loralei sagged as she tried to slide down from the table, she wasn't going to be able to do much to defend herself. The prince had already exhausted her far too much with his exercises.

Still she tried, his warrior queen, growing a wall of ivy behind them as they began to make their way through the maze of tunnels. They had no way of knowing if they were heading in the right direction, but he hoped that between Loralei's sense for where people were, and the few ghosts who had remained with them, they would be lucky enough to get out without facing any more guards.

If only his life were ever that simple.

Guards found them around the next corner, their footsteps so quiet against the dirt floors that Mozare had not heard them coming. He stepped in front of Loralei, A pitch black blade in each hand. The ghosts around him charged, no longer waiting for his order to pursue their tormentors.

Some of the guards fell to the ghosts, others to his blade. He did his best to keep his own body between Loralei and the guards surrounding them, shooting daggers of darkness into the bodies of those who were outside the range of his swords. His hands still soaked with blood even as his blades deflected it.

Two guards reached for him at the same time, trying to pull him away from Loralei. Then one of them was skewered, roses growing from his stomach where a vine of them held him against the ceiling of the tunnel. His blood dripped on Mozare as he turned to the other attackers, swiping one blade through his chest and the other across his throat.

"You need to get out of here." He said to her as he decapitated the guard, planting one foot firmly against his chest so his headless body fell into another guard, buying him a second. "Find Cassimir's father and get help."

He spared Loralei one glance in the melee, just enough to see that she had no desire to leave him. Just enough to see her listen to him anyway, ducking under a guards open arms and trusting him to stop the guard from reaching her.

"You filthy, vile creatures." The prince spoke from behind him and Mozare tensed. He could still hear Loralei's bare feet slapping the floor as she ran away. She needed more time. Mozare had to buy her more time.

He turned slowly, his blades in front of him, his ghosts behind him. Fear burst into the prince's eyes for a second before rage once again overcame him. His once meticulous robes were ripped to shreds, blood soaking the ripped edges. The glasses he'd been wearing now sported a broken lens, and blood trailed down his face from a jagged cut on his forehead.

"Don't like what vengeance looks like? Were the consequences of your own actions too brutal for you?"

The prince scowled. Mozare returned the look with a smirk, putting all his energy into being cocky, instead of worrying about the fighting at his back or if Loralei had made it out of the catacombs safely on her own. If she would be able to get help in time. He felt his power draining. He had never drawn on so much of it at one time, and though he tried to maintain the facade, there was limited time until his warriors and his weapons were all gone.

"I would say this has provided a very interesting revelation about your gifts, but it has been such a great inconvenience to my work that I cannot even enjoy this display of power." Mozare was pretty sure the prince's words were going to make him sick. "If you wouldn't mind making your way back to your room, we can forget this little excursion ever happened."

The prince must've been insane. If the past few days of torture and experiments hadn't been enough to prove that fact, the idea that he thought Mozare would return to that room of his own free will solidified it. He'd rather die, rather fall on his own blade here in front of the prince than ever be under Akil's control again.

The prince must've seen something in Mozare's face, anger or resolve he didn't know. He didn't have the energy to even worry about what his face might be giving away.

"You can run. There aren't any guards left to stop you. We both know that I am not a match for you with or without your powers. But know this. I have the resources of an entire empire behind me. There is nowhere you and that disgraced wretch could go where I couldn't find you. Nowhere where you will ever be safe. You will spend every day of the rest of your life looking over your shoulder and waiting for me."

Mozare ignored the sounds of footsteps racing towards him. Ignored the warning bells in his own head that suggested he was going to make a bad decision. Ignored everything except his next steps.

He only needs two to bridge the space between himself and the crown prince of Taezhali, one push of his arm for the blade of his shadows to push through his chest. One moment for his shadows to disappear completely, leaving only a bloody wound, and the sound of screams behind him.

64

MOZARE

Mozare was fairly certain this was the last time he would wake up in a prison cell. Only fairly certain though, because he didn't know exactly how trials worked in Taezhali, so he couldn't predict how fast the emperor would be having him executed.

At least this time, there was no one in the cell beside his. Loralei had been with Cassimir's father when they had found him, just after he had plunged his blade through the prince's chest. Even now, with the consequences of his actions staring at him, he couldn't regret killing Akil. He had bought Loralei her freedom, and even the price of his own life didn't seem like too high a cost.

She disagreed, and had yelled at him profusely the first moment they were alone. But she was not allowed to stay in the prison. She was a witness to the horrible things the prince had done to both of them, and she was needed if he was going to have any chance of making it out of this sand blasted kingdom alive.

He wanted to tell them that it wasn't worth fighting. No emperor, no matter how weak the prince may have believed him to be, would ever pardon the man who killed his son and heir. Mozare didn't expect their efforts to do anything but make his death harder on the people who cared about him.

At least this cell had a window. Darkness didn't bother him, but he hadn't wanted his last views to be the vile walls in the catacombs where he now knew Akil had been keeping them for his experiments. This cell was clean, and food and water had already been brought to him twice since he had woken up. This was an honorable way to die, which made it so much easier for him to accept his fate.

Guards came a few hours after midday to fetch him from the prison. He didn't fight them as they cuffed his wrists in thick chains and formed a square around him, guiding him through the winding hallways that would lead him to the emperor's throne room.

He thought he would feel fear when Ilona finally came to claim him, but nothing but peace radiated through his chest, and his steps were even as he walked to the middle of the room despite the nobility gathered to gawk at him. He searched only for her, for the pair of green eyes that would center him. To Loralei, who despite their differences had learned to love him, had shown him that he was worth so much more than he had ever thought. Who he had come to love as well.

They connected the other ends of his chains to loops in the floor that had not been there any of his previous times visiting the throne room. The distance between the loop and length of his chains forced him to kneel, arms spread wide at his sides. It was meant to be humiliating, but he didn't care. He couldn't do anything but try to reassure Loralei that this was his choice, that it was his honor to die for her.

He didn't want to look away when the emperor started speaking, but one of the guards roughly shoved his head forward, forcing him to focus on their ruler.

The emperor didn't look like he was mourning, despite the fact that his regalia was now all in black. There was no show of opulence, no abundance of golden chains. Even from a distance Mozare could see that no rings adorned his fingers.

Mozare couldn't tell what emotion swirled on the emperor's face, no longer concealed by his mask of etiquette, but it didn't look like grief. If Mozare were not already on the brink of death, he might bet his life that the look on the emperor's face was actually relief.

"Death is not a suitable punishment for you, as the death of my eldest son is not the only crime you have committed this day. You have robbed this country of its future and ripped its birthright straight from his hands." The first of the emperor's words rang through a silent hall, but as he continued to speak, the others around Mozare began to whisper back and forth.

He was a dead man already, so he didn't bother trying to learn anything from their whispers. There was nothing left to save him from this fate. He had used all his luck, good, bad or otherwise, and he had to face that. Hoping would only delay the inevitable.

Mozare heard heavy footsteps approach from behind him, a second guard joining the one who kept him from turning his head to look behind him.

"For the pain you have caused my subjects, that pain shall be returned to you. Lashes were a fitting punishment last time, though I see you've healed nicely. My punishment to you now is a lash for every one of my subjects, for as long as your body can withstand it."

He heard someone scream, heard *Loralei* scream. He pulled his head away from the guard long enough to look at her and watched as she was grabbed by her arms and held back. Kept away from him. He was grateful for that. Loralei would have interfered, would have tried to take this punishment with him, and he wanted nothing more than for her to live. To be able to someday move past this darkness and find her own light. Just like she had given him.

With the chains already on his wrists there was no use trying to pull his shirt over his head, and he wouldn't need the fabric where he was going. He heard the metal of a knife releasing from its sheath, and then his back was bare to the warm Taezhali sun streaming in through the ceiling's windows.

This was not a bad place to die, with the sun on his back and love in his heart.

The first lash hit, and he focused on Loralei, on showing her the love he never declared, all the feelings he hadn't had the time to act on. He didn't keep count, didn't worry about how many times the whip cut into him or how the warmth on his back quickly became wet, his blood soaking into the waist band of his pants.

He only watched her.

65

SAIDEN

It took them twelve days to get back to the palace. Without the fear hanging over their heads, Saiden and the siblings took their time to travel through the towns they passed. They rested too, spending the nights dancing at festivals and watching the stars cross the sky. They didn't have to run or chase caravans or interrogate bar patrons.

They were some of the happiest memories she had, and she smiled as she stepped across the threshold of the emperor's palace, Cassimir flashing his signet ring to show the guards who they were. They all inclined their heads as the trio passed, a look on their face that made her skin crawl.

"Something's wrong." She didn't focus her comment at anyone, speaking before her brain had fully caught up with what was going on.

"The halls are too silent." Eleni agreed, huddling closer between the two of them. Saiden used the same trickle of her power that had led her to Eleni in the pirate's camp to look for Mozare, pushing her consciousness through the labyrinth of a palace until she found him, kneeling in the emperor's throne room.

Shocked, she looked at Cassimir before taking off at a sprint, following the pull of her power down long hallways turning so many times she would never be able to find her way back out of there on her own. Cassimir and Eleni were running behind her, their footsteps echoing through the halls.

The guards were hesitant to open the doors, fear clear on their faces as she appeared red faced and out of breath. It took Cassimir ordering them aside before she was able to push the solid mahogany doors open, interrupting the trial happening on the other side of the door.

Her brain tried to take in everything she saw, her thoughts racing with all the information at one time. The emperor wore regalia all in black, the cloth hugging his bony frame underneath it all a deep blue. Besides him, the place his son Akil would've been standing was now occupied by the younger prince Khari, a golden circlet on his brow. Cassimir's father was at the emperor's other side, a hand against his chest as he took in his daughter, safe and returned to him.

In the middle of the room, Mozare's back was bare, his arms held away from him with thick chains of rusted metal. His back was a mess of old and new scars, lashes that she could tell had cut deep to the bone. Light flooded from her chest, her feet moving without her brain acknowledging the truth. She didn't even have to pull a blade, she used her bare hands to break the chain links, her mind detached as she saw Mozare slump against the marble floor.

Loralei was in the crowd, pushing through the rest of the nobility that had come to watch what she was now sure was meant to be an execution. Rage burned through her chest. She hadn't escaped the tyranny of her own country so a foreign ruler could kill her best friend. Her brother. She pushed through the guards that had moved to the base of the steps leading up to the emperor's throne. Threw them aside as if they weighed nothing.

Shadows slithered through the bright light that still pulsed from her chest, making it impossible for them to find her. Impossible for anyone to stop her as she pulled the emperor from his gilded throne, and threw him to his knees in front of her. She heard the stone crack, and finally she pulled a blade, a small dagger she had bought from a merchant on their way back to the palace. Gems in the handle glinted red as she rested the tip of it at the hollow of the emperor's throat.

She let the hall settle, let natural light shine through again so all the gawking scared nobility could see that she had reduced their once mighty emperor to nothing. Had him crying on his knees, no longer strong and mighty, but terrified.

She leaned in close. "What were you going to do to my friend?" She didn't recognize her own voice. The anger and worry that she had felt long before she had set foot in Taezhali, all the years of hatred and isolation pushed to the surface of her mind until her thoughts were dyed with the remembrance of it.

Cassimir's father answered her, standing behind the emperor, palms up as he took a cautious step towards her. "Your friend has been charged with the murder of the emperor's heir apparent mistress." He sounded almost like Cassimir, but there was fear behind his words. Cassimir had never feared her. She wondered briefly what he thought of her now.

"Mozare would never kill someone without just cause."

"Just cause does not matter." The emperor spat at her. "The blood of the empire has been spilt and someone must pay for it."

"Then I assume he was given fair trial. There are enough law books in that library of yours."

She applied the slightest pressure to her blade, watching blood bead at the emperors throat and slowly drip until it bled into the deep blue of the emperors tunic. Fear stained his eyes, like cowardice stained his heart. She saw how easy it would be to push her blade through his neck, to take her friends and flee before anything could be done to stop her. But she wasn't their monster either.

She sheathed her blade, keeping her feet wide in case one of the approaching guards took it as a sign to try and restrain her.

"No mistress he wasn't." Cassimir's father could not see the betrayal that flashed across the emperor's face, but Saiden did. She moved to sit on his throne, ignoring the shocked gasps from the nobility still crowding the steps, trying to watch and see how everything would unfold.

"Then he will get the chance to speak now."

She finally looked at Mozare, at the pain written on his face that was touched now by hope. Loralei was holding on to him, letting his weight lean into her. "I was kidnapped a few days after Saiden and Cassimir set off to rescue the emperor's niece. The crown prince was interested in my gifts, wanted to see if there was any way for him to steal and recreate the power the gods have gifted to us." He stopped, coughing into his hand.

"Loralei came to rescue me. We thought we would take leave of the palace and wait for Saiden to return before leaving Taezhali altogether. The hospitality of the southern kingdom isn't very apparent from the catacombs." Even now with Ilona's hand reaching for him, Mozare still joked. Saiden had to suppress a smile of her own. "The prince was there, he was waiting for her. 'It wouldn't do' he had said, 'to have just one half of their power, when both were within his reach'." Mozare paused to cough again, and blood splattered the marble in front of him.

Loralei's hands moved up his sides, and Saiden realized through the bond of their gifts Loralei wasn't just there to support him, but she was healing him, in front of all these people who wanted him dead, she was giving him a fighting chance.

"He ran experiments on us, testing how far our powers would stretch, how they worked when in pain, or exhausted or starving. When I would not cooperate he would torture Loralei," he said her name like it was the beginning and end of everything good in his life. "And the prince's men would torture me when she would refuse."

"It took time, but his experiments were making us stronger. I waited as long as I could before trying to escape." A tear slid down his cheek. "Then he tried to kill her." His voice broke, "and I knew I wouldn't survive it. No escape was worth it, if I couldn't take her with me. I broke free, and I used the power Akil had helped me build and I suffocated him in his own nightmares."

Saiden waited for his words to settle throughout the hall, waited and watched the way the nobility's faces shifted with emotion. Kept an eye on the emperor who snarled at Mozare and Loralei from his place kneeling at her feet. She opened her mouth to speak, but stopped when another voice spoke from beside her.

"There has been enough blood spilt in the palace of Taezhali. Though we are heavy of heart at the loss of the prince," Prince Khari spoke from beside her, his calm voice carrying over the crowd of people who stopped their whispers to hear what he had to say. "We shall have no more blood spilt in retribution. The foreigner is to be freed to the custody of his friends, who will be given until evening tomorrow to leave Taezhali."

She waited for the emperor to contradict his younger son, hand hovering over her blade and waiting for the order to have them arrested or killed. No objection came. The people faced their new heir and they knelt. She looked to the back of the room and saw Cassimir, his eyes on her, as he kneeled as well, never taking them off her.

She stepped down from the throne, ignoring the emperor from his seat of hatred, and went to get her friends.

Saiden didn't let herself feel relief until they were back in the relative safety of Cassimir's suite. She knew the emperor could still choose to send guards after them at any minute, that he could still choose to have them killed in private, but there was a familiarity and a sense of peace within these walls that made that danger feel far away. As soon as their escort had left them, she pulled Mozare against her, relishing in the fact that they were here, that despite odds that seemed perpetually stacked against them, they were whole and safe and together again. He tucked his head against her shoulder, and they stood there for what was likely more time than appropriate. She couldn't bring herself to care.

Behind Mozare, Loralei stood with her hands clutched in front of her, awkwardness hugging the frame of her body, much thinner than the last time she had seen her Queen. She reached a hand out to her, a thank you for saving his life. At the same time it was gratitude and relief that she had made it out too. She had never been one for hugging, but she pulled Loralei into their embrace, holding her two friends safe in her arms.

She gave herself another moment to bathe in the relief she felt before stepping out of the embrace. The prince had given them time to get their things, but not much and there was a lot of work to still be done if they were going to be heading out of Taezhali by nightfall tomorrow.

THE BLOOD-CURSED

A knock sounded at the outside door of Cassimir's suite. She braced herself, hand reaching for the remaining kindjal blade from the set he had gifted her, and waited. The room swelled with tense anticipation as Cassimir went to open the door. From what Saiden could see around Cassimir's large frame, there were no guards on the other side of the door, though she doubted they would have knocked. It was just a single servant woman, who handed him a bundle of papers before bowing and heading off in a different direction.

Cassimir looked through the papers before handing the full stack of them to Saiden, taking her hand and leading her to the small kneeling table in the center of the room. He didn't let go of her hand when they were sitting either, keeping it tucked within his, thumb rubbing small circles on the tattooed back of her hand.

"They're letters from Rhena." She had once again forgotten about the younger girl who had put so much trust in her. Forgotten that while her friends in Taezhali were threatened, Rhena still lived trapped in a country ruled within the brutal grasp of a tyrant with no right to his throne. Her skin tingled as panic coursed through her and she opened the first letter.

The first few were simple updates, information on the drills they were running in training, the new guard rotations, the efforts to find and recover the traitors who had stolen her from the kingdom in the cover of darkness. She wanted to laugh, trying to imagine how Revon had framed her mother's death and Saiden's loss of control as something that was an attack on his power, instead of his desperate reach for more.

She opened another letter, the handwriting no longer neat, the letters rushed and tearstained at the bottom of the parchment. She had to take a deep breath before she could read it.

To my sister,
    I'm growing more and more worried that I haven't heard from you. Are you getting my letters? Things are not well here, and we need you to come home. I need you.

Revon has been hunting anyone who might be a counter revolutionary and executing them, whether or not he can find proof of guilt. He's gone mad. As if he were not mad enough when he tried to control you, he's now too far gone to be saved.

When the people he accuses are gifted it's even worse. He's not willing to execute them, but he also can't let them get away without punishment. Just this week he used one of the recruits from my training class to make an example of those who might try to dethrone him.

You wouldn't believe the things he's done, since the horrible things he did to you and your mother. He brought this boy to the middle of the barracks and forced everyone to attend, to watch as his newly appointed general carved the boy's skin from his body.

Saiden had to stop reading, had to push against her powers to stop the anger from burning the parchment to ash before she had a chance to finish reading Rhena's letter.

If you are getting these letters please write back to me. I need to know that somewhere out there you are safe and coming back to help us.

Your maus.

Rhena was panicked, Saiden could feel some part of her still connected to her chosen sister even with the distance between them. The paper wrinkled in her hands, curling at the edges. She could smell the beginning of smoke, and she threw the paper on the table, trying to pull her hand free from Cassimir's worried that she would hurt him; but he wouldn't let go. On her other side, Mozare grabbed her hand, Loralei holding tight to his other.

Eleni came and sat next to her, resting her head against Saiden's shoulder. She could feel her breathing against her back, and used the calm rhythm of it to center herself. Rhena was in danger, their kingdom was suffering, but her friends were here with her, they wouldn't abandon her now.

"We have to return to Kaizia." She wasn't sure where they were going to go before, when the prince had announced their exile, but she knew now. This was their responsibility, this was their fight.

66

RHENA

Nearly two months went by before Rhena got a letter back from Saiden. In that time her mind had already gone over the worst case scenarios a couple thousand times. Her bag was packed and she was ready to flee. Realistically her days in Kaizia were numbered so long as she kept acting against Revon's orders.

But she wasn't going to stop doing what she believed was right because of a few death threats from her king.

Not that he had threatened her directly, she had been too clever for that. But Rhena knew, even the cleverest mouse still got caught when it became too greedy. There were simply too many prisoners and not enough time or resources to get them all out.

Her tears traced paths identical to the spill of blood on the marble floors of the hall every time she failed. But only in private.

The vines in the corner of her room had begun to shrivel at the edges despite the number of letters Rhena had put through it. And the fact that she didn't know what that meant was terrifying her. When Saiden's letter finally uncurled in the vines, Rhena was half convinced she was imagining it.

Only holding the worn paper in her hands and pressing it against herself could convince her that she was finally hearing back from her family.

> *My little maus,*
>
> *I am sorry we let you go so long without hearing from us, but the situation was not ideal. Know that you have been in every thought and every prayer I've had while we've been gone. I have plenty of stories to tell you when the world is right again, but for now just know, we're on our way back to you.*
>
> *Your big sister.*

Rhena's eyes stung with unshed tears. And her chest burned with the last spark of hope she had so carefully protected, finally allowing herself to think things might actually start getting better. She wouldn't have to be the only one fighting for the soul of her country anymore.

She could finally admit how tired she was. How desperately she clung to the idea of returning to easier times, even while she continued to fight.

They were coming home.

EPILOGUE
ELENI

Eleni and Cassimir went back and forth on whether or not she would be allowed to come with them to the Northern Kingdom. She saw no reason why the rest of them should be allowed to risk their lives and she be forbidden to do the same.

They were her friends, and Cassimir was her brother. He and Saiden had risked their lives to rescue her from the Isle of the Severed Key, it seemed only right that she went with them now, and offered whatever help she could.

"I am an adult Miri, you can't always be the one to decide what I do with my life."

"I almost lost you Eleni. What was I supposed to do if I never got you back?"

"You went to a foreign kingdom already once to fight their war, what am I supposed to do if you do not come back this time? Don't think I missed the scar on your chest." Cassimir at least had the decency to look sheepish. She understood that he wanted her safe and far away from the danger they were bound to be charging into, but a safe life had not protected her mother, and she was tired of being locked away and treated like she would break at the first test of her strength.

Their friends had filed out of the room when it became clear to them that this conversation was a fight that needed to happen between the siblings, and she was grateful for the privacy, although she was also fairly certain they were just waiting on the other side of the door listening in anyway.

"I have military training. I knew what I was getting into. You don't."

"I can heal. I'm useful. Certainly more useful with you and our friends than sitting here in a palace where I am nothing but a reminder of loss."

Cassimir ran his hands through his hair, a habit he had picked up from their mother that made her heart hurt for a moment. He was pacing their suite, sure at any moment to leave a permanent trail in his wake.

Someone knocked on the door, and Cassimir shrugged before he went to answer it. On the other side of the door, Saiden waited, her hand still lifted as if she was going to knock again. Behind her Mozare and Loralei crowded by the door, though at least the Queen pretended to be busy cleaning her nails.

"Might I make a suggestion?"

Eleni stiffened. She had no way to know if Saiden was going to be on her side, or Cassimir's. Whatever she chose would be the deciding vote.

She walked in behind Cassimir, stopping beside him and running a hand down his arm to entwine their fingers together. Eleni felt her fight dying before Saiden even began to speak.

"I think Eleni should come with us."

Words bubbled behind Eleni's lips, all her arguments for why she should be allowed to come ready, except that she didn't need them. Saiden was agreeing with her.

Saiden turned to Cassimir, "With conditions of course."

Eleni's shoulders sank, but she was ready to listen.

"You'll take the time while we are traveling to train every day. You'll have to keep up with my training regimen, which won't be easy. And when it comes to it, you will follow what the rest of us say if there is any danger. We have years of training, of honing our instincts. There can't be any arguing once we get to Kaizia."

Eleni could deal with these conditions. She was already planning on asking to train, she wasn't foolish. Her talents for healing would be useful, but war required fighting, even if she just had to defend herself.

"I agree."

Saiden threw a wink at her over Cassimir's shoulder as she went to let the rest of their friends back in.

Eleni watched the others pack the few things they had managed to bring with them, and summoned servants to bring them more. More clothing, more food and more weapons.

She could feel her brother's eyes on her the entire time, no doubt wondering if it would be possible to tie her up and leave her here while they escaped and made their way to certain danger. She walked over to him, placing a gentle kiss on his cheek, relieved that Saiden would not let that happen. And while she hadn't spent as much time with the dethroned Queen, she could see herself in Loralei's eyes, and knew the other girl would fight for her to come as well.

"How are we getting back to Kaizia?" Mozare stopped them to ask.

Saiden answered. "Leave that to me. I have a plan."

BONUS SCENES: REVON

Little Revon still couldn't quite believe his luck. Of all the children in this land when Ilona and Keir had sent out their people to search for the next ruler, they had been led to his door. Every morning he woke up to pampering and a full plate of warm food hand-prepared just for him.

Even in his wildest dreams, he hadn't pictured himself in a life like this.

But it was his life, and at eight years old he was prepared to live it to the fullest. The only thing he missed in the palace were the neighborhood children he used to play with, but he had managed to get some of the guards to turn their responsibility for watching him into an opportunity to play.

If he was going to be king, he might as well start practicing now.

He missed his mother too, if only in the darkest parts of night when his bed was empty and no one came to sing him to sleep. It was then that he took out his memories of her, and played them until he drifted off into dreams where she might visit him.

His advisors left him alone for the most part. After the parade they had thrown for him, there was little else to use an eight year old for in a palace, and they were more than satisfied to run things in his place.

BONUS SCENES: REVON

Revon only occasionally checked on them, sneaking through the walls to listen in on meetings when they weren't expecting it.

That was the most fun part of being in the palace. When he had discovered the tunnels behind his bedroom wall he had spent hours playing an elaborate game of hide and seek with his guards, running until the construction of the palace forced him to turn around and go a different way.

Months went by where the only people who paid Revon any attention were the palace guards assigned to watch him and the kitchen maid who came to have breakfast with him. He knew that she was there to make sure he learned proper etiquette, but after a while they spent their breakfasts with him chatting animatedly about whatever new thing he was exploring.

She was the first person Revon told about the mysterious things he one day found himself able to do. To Revon, who knew very little about the world, the small black cat was a wonder. But when he summoned her to the table, his kitchen maid nearly fell from her chair.

"Blasphemy." She shrieked, "guards."

His guards rushed into the room, frantically scanning for danger, but when they couldn't find anyone threatening the young king, they finally noticed the small trail of shadow coming from his hands, and the cat he had summoned nibbling at the leftovers on his table.

They surged forward and Revon moved to protect the little creature, not understanding that they were coming for him. Each of them grabbed one of his arms, despite the fact that he was easily less than half their size. They were terrified, and their fear only made things worse for Revon as they dragged him from the room.

His advisors were already assembled and well into today's argument when the guards interrupted them, shoving Revon to stand where they could all see him.

Out of breath, the larger of his two guards huffed as he began to address the group of men, all of them staring, half in anger, at their interruption.

"The boy is an abomination. He's unfit to be king. We caught him calling on Ilona's magic this morning with no remorse."

Half of his advisors froze, while the other began yelling at each other, each call more frantic than the last. The only thing that was clear to Revon, was that he had been mistaken in trusting the kitchen maid. Surely this was a misunderstanding.

He tried to address the men, but his small voice couldn't be heard over their yelling. He didn't think they could even hear each other with all the noise they were making.

When they finally calmed long enough for him to speak, his words became his own damnation. "The goddess gifted me. But she also chose me to be king. Is it so wrong to be both things?"

"He admits to it."

"With all of us as witness?" The men started shouting again, until the oldest among them, Brogan stood, ushering them all into silence.

"The young man can no longer be king. By the laws that govern our nation, we cannot endorse a ruler with this kind of power. And so he must be removed from the palace at once. His name stripped from our records. It must be as if the child has died, if we cannot make it look as if he were never Chosen."

No one spoke now. No one argued for him, or his right to stay at the palace. The guards came back to his sides, gathering him up again and removing him. They gave him only his cloak before rushing him out of the city.

He had no home, and no crown. He couldn't return to his family, he wasn't sure he'd even know how to get home. He hadn't been paying attention to directions in the long carriage ride that had brought him to the capital city.

And now he was lost. In more ways than just one.

Revon couldn't remember if he had ever seen so many people in one place before. Aside from his introduction to the town, they had never had a reason to call an assembly in the fourteen months he had lived in the palace.

But now they did.

Despite being young, Revon knew to keep himself hidden, calling on the meager talents as a shadow summoner that had put him into this mess in the first place to distort his image. No one was looking at him anyway. He was a dirty child in a crowd more focused on his death than a grubby homeless kid.

The small shadow cat that had gotten him into this mess rubbed against his legs. If only he had gotten enough magic to do something big, then maybe he could change everything that was going on. But all he got was a sidekick he couldn't seem to make disappear.

Oscan began speaking at the podium. He doubted they realized he knew their names, but he had each of his once advisors's faces burned into his memory. Revon wouldn't forget the terrible things they did to him when they found out about his powers. How after it all, they had still decided to fake his death and send him out into the world on his own instead of admitting the gods had picked a Gifted king.

Who were they to decide that Keir and Ilona had been wrong?

His voice, augmented by technology Revon didn't understand burst through the open pavilion. "It is with heavy hearts that we come here today to announce the passing of the young king-to-be Revon. During an armed invasion, his would-be assassin infiltrated the halls of our sleeping castle and killed him in his sleep. We do not believe he suffered, and we know he rests now in the gentle embrace of our goddess."

"We urge you in your grief to remember them, and to pray. For they know their plans for us, and they are greater than any we could imagine. In his short life, Revon was a faithful servant, all the way to the end."

The people around him began to bow their heads. They believed every word of the lie he was spreading. Revon had half a mind to scream, to prove to these people that they were lead by a bunch of liars. But he'd listened to enough of their meetings to know how to play their game. And he was young, he had time to be patient.

That crown was going to be his.

Revon was twenty four the next time someone was chosen to wear the crown that should've been his. A little girl, her skin as dirty as his had once been. He'd never left, the call to power was too strong in the capital, between his proximity to the barracks and the palace.

He couldn't be seen near either, he wouldn't risk the kind of punishment they might inflict now that he was no longer a child. Revon knew they wouldn't have a problem killing him now that he wasn't an innocent faced boy.

It wasn't as hard to acknowledge it now as it had been when he was a child. When he thought the world was good and its people were too. Now he saw the truth of it wherever he went, the darkness inherent to everyone around him.

And he himself was full of a rage that helped to dull any pain he might have once felt. Vengeance focused all his sense. Even his powers were harnessed now, although he still felt the phantom of the cat at his ankles whenever his brain succumbed to doubt.

He'd spent a long time without a home, until he'd stumbled into the ruins of barracks he'd only heard about in passing during his brief stay at the palace. When weeks had passed and no one had claimed them, he decided they were his.

Revon was going to build something to rule over. It was the only thing that would quiet the indignation in his mind. And slowly but surely he began to pick out others like him, wronged by this system, and turn them to his side.

The new choosing put a wrench in things. Some of his followers might believe it was right to replace the board of advisors, but he didn't know how many of them would want to fight the gods will.

He needed to turn their minds against her.

And eventually he would turn the entire country against her, he would make them all fight for his side. He would rule, no matter how much blood he had to spill to get there.

The key to everything found Revon nearly ten years later. Stumbling through the woods without a care for what was around him, Revon saw opportunity the first time he caught sight of the boy.

He kicked a tree, his voice only loud enough to just carry to

Revon's stake out spot. "They shouldn't have that power." He kicked the tree again, huffing. Revon did his best to move closer to the boy, the power in his chest rising in response to the boy's own gifts.

Revon could feel that this child was powerful. And he recognized that anger too. It was exactly the kind of anger that was valuable to Revon. The moldable kind. Revon saw the potential building in front of them.

"Who shouldn't have that power?" Revon asked, risking his position as he stepped out from behind the tree line.

The young boy pulled out a small blade, but he was so skinny Revon didn't think he was an actual threat. Even with the power roiling inside him.

"Who are you?"

"Revon. I'm a freedom fighter." Revon repeated his question, "Who shouldn't have that power?"

"Who has all the power?" The boy asked, and Revon had to stop himself from smiling. "And still they turn from the gods. They mock us and their gifts."

"What's your name child?"

The boy looked him up and down, and he felt his judgements. But he must've been enough because the boy did finally answer. "Mozare."

"Would you like to help me bring glory back to our gods?" He knew the boy would nod, and he would not put that trust to waste. He would not put this gift from the gods to waste.

GLOSSARY

Sahadi: sister
    Syhedi: brother
    Hramam: form of currency
    Preeyapet: beloved

ACKNOWLEDGMENTS

The journey to this finished book has not been an easy one. It may not have gone through as many challenges as the characters inside it do, but we definitely hit some rough spots where things didn't look too good. I am so eternally grateful to everyone who helped me preserve through those challenges and get this book into your hands. I love this story so much and it is so heartwarming to know it's in the world, hopefully finding the readers who need it.

The biggest thanks to my bestie Jessi Elliott who listened to hundreds of hours of rants and answered even more of my questions. You have kept me sane during this process and I love you so much. I', so glad our friendship made it out of the internet.

To my mom, you've probably listened to nearly as many rants. Thank you for believing I could make it through this process no matter what that journey looked like.

To my twin, thank you for seeing the positives when I couldn't. For handling the panic and the moodiness so I could take a break from it.

To my cousin Catie, who once again was an invaluable reader of this story and helped to correct the storyline and continuity problems between this book and The Legionnaire.

To Lauren Geary, my Aunt Laurie, Deirdre Falla, Tammy Goodwin, Christina Valentine, and Aimee Pozorski. Thank you for giving me marketing advice and at times pushing me out of my comfort zone to try and get this series to readers.

To my dad, who listened to story ideas and did not judge me. Even though he probably should have at some point.

Thank to every person who reached out when I announced I was going Indie and offered support. Especially to Jayme Smith who has checked in on me regularly just to offer her help.

I love this story with all my heart, and I only hope you do the same. Until next time, one last thanks to you, dear reader.

About the Author

Samantha Traunfeld's love of stories began when she was about 12—back when she could read a whole book in a day, and wrote lots of stories featuring cute ghosts. Now she writes stories about badass women, sharp weapons, and banter-y relationships. When she isn't writing, she's usually cuddling her dog, starting a new craft project she might not finish, or trying to figure out how video games work. There's a 94.6% chance you can find her curled up in a bookstore somewhere (math is not her strong suit), but if you don't, you can find more information on her website: samanthatraunfeld.com.

instagram.com/sam.traunfeld

Milton Keynes UK
Ingram Content Group UK Ltd.
UKHW041947091024
449514UK00018B/153/J

9 781965 436004